ALEXE

OLEG SAPPHIRE

THE HEALER'S
WAY

With our best wishes,
A. Kovtunov

Enjoy
the
adventure!

BOOK SEVEN

PUBLISHED BY MAGIC DOME BOOKS

The Healer's Way
Book # 7
Copyright © Alexey Kovtunov, Oleg Sapphire 2024
Cover Art © Linni 2024
Cover Design: Vladimir Manyukhin
English translation copyright © Jennifer E. Sunseri 2024
Published by Magic Dome Books, 2024
ISBN: 978-80-7693-864-9

ALSO BY THE AUTHORS:

AN IDEAL WORLD FOR A SOCIOPATH
A LITRPG SERIES BY OLEG SAPPHIRE

GHOST IN THE SYSTEM
AN APOCALYPSE LITRPG SERIES BY ALEXEY KOVTUNOV

THE ORDER OF ARCHITECTS
BY OLEG SAPPHIRE (WITH YURI VINOKUROFF)

THE HUNTER'S CODE
BY OLEG SAPPHIRE (WITH YURI VINOKUROFF)

THE VILLAGE
BY ALEXEY KOVTUNOV (WITH DMITRY DORNICHEV)

TABLE OF CONTENTS:

CHAPTER 1

WILLSON DASHED ABOUT HIS HOME in a panic. A sack in one hand, he scooped up whatever he could and stuffed it in, and then he repeated the process with another sack.

"Hey, let's enjoy some of these treats! They're delectable! You must try the smoked sausage. It would be a crime not to!" Despite the frantic rush he was in, his guest kept urging him and his sister to stop and eat something.

And, in fact, his sister Mirabelle pause to sample some of the treats. She drank a little wine, too, but then she abruptly came back to her senses, and went back to preparing to flee. After all, a punitive squad was due to arrive, and that meant certain death! Death to almost the entire city.

"Hey, you two! Stop it!" exclaimed the Healer

yet again. "Look at this!"

"Look at what?" Willson asked, spooked as he looked out the window. "What's out there?"

"Look over here!" Mikhail said, fishing a bottle out of his bag and with one deft movement pulling off the metal cap. "See how easy that is for me to do?"

"Arrrgh!" groaned the Artifactor as he continued his packing. Only the most valuable things, materials for artifacts, gold, documents...

"Oh no! We're too late. Why are you in such a hurry?" Everyone in the city felt a sudden surge of necrotics. The wave rolled over several kilometers, meaning....

"Dark portal..." Mira stammered.

"We're finished!" Willson squeal, but his sister grabbed him and dragged him toward the door.

"Let's go!" she yelled, and jumped outside.

"Hey! I haven't finished eating!" Mikhail was indignant, but he had no choice but to follow them. He grabbed the open bottle, and also a hunk of smoked sausage. "By the way, you're making a mistake, refusing these treats."

"Did you feel it?" Mirabelle asked.

"I felt it. It hot and spicy, but I like it," said Mikhail, looking at Mira, and comprehending then that she was talking about something else. "Oh, you're talking about the dark portal? Well, yes, it opened, but what's the big deal?"

"That's a punitive squad!" she exclaimed. "We have to get away as far as we can and as fast as possible..." she said. "Otherwise they'll destroy this entire city. But... If there are only three of them, we have a shot at fighting back."

She was worried about the city because, in part, her brother had many friends here, and he'd be devastated in the event of a massacre. But yes, this trio of punishers had to be defeated. Usually the Order of Death sent exactly three, that is, a single squad.

"If you really believe what you're saying, then you really don't have any chance," said the Healer, distracting her from her dire musings. She looked over at him and saw that he was waving the sausage towards the gate.

"We're f*cked!" Willson threw up his hands, seeing six death mages heading their way.

"You are so right," said his sister.

"Oh, better still! Six of them!" smiled Mikhail, taking a bite of the sausage and washing it down with a slug of wine. "It's not much of a challenge, but it's something, at least."

Mirabelle suddenly turned pale, and Willson was ready to pass out he was so scared. But then, Mira got a grip on herself, and she squared her shoulders and adopted a fighting stance. She had some grievances against this Order, and she wasn't about to give up without a fight. That being said, she knew full well that they were doomed. Two squads of punishers....That was huge.

Sure, Mikhail had killed two not long ago, but Mira believed that this had been possible only because he'd taken them by surprise.

Willson was as if rooted to the ground, and

stared vacantly in front of him. His life had already flashed before his eyes, and so now he had nothing else to think about. He'd recalled all the happy moments, and felt regret at not managing to create the perfect artifact before he died.

"What?" he muttered, suddenly coming to his senses. He felt like he'd surely died, but....where was he? Either he'd gone to hell, or else someone had brought hell to him right here.

All around him he heard rumbling and saw flashing lights, and screams broke out. Funny sounding screams. Not that it was funny, because he was only now coming to the realization that his nightmare was just beginning. He, Willson, had to serve this man.

It was this Healer, who, although he looked like an ordinary guy, and a young one, at that, was in the process of fighting five senior death mages at once. He wasn't just fighting them; he was also making fun of them! Why else would he make them sound so funny? Take that wise old man in a black robe who would make any ordinary person shrink in horror — and now he was squeaking like a teenage girl! Likewise, all of the other death mages had girlish voices.

"Cloud of Death!" squeaked one of them, and with his comrades prepared to cast a spell together.

But just then, Mikhail's face changed. He had been laughing, having a good time. And he still held aloft his smoked sausage. But now, he was serious.

"What on earth are you morons thinking? The Cloud of Death would kill the whole city, idiots!" he growled, and then....Then Willson closed his eyes. And he opened them only when Mikhail approached him and offered him a drink. "Here! You'll feel better right away, I promise!"

"B-but..." Willson looked over the Healer's shoulder and saw five corpses there. His sister was almost done with the sixth one. "W-who are you?"

"You've lost your memory, is that it?" — Mikhail passed his flickering palm over the Artifactor's head and shrugged. "No, your brain seems to be intact."

Before, Willson didn't think things could get any worse. But he was wrong. He needn't fear the Order of Death; rather, he should have feared *for* them. After all, Mikhail clearly had their number. And Willson also realized that he'd best forget about some of his plans for now. And not just his current plans, but also any plans he had for the future. He'd been toying with the idea of somehow terminating his contract with the Healer. But no, it was best that he banish such thoughts for the foreseeable future.

*　*　*

"So why were they so uptight about you two?" I asked, impressed by the zest with which Mira did her adversary in. She'd gone a little overboard whilst killing him, the damage was so bad.

The girl looked up from the decayed ashes

that were all that was left of the rather strong death mage. Right...But she could have simply made him expel his lungs, which is what I had done to my lot. And not through the mouth, either. No, I'm not cruel, not at all. I'm a Healer, after all.

The death mages were actually rather strong. I didn't expect mages of that caliber in this outback. Magisters, no less. But what I knew for sure was that these guys had nothing to do with death, and so their glory was a complete facade. On the other hand, someone, some small entity, was definitely feeding the forces of the Order. It was linked to death somehow, but only indirectly and in passing. They probably performed some regular sacrificial rituals and stuff like that. That's what made them stronger, as it would replenish them. But it was their strength that gave me an advantage. All in all, fighting this punitive squad was nothing but fun. What was great about this world was that I didn't have to hold back in public. I didn't have to worry about revealing too much about myself and then being hunted.

Half of the cursed power of death magic simply flowed off me like water off a duck, and I absorbed the rest into my body with the help of vital magic. The most important thing was to dose the energy correctly, and I didn't need a lot from my reserves to do that.

I took a look at the dead punishers, and realized how it was they had such fearsome reputations here. Each of these men possessed an offshoot of death magic. Yes, just as I thought, they fed on sacrifices; now there was no doubt about it. They drew strength from tormenting and torturing innocent victims, and I verified this with Mira, who had normal death magic, the standard type.

No, she hadn't mastered necromancy, but it was the same source of energy. Theoretically, she could raise the dead just like Vika, except that in actuality she couldn't. She'd selected another school to develop. She could create a personal shield, and attack with arrows of dead dust and death rays. And much more.

She could grow stronger by fueling from the same source as did the now-dead punitive squad. But what would happen if they stopped making sacrifices? The punishers would lose power, while, in contrast, Mira controlled her own energy at will, and didn't need any sacrifices. Fifty years from now, she could, say, take a break from it all, and she'd still be strong.

That's the problem with sacrifices. And not the only problem, because, after all, those who relied on them for power always needed to be on the lookout for new victims.

"So, tell me, why is it you don't like these guys?" I asked Mira as she went over to sit down next to her brother on the ground.

The city seemed to have fallen asleep in broad daylight. All of the doors and windows were closed, and there wasn't a soul out there on the streets. Even the city guards were gone, and the only sound was that of a whistling gust of wind herding rubbish down the street.

"This is all because of you!" she yelled, dumb-founding me.

"Okay, I'm not going to argue with you. But what's your thinking on that?" I said, after a pause.

"I had a little fight with them," the girl sighed, and again I didn't follow.

"Very interesting, but you lost me there. Could you provide me a little context to all this?" Candidly, I couldn't believe that all this was my fault. However, I wanted to understand Mira's train of thought. And I immediately realized that I wanted too much. I could never understand the girl's train of thought even if I happened to be the greatest Archmagister of Mind Magic

"What is there to say?" Willson saved me. He'd been silently listening to us, and finally got sick of it all. "My sister is wonderful, strong, a joy to be around, but she is also quick-tempered. And when you told her she was going to die, she rampaged through half the kingdom, annoying everyone. I actually felt sorry for the Healers," he said with a shudder, recalling how she sought out a Healer who was an Archmagister. She could not find one who had that kind of power, but she'd managed to seriously annoy the Magister Healers. And so one twisted freak told her that her condition could have stemmed from the magic of Death Bringers.

"I'm still at a loss. But all of this is ever the more interesting," I spoke into the ensuing silence, because it seemed as if Willson thought he'd an-swered my question.

"Well, once upon a time, she participated in a tournament and reached the final competition against one of them. Then she lost. And so he might have cursed Mira with an affliction, although that would be strictly prohibited by the tournament rules."

"So then what happened?" I sat down to relax as I listened. I loved stories like this. I also fished more treats out of my backpack. It wasn't my way to not enjoy some food while listening to tales.

"Well, that's all there is to it!" The Artifactor shrugged. "She tracked down the winner and tore his head off. Literally... And what's strange is that he swept her away in the tournament, but when she tracked him down to wreak vengeance on him, she didn't even get a scratch."

"She's a dangerous woman..." I nodded, taking a bite out of a sandwich.

"That's putting it lightly," Willson said. I again offered him a bite, but he again refused. He was still in deep shock, and it would take him awhile to recover.

"How about you, Mira? Want a bite?" And she happily extended her hand. "How about a little wine? Hmmm...?" She gratefully accepted that, too.

Thus, for the next twenty minutes I simply served Mira food and drink as she stared off into space while eating whatever.

This included all the sausage, as well as the cheese. We ran out of the bread first, and I was curious to see how much she could stuff into herself. It turned out more than what I'd brought with me. Eventually she reached out for more, but there was nothing left.

"Aren't you worried about gaining weight?" I said, looking at her perfect figure. Most people who looked that fit put in hard work every day for years on end.

"Nope..." she shook her head. "I don't have to worry about it."

"You've just put on four hundred grams," I said, having conducted a swift diagnosis.

"Because of her magic, she has an excellent metabolism," Willson chuckled. "Our parents had to struggle to feed us. I wasn't a problem, but Mira inhaled everything on the table, and would start gnawing on the wooden dishes."

Silence ensued for a few minutes, and then both Mira and Willson began stirring again. Meanwhile, I searched the corpses, and turned them into dust. There was nothing of value that remained once they died. I had to destroy their artifacts during the battle, and had no use for their clothing. Let them lie there; perhaps those who lacked the means to buy clothing would appreciate their threads.

In fact, killing these punishers was actually a serious crime. At least their Order thought so, and now they were going to have to bend over backwards to find Wilson. After all, not just the first two, but also six more death mages had dies while out to get Willson. And no one knew about me.

Of course, Mira was also in trouble, but she

wasn't an easy target, and wielded a lot of influence in this world. She was just fine in the capital, as no one there would dare to cross her. Once she was at the side of the king, nobody would openly attack her. Yes, he paid tribute to their Order, but they weren't foolish enough to be impudent with him. So I didn't have to worry about the girl, but Willson...

"I think that your jig here is up!" I concluded. "You have no options."

"Gosh, thanks. I was just starting to calm down," he said, turning pale. "What am I to do? I have to go back to the capital; it's at least a little safer there. If I stay here, well, I'm done for..." he said, thinking out loud. "And why, why? Because my sister is so hot-headed. Impulsive and aggressive. And also..." he plunged into his thoughts.

"What?" I asked, but he just waved his hand.

"Nothing..." he seemed to be upset at the trouble he was in. Even in the capital he could be killed. It was one thing to attack Mira there, and quite another to attack a not-so-influential Artifactor from the outback.

"Okay," I smiled. "Truly, I am to blame here. I didn't need to mention that Mira is dying."

"Actually, she's not dying, rather, she was dying," Mira said, raising her index finger. "I finally found Healers who could successfully treat me."

"Is that right?" I asked dubiously. "So they cured your sore knees and that's it; you thought they'd cured your malady!? Oh, well," I shrugged

"How did you know that? About my knees?"

she asked.

"I've just touched you, not once, but twice. That's all I need to fully diagnose you." I was offended. She, after all, knows that I am an Archmagister. Or perhaps not? But, okay. "Anyway, you're still dying. It's just life," I shrugged. I could also tell her that her malady wasn't due to the Death Bringers, but why bother? Let her give them hell; I didn't like them.

"What bastards..." hissed Mirabelle. "I paid them fifty gold pieces, and they..."

She began to list what she was going to do to punish the thieving Healers, while I turned back to Willson.

"You can join me at my castle for now. After all, we have a contract, and according to it I must provide you with all possible assistance. I can hide you from the Death Bringers; they definitely won't harm you in my world."

"No way! Another world? Never, not for anything! I'd rather die in the capital than go through the portal!" Wilson wailed and looked for support from his sister. "Mira, you tell him! It's not possible!"

"Agree to it," she frowned. "They really will finish you off, Willie."

For some time the Artifactor tried to collect his thoughts. He was sure that his sister would be categorically against it and would not allow the evil Healer to drag him to his lair. But, to his surprise, Mira herself insisted that he go. So then he reluctantly went back to packing.

Although they'd taken out one punitive squad, that didn't mean more wouldn't soon follow. And it wouldn't take them long...And so it took very little time for Willson to pack up. What he couldn't take with him, he delivered to the trading post for sale, and then, finally, we headed for the portal.

"Okay, brother, work well, don't forget to eat," Mira hugged Willson goodbye, and then looked at me. "And you...

"What?" I asked, eyebrow raised.

"Nothing," she waved her hand. "Just take care of him!

I could only shrug. What did he have to worry about? I had delicious food, interesting work, a nice comfy abode, television, and work...Oh, guess I mentioned work already. But work was good, as busy hands stopped a person from engaging in all sorts of nonsense. Work hard enough and you didn't have the strength for anything else.

Once through the portal we headed straight for the castle. Willson was again quaking in fear, but now he was full of questions. He was clearly afraid of this world, having heard lots of scary stories from travelers.

"Don't worry so much. In this world I'm a count, the head of a Family. No Death Bringer can get to you here," I tried to calm him down.

"Is a count like a lord?" he asked, and exhaled with relief.

"Yes, something like one of your lords, but with only five hundred people in his county. And oh, a lord whose neighbors are all out to get him. Something like that, give or take," I grinned, watching the Artifactor's face change.

"I'm definitely finished!" he sighed.

We didn't have to walk far before transportation arrived. I'd called for it right away, as we both couldn't ride my Corgi horse. Once we arrived at the castle, I led Willson to his new abode.

"Here you go," I smiled, gesturing him in. "For the next month this will be your new home." By then, Mira had said she could resolve matters with the Order of Death.

I could tell that Willson wasn't too impressed with the room. But it was, in fact, the only one I could offer him right then. I then summoned Chernomor and Vika to meet him. They stood in the doorway and looked with interest at Willson.

"Meet my friend Willson!" I said, indicating the frozen Artifactor. "He'll be staying here for a while due to family problems at home. Serious people are hunting him, but they won't hurt us. So I urge you to provide him a warm welcome and do your best not to offend him."

"Hello, Willson!" They both spoke at once without any enthusiasm. Willson waved in response, opting not to speak to this alien twosome.

As soon as they left, the Artifactor managed to scrape together some courage. Hands on his hips, he frowned.

"Mikhail... I understand, it's a temporary measure, but... It's like I'm back in my student years! Only there the room was three times larger than this kennel!" he complained.

"Well, excuse me, a servant used to live here," I didn't mention that he later moved to more comfortable housing. But I couldn't kick anyone out because of this new guest! As long as all we had was this room he had to make do with it.

"Did I understand correctly that you need artifacts??" he asked, and I nodded in response.

"Yes, that's in the contract."

"If you need artifacts, then I need good working conditions," he extended his hand forward and began to count off on his fingers, and I, crossing my arms over my chest, began to listen. "A place for gymnastics, a jogging track, a comfortable restroom, a space for meditation, a separate dining room..." at this point the fingers ran out, so he switched to his second hand. But there, too, the fingers didn't last long.

"If you need me to, I can add twenty or so more fingers to each hand. That would make it easier, I'm sure," I grinned, and he looked startled and hid his hands.

"I'm not finished! Tables for preparing solutions, a comfortable bed with a soft feather mattress, a massage therapist...

"Stop!" I cut in. "Don't be ridiculous here! You've never needed a massage therapist before."

"Maybe not, but I've always wanted one!" he replied hotly. "And until I have proper housing, I won't make artifacts, period!"

Well, I guess I asked for it. I sent Kooky to my study to fetch something, and when he got back, I slammed a huge pad of paper onto the table.

"Here! Draw!"

"What? Draw what?" he asked, picking up the pen.

"Everything you need. Draw it, write it down, whatever you need, and I'll make it happen," I said, serious now. "But if you don't make any artifacts... The Death Bringers will seem like pissed-off kids next to me. You'll need a rolling walker to get around."

"Are you going to break my legs?" Willson asked, alarmed, and I had to laugh.

"You'll have to roll a cart in front of you. And groan at every bump; I've already thought about how I'm going to do it."

"What do you mean?" He clearly didn't realize that I could grow a certain part of him to obscene sizes.

"So draw....draw it," I nodded toward the paper. "Just don't leave anything out."

Shrugging then, Willson fired up his imagination, and began drawing, sketching, writing. Whatever he could think of. Did he think that I wouldn't be able to fulfill his demands, and that he'd perhaps have time off from work? But no, this time I had him. Little did he know that in another month he wouldn't want to leave.

Ah, but he had a good imagination. First, Willson depicted a huge square five-story tower, then he began to describe in detail what should be on each floor. Lamps, heat, tables, a Jacuzzi, pools for cooling artifacts and, conversely, for heating.

But the latter looked quite small, and a fire could be lit underneath each of them. Quite convenient, by the way, but I would heat the water with electricity.

Furnaces in which metal would be melted, all kinds of furniture for various purposes, some pots, both clay and cast iron, instruments for carving, for working with stone. Willson pictured a lot of items in the rooms, and ultimately left two entire floors for relaxation. And on the very top floor, there was a bathhouse and a massage table exactly in the center of the main room.

He finished only eight hours later. From time to time I had to clarify what was what, because it was not always clear from his artwork. He also put in explanations at my request. The list was quite extensive, and all of this stuff would have to be purchased by my people. The notes ended up being completely covered in drawings, and I even had to bring him more paper. But as night fell, Willson tiredly leaned back in his chair and stretched out with a satisfied smile.

"That's it!" he sighed.

"Are you sure?" I felt like there were important omissions, just the same.

"Yes, that's everything," he smiled, content. "I've thought through every detail, so it's up to you now!"

"Well, okay," I smiled. Too late for him to tell me he wanted a television. He could have at least strolled around the castle to see the benefits of civilization that were to found here. "And about the last point, why a masseur and not a masseuse?"

"Oh, are there such people?" He snatched the notes from my hands, and I shrugged. "Damn, I should have asked for two masseuses..." But I took the notes back and headed out. Too late for that.

I went to my study, threw the notes on the table and exhaled. Yes, he had quite the list of demands, but it was okay. Willson was in for a surprise.

Next, I turned in for a night of sleep, and the next morning I summoned everyone who could help in arranging the artifact tower. Georgy, Vika, Chernomor, Timothy, and an entire team of specialists. As soon as everyone had gathered, I laid out Willson's demands on the table, and asked what they could do to help.

"Well, stoves are not a problem," Victoria said immediately. "The mages can make the base, and we have everything else in storage," she said, studying the list. "But why does he need four bedrooms?"

"I don't know," I shrugged. "Maybe he wants to invite his relatives to join him."

"Or a masseuse." smiled Vika, pointing to the last items on the list.

"I can help with that," Georgy said. "I'll have one here by tomorrow. Just one clarification. Do you want one that's intact, or one that needs help before she's intact?"

"Feel free to bring me one without hands," I said, gesturing dismissively. "If she knows what to do, and is loyal, then I can grow her new hands."

"What if she's ugly?" Apparently Georgy had someone in mind.

"If she's ugly, I can make her beautiful," I said. That way, if Willson didn't come through for me, I could make her ugly again. More motivation for him to get to work. "Okay. Chernomor, what do you say?"

"What is there to say?" he said, pointing a thick finger at the drawings. "We'll install cameras here, here, and here. A couple of coils of wires, half a day of work, and there will be round-the-clock surveillance. But I would slightly modify the location of the windows so that we can install machine guns and cannons there.

Everyone began to express their minds, each focusing on what they planned on doing, and right in the middle of the conversation my phone rang.

"Oh, Snegireva is calling," I asked everyone to be silent and answered the call, turning on the speakerphone. "Hello!"

"You..." the viscountess growled. "How dare you? Wasn't it enough for you? You plundered my mansion, and now you're sending your Suits out at night to prey on me? How can you look at yourself in the mirror? I'm offering you one final opportunity to return all that you've stolen, compensate me for my losses, and return the mines to the baron. And then, you must meet me in person to discuss what comes next. Otherwise, you'll seriously regret it! Do you understand?"

"Aha!" I had to smile.

"You've pushed me over the edge, and I have

nothing more to lose! See what happens if you decide to mess with me again!"

"Okay, later!" I hung up and looked at the others. They stood with their mouths agape, and Chernomor frowned. But he frowned all the time, so this was nothing unusual. "Well? Let's continue! Who will purchase mattresses? Timothy, do you have anything in stock?"

"Mikhail.....what....what was that?" Victoria was puzzled.

"That was... Now... Well, what?" I snapped my fingers, trying to remember the word. "It's right on the tip of my tongue! "Georgy, you told me that word...what is it? It's pathetic, really, but it would be just right now."

"Haters?" he responded hesitantly.

"Yes, that's it! I jumped out of my chair. "Vika, that was a hater calling!"

"I'm not talking about that," the countess shook her head. "What were you doing to push the viscountess to the brink like that? Now she's making these crazy threats!"

"Hmm..." Chernomor cleared his throat. "Well, the Suits have been flying around her lands for two days now razing everything to the ground. I'd be ticked off, too."

"Well, why should our Suits sit idle?" I said, spreading my hands. "We have Suits, so let them work! By the way, a bird whispered to me that there's another task for them. Remind me, and we can talk about it later. And one more thing... Any news on the hunt for more operators?"

"Mikhail, of course I understand that your abilities are extraordinary," Chernomor scratched the back of his head. "But there simply aren't many disabled Combat Suit operators in the Empire."

"Yes, I see now that there are in existence more Suits than disabled operators," I sighed.

"Well, if you need one fast, I know on old man who could help out. Only he's over ninety years old, and there's something wrong with his head," Chernomor suggested. "Can you restore his youth?"

"Both his youth and potency. But he has to be worth it," I said. Now, I'd make do with whomever.

Anyway, we finished allocating the work load for the Artifactor's tower, and I gave everyone two days to get their part done. Hopefully, they'd finish even sooner. And just like that, my study was again empty as everyone left to do their share of the work. The only thing left to do was get the tower built. But for this job, I had other specialists. I called the earth mages, and soon they were looking at the tower the Artifactor had depicted on paper.

"You understand that we still haven't finished the lake, right?" Ludwig asked, and I nodded. "Likewise with the underground parking facility."

"Yes, I know that you are slackers," I sighed and plopped down in my chair, picking up a cup of now cold tea. I could only hope that Kooky hadn't bathed in it... "But I haven't managed to find any other Earthbenders yet."

"Actually, that's offensive," said Giovanni.

"Well, if that's so, prove me wrong. Here are the sketches; this tower should be attached to the castle. And fit into the big picture. It must also be very, very strong, so that it does not crack even from a direct hit from a shell." --I wondered if they knew what an artillery shell was? Not that it mattered. "You can use crystals, black diamond, whatever."

"I can tell you right away that we need at least a week..." Ludwig began to say, but I interrupted him.

"You have, at most, a night to get this done," I smiled, enjoying the look on their faces. "Get going on it."

"But....we don't have that much energy...We can't do it that fast!" They chorused their displeasure, but I was deaf to their indignation.

"You can do it. You just have to try, that's all!"

"Give us at least one reason what the rush is," Toren couldn't stand aside.

"I stole an Artifactor, and most importantly, unlike you, he is idle now, without work. And the longer it takes you to build the tower, the longer he'll be sitting around twiddling his thumbs."

"That's an ironclad argument," the mages all nodded. "But first of all, we need energy. And secondly, we demand a three-day vacation afterwards. So there!"

"I'll share the energy myself and give you two days off," I nodded to them.

"Three days!" Giovanni was incensed, "And not a day less."

"Two!" Under the contract I didn't have to give them any days off, and so I was already being generous.

"Three! And freedom from drinking with Cherepanov!" That was Ludwig, and I had to agree with him.

"You two are freed, and let Toren drink with him. Do we have a deal?" The mages were happy with this, although Toren didn't yet fully understand what he'd just signed up for.

"Who is this Cherepanov? Although if he needs a drinking friend, why not? I am for it!" He was happy at the thought.

I'd sacrificed Giovanni and Ludwig to my fish supplier. Moreover, my strategy was brilliant. He was satisfied and I no longer had to waste my time. We'd had to come up with a story about how I had enchanted stones from the Interface world, and they had to pretend that they were professional builders. Cherepanov was wondering how the restoration of my castle was being moving along so quickly.

And while Ludwig was fluent enough in the local language, Giovanni knew only a few common phrases. Toren, though, would have nothing to say. But this was no hindrance to Cherepanov. He was happy to do all the talking as long as everybody drank.

They all left then to get to work, and I could finally sit back and relax. Everything turned out even better than I expected. Now I could get together all of the resources right here, rather than having to haul artifacts through the portal.

Willson had given me a list of what he needed, and it wasn't anything special. He just needed it all. Creating artifacts was a complex and rather strange process. For example, they could be made from wood, bones, or even metal. Depending on which element went into their makeup, they would function differently.

Thus, a lot of materials were needed, in great variety. From now on, the peasants wouldn't be throwing away their fish bones. Now they'd have to clean them, dry them and send them here. The same with birds, and with many other things. Gold, different types of wood, and for each artifact you needed something else, and the age of the material also mattered. Although I did not yet know how good my Artifactor was, nor how wide his range of recipes was. But I'd soon find out, and if need be, I could find another Artifactor. I had enough wine for it, so to speak.

After issuing orders to the peasants, I summoned the operators. I'd asked Chernomor to remind me, but he somehow forgot to do so. I and the operators went to find him, and then we began discussing the plan.

Although the viscountess was weak now, she definitely still had it out for me. And not far from our borders, Kooky had come across a storehouse of military hardware camouflaged in the woods. This included some interesting new items. At present the guard comprised only fifteen lonely men. The Suits would handle them, while Chernomor and his strike force would swiftly steal the trophies.

Hearing the pigeon describe the new artillery there, Chernomor said "Those must be three new Sharoshkas. They have electronic locks that can only be opened remotely using a special key"

"Can they be unlocked from inside? Without a key?" Chernomor nodded, yes.

"Kooky, you know what to do."

"*Cooo!*" responded the feathered one, shaking his head. "*Coooo-coo-coo!*"

"What are you saying? You just have to press a button. That's it! You've done this a hundred times," I was indignant at the pigeon's impudence, but he remained adamant. "Okay," I pulled out a bag from my pocket and threw it in front of Kooky. "Fly off now."

"*Cooo?*" he kicked the bag and shook his head again. "*Coooo-coo-coo!*"

"Before you complain, open it and see what's inside," I smiled. Kooky looked at me suspiciously, but went ahead and peeked inside.

"*Coooo-coo!*" He hugged the bag close to him. I knew that he loved pumpkin seeds. I made a point of collecting them in the Interface world.

* * *

Next morning
Artifactor's room

Willson went to bed, but slept poorly due to feeling disgruntled. The thing was, this was almost a closet he was in, devoid of any amenities. And there was a square hanging on the wall. It wasn't a painting, and so what was it for?

And he didn't have any clothes. Actually, he did, but they were all from his old world, and Willson detested standing out in public. Generally, he opted to dress as inconspicuously as possible

He spent half the night thinking about who was worse: the Death Bringers or this count. But one way or another, now he had to fulfill the contract. If not for one small "but". He had to slip out of here and escape, but right now Willson had nothing with which to fashion artifacts. What remained were just small reserves with which to buy off the count. And what was going to happen next was anybody's guess. Maybe it was crazy of him to freak out like that and request the ideal laboratory. Only the Order of Artifactors possessed something roughly like what he'd ask for, but inferior in quality. But it was the count's fault for telling him to make up a list of demands, so let him deal with it. What a shame that he'd only asked for a single masseuse instead of two.

Gradually, Willson's mood began to improve.

Thinking about it, he realized that things weren't all that bad. At worst, he'd have to work, but he loved his work. And how long would it take the count to build him a tower? Half a year? A year? Even if for now the count gave him another room, it would take at least a month and a half for him to equip it. So, whatever the case he'd just rest up here in peace while Mira dealt with the Order of Death. Thinking thusly, Willson finally drifted into a luscious sleep.

And the next morning, upon awakening, he headed out for a run. He again remembered that he needed normal clothes, but for now he had to make do with what he had, at least until he asked the count for new threads. But at the door he ran into a maid. She was, in fact, a most attractive, pretty girl. Such charming young women were extremely rare in his world. He actually thought that his sister was the only truly beautiful woman in their kingdom.

"Sir, may I offer you some breakfast?" she asked with a smile, throwing Willson into confusion for a couple of seconds. He was no longer used to having servants since moving from the capital to the hinterlands long ago now. "Or perhaps just some coffee?"

"What is coffee?" he asked.

"I was warned that you might not know," the girl smiled again. "Follow me, and I'll show you around."

Willson had no reason not to do just that, his run now forgotten. So he trailed after the maid,

and after they made their way through a few cor-
ridors, she led him to the dining room. And before
he knew it, he happily took a sip of the aromatic
drink.

It was only half an hour later that he recalled
that he had been running every morning for
twenty years now. And he didn't want to stop the
tradition now, and so after consuming his third
cup, he stood up and asked to be shown out.

And once out the door, he was a little surprised.

"Sorry, but I don't recall that tower over there.
Is it new?" He was looking at a huge extension to
the castle. In fact, the tower was taller than the
main building, so it was impossible to miss. Moreover, it looked suspiciously like the one he had recently drawn on paper.

"Yes, of course it's new. Last night the es-
teemed mages built it. It is beautiful, is it not?" The
girl gazed in admiration at the tower. It was even
better than the one Willson had drawn.

And now, looking at it, he was stupefied.

"Mages?" he asked. "What mages?"

"Didn't you know? Count Bulatov has three
earth mages in his service!" said the maid proudly,
straightening her shoulders while the Artifactor
wilted a little.

"Really, what rank are they?"

"Oh, I have no inkling," the girl said, waving
dismissively. "Some kind of Magisters or Junior
Magisters like they have over there. Something like
that..."

"Magisters..." whispered Willson, his head spinning. Fortunately, the maid grabbed his arm before he collapsed. "You'll forgive me, but it's very interesting how it is that you, a maid, know so much. Is your count that stupid? Isn't he afraid that someone will talk? Then he'll be finished."

"Don't you know?" the girl was even more surprised. "The people who work here for Count Bulatov would never talk about him to others. Never!"

"Oh, Willie! You're awake!" he heard the familiar voice at his back, and turned pale. "Congratulations! The tower is ready! All we have to do now is install the equipment and furnishings."

"Well, that's no small matter," Willson turned to Mikhail. "How long will that take? Three or four weeks?"

"No, of course not! All will be ready for you the day after tomorrow, and then you can get right to work." said the count with a broad smile. "Listen, you look kind of pale today. Do you want me to take a look at you?"

CHAPTER 2

I ENJOYED SEEING WILLSON's reaction. He was such a cad, really, to expect a little vacation while we put up his tower, and he was astonished at how swiftly it went up.

Solid Earthbenders are rather rare in his world, too. That is why all I had now on staff was three thus far. Too bad, really, that the lord who'd provided me with my three couldn't find others.

After greeting Willson, who seemed to have forgotten about his plans to run, I proceeded to my study. All night I'd had to help the mages by providing them energy, and thus, I myself did not get any rest. But when did anyone care?

I'd gone out there just to offer my help. In the end, the mages were tired, but happy, and they eagerly showed off the new tower, telling me about every little detail, and assuring me that the tower was virtually indestructible. Even if the castle fell, the tower would remain standing. To bring this about, I had to expend a lot of valuable strengthening crystals, but at least Toren didn't have to use his black diamond. He said it would be too much. By the way, he was in charge of the fortification system; his colleagues readily delegated this task to him.

In the end, the tower was far better than what Willson expected. He had no idea what we could do, and so he failed to request any embellishments, such as interior design work or adornments on the facade. Of course, Ludwig insisted on adding his decorative touches. Thus, the color of the tower matched the color of the castle. And they did a great job on other stylish elements.

While Ludwig was busy with the interior and exterior of the tower, Giovanni dug passages underground. There were seven stories about ground, and six more subterranean floors. These would in part comprise storehouses equipped with freight elevators. To this end, the mages created shafts, and large garage doors, all according to design. This, despite never having seen service elevators and such. Magic functions differently from straight up engineering.

Now, from afar, the castle looked as if a massive tower had been added to it. It was as if attached to the castle, or else, vice versa, the castle was attached to the tower. It was, in the end, a huge edifice.

Really, it was a little strange. Now, the castle

looked rather miserable, small and scary, although before it didn't. We'd just have to finish building it up, too. But this, too, required monumental amounts of building materials.

Not just stone, either. For constructing edifices, more than rock was needed, after all. Wood, metals, and much more were required. And then, whatever was built also required furnishings of some sort. Generally speaking, that's why Georgy was always busy. Not the he minded. In fact, he relished doing a great job.

For example, there were stores that sold building materials for the masses. Such enterprises weren't usually run by aristocrats, but by wealthy peasants or merchants. But the wealthy commoners usually had patrons, those being aristocrats. Thus, at present, I couldn't shop at such places.

In general, I noticed that in this city, the nobility always took a cut out of any more or less successful business. I hadn't yet examined how this had come to be, but there had to be a reason for it. If they didn't get a share in the venture, the aristocrats would no doubt do what they could to undermine these enterprises. It was, in effect, officially sanctioned corruption of the worst sort.

I found Victoria and asked around about the Necromancer. After all, two days had already passed, and he should have come back by now. I really didn't feel like hunting him down.

"No, he's not back," shrugged Victoria. She didn't seem to be too concerned about him, saying

"I still have plenty of his materials to study. He wrote up several lessons for me, and I'm learning a lot of new techniques."

"I'd like to see them," I said, curious now, and sat down beside her to read a small handwritten book. I love stuff like this, little booklets containing specific spells or segments on magical techniques. Everything was concise and to the point.

And indeed, I'd found a pretty good Necromancer. He had a novel approach to the craft, and clearly knew how to create new spells on his own. To do this, he had to know how his native energy worked.

And this is what he was teaching Vika to do. She had never used magic before. Although this was not surprising, because in this world people used only their Gift, fundamentally ignoring magic. Although one could say the Gift was magic.

In fact, if one had a Gift, they could perform magic, especially if it involved their Gift. In the other world, for example, only warriors used just their Gift, although many who were fortunate enough to be born with an element would end up studying the art of Sorcery. It is a difficult science, and required complete dedication and lifelong study. But it was worth it...

But, yes, there were lazy people, even there. There were those who, even though they were gifted with an element, opted only to serve as warriors rather than focus on developing any knowledge of magic. Even so, such types were strong warriors who could fully use their Gift in battle.

It was, actually, all rather complicated. In my opinion it was more difficult to use one's Gift in long-range attacks. For example, those with the Gift of Flame could create fireballs without using any spells. But this would cost them in terms of the power they generated.

"Thank you so much for providing me a teacher," said Victoria, setting the spell book aside and looking into my eyes. "My father always tried to find someone who could teach me. Even when it all started to go downhill for our Family, he never stopped trying, although in vain. And, I just wanted you to know that only now do I understand how all of my past knowledge pales in comparison to what I'm learning from Belmore."

"But of course, Vika," I smiled. "You were trained to wield the Gift, not magic." She only recently learned that these concepts, although similar, were still distinctly different. "If only you knew the diversity in the types of magic in the world..." I shook my head, thinking about it. It's true what they say: everyone has their own magic. Any mage who'd developed their powers could invent their own type of magic, tailored specifically for him.

"For example, look at this," I said. I took paper and a pen, and drew several magical ligatures, a circle, and linked it all with seals of strength, conductivity and magical saturation. Because I drew all of this with a pen rather than using my own energy, the spell wasn't activated, and so no worries.

"What is that?" Victoria looked in fascination at the perfectly constructed complex structure that made up the magical circle. "This is..."

"Yes, I can create this using vital energy," I smiled. "Actually, before I could. Now, this type of thing could kill me," I sighed, realizing how constrained I was right now because of my weak body. "You see, like you, I have to develop myself from the ground up."

I'd drawn a Dark Worm. This spell belongs to the school of Reverse Healers, which specializes mainly in assassinations. Adherents of this school are intimately acquainted with all human systems, and by creating such a worm they can easily manipulate someone, directing the magical creature to attack only the most vulnerable points. Usually this creature simply climbs into a person and destroys his nervous system from the inside.

"By the way, Necromancers, too, can have a lot of fun. I alone know about fifty different schools. And before I found the right one for you, I had to go through as many as ten of these Necromancers — yes, I had to wander around a lot. But it was worth it. What I like about Belmore is that he doesn't like the stench of corpses, which is why his magic creates skeletons, not rotten zombies."

Vika and I sat and talked a little more. I told her about the various Necromancers I'd known in my past world. I told her one story about an old friend that made us both laugh. He was a very strong Necromancer who wasn't prone to being a psychopath, unlike others. He loved music very much, and therefore created a dead orchestra especially for himself. I remembered how people ran away in fear when the dead elephant trumpeter began his part. But I must say, their music was quite good. And the skeleton choir also had their own special sound. Although, to be honest, this entire choir relied heavily on their soloist Lich.

"Listen, doesn't it seem like this lull in attacks we're in is kind of suspicious?" Vika suddenly remembered that we were surrounded by enemies. Literally, all of our neighbors.

"Why do you think we're in a lull?" I asked. "It's only that our partner in business is helping me out a little with a certain adversary," I shrugged. For whatever reason, the duke didn't even mention it to me. All he did was demolish my enemies, and no big deal. "Pigeon intelligence reported that Konakov stopped Dushilin's army not far from his borders. And in so doing, the duke expanded his landholdings," I chuckled. Naturally, one expected compensation after such battles.

"I didn't realize that the pigeons flew over his lands," meaning that she felt that they surely already had enough to keep track of. Especially as we faced no threats from the duke, so why waste Kooky's time?

"They fly where they will. The duke is a great guy, kind and considerate. Not to his enemies, of course, but in general, yes. And on the roof of his mansion is a dovecote. Kooky has recruited twelve pigeons from there," I shrugged, stealing a piece of candy Vika had tucked away, to her displeasure.

"That's not mine, by the way. It was just lying around..."

"Right, in your drawer here," I grinned. "Do you really think that, just because I'm a Healer you don't have to worry about gaining a few pounds?"

"Let's talk about the pigeons. Were you serious just now? Or joking?" Apparently Vika was intrigued at learning that Kooky had been recruiting an entire contingent of pigeons. Or was she alarmed at hearing this?

"Who knows... Maybe I was joking...," I said thoughtfully.

But no, because, in fact, the network of pigeon intelligence agents was growing by the day. But there was no need for everyone to know about this. So, after talking a little more with Victoria, I went about my business. Or rather, rest. And so as not to waste time, I turned on the TV and sprawled out on the sofa. News in this world was always interesting. And the format itself, when you can sit at home and watch what was happening in this country and the world, was very convenient. Only little by little doubts began to creep in that not everything shown via this medium was as it seemed. They were great at lying, such that you really wanted to believe them. At first, I took everything said on TV at face value, but now... In any case, this was an interesting part of my responsibilities. True, there wasn't anything new in the news today. It was the same old same old, meaning the ongoing war, with the assistance we were providing to our allies, and portals opening up all over the country, with some journalists upset that neighboring countries didn't have many portals.

What was their problem? The portals were great! It was how the people of this world could grow stronger! The way to develop one's Gift was to fight these offworlders. Did no one understand this? True, it wasn't easy, what with having to spend on weapons, as well as guardsmen and troops.

Anyway, as I watched the news, Timothy walked in. I could always make time for him, because he was like this invisible man who only showed up when absolutely necessary. And he performed his duties in exemplary fashion. Really, I'd selected the perfect position for him, and he was providing far more benefit by managing our support structure and warehouses than he could by piloting a chopper.

"Ahem..." he cleared his throat, not daring to start a conversation. He shifted from foot to foot for a couple of seconds, but then he finally spoke. "Mikhail, here's the thing. It's high time that I brought something up." I nodded at him to continue. "Do you remember my granddaughter?"

"How could I forget her?" I smiled, because it was through her that I'd met Timothy. "She loves cake and her business."

"That's an understatement," Timothy laughed. "But I wanted to ask, can I bring her here to the castle? Before, we decided it was too dangerous, but now the situation has changed."

"I can't see why not," I shrugged. In fact, we

could have brought her here sooner, but due to all I had going on, I forgot all about little Marina.

Timothy had found a good temporary home for her. Some kind of imperial boarding school for girls, and judging by the description, one of the best in this region. Excellent teachers, good living conditions, quality food, care, safety. What more could she need? Well, that would be a close relative, that being her grandfather.

"So when can we pick her up?" — the wrinkles on the old face smoothed out with a smile, and his eyes sparkled with joy.

"Well, how about right now?" I got up from the sofa and threw on a light jacket. I had nothing urgent to attend to right then, so why not go out and about?

"You don't have to do it, Mikhail," Timothy protested. "You have enough other worries. I'll pick her up myself and bring her here."

"Oh, calm down," I waved my hand. "But you take the lead."

Timothy had arranged for transportation in advance, and so a SUV was ready to go right outside the castle. But along the way I called Chernomor, and we took a convoy of sorts along with us. This included a bus with guards behind us, and also a van.

"Why do we need the van?" asked Timothy, and I chuckled.

"Well, I can't have a Combat Suit traveling by bus, can I?"

Hearing this, Timothy tensed up. He must

think that since I was bringing so many guards and such along I must be expecting an attack. So all along the way he kept stealing glances at me, while I just sat there staring out the window.

No amount of security was too much. Especially when it concerns not me personally, but my people. I expected that they all knew by now that I wasn't an easy target. And, in fact, anyone who tried to again rip me to shreds with bullets from heavy machine guns was in for a big surprise. You see, I knew full well how to take mistakes into account, and therefore I had a couple of aces up my sleeve for any similar attempt on my life.

And Timothy was definitely on my team. I didn't for a minute question either his loyalty, or his value to me. He flew under the radar a lot, but that was a plus. And he dealt with masses of issues put forth by our staff, all on his own. Requests from peasants, from the guards, and, the icing on the cake was that all the trophies we collected also ended up on his table. And he'd enter it all into the database and distribute everything among the storehouses and to whomever could best use them. Best of all, I had nothing to do with any of this. I didn't even have to think about it. Timothy even had access to our treasury, and he could, if necessary, task Georgy with picking up this or that, all without wasting my time.

In short, Timothy was an invisible, but integral cog in the huge, rattling, dangerous structure that made up the Bulatov Family. And I'm sure that during his past military service he was not a pilot, but a combat hamster. Only now, looking at the bags under his eyes and his extremely tired demeanor, I understood that he needed help. The number of organizational issues was only growing, with more to deal with at the warehouses, and it was all getting to be too much for just Timothy to handle.

So where could I find help for him? I had to locate more loyal people. Okay, I'd have Georgy help me. I had no idea where he found so many wounded and disadvantaged. But in any case, that is who ended up serving the Family the best.

Lost in my thoughts, we arrived at the boarding school before I knew it. The complex of buildings was surrounded by a three-meter stone wall, with wide gates and a sign up above:

B.A.L.L.S: Bodana's Academy for Little Ladies

"BALLS?" I said, turning to Timothy. "Are you sure this place is for girls?"

"No, not BALLS, but B-A-L-L-S. That's Bodana's Academy for Little Ladies. Countess Bodana Ivanova is the philanthropist behind this establishment," said Timothy.

Right. B.A.L.L.S. The acronyms used for the institutions in this world never ceased to surprise me.

But in fact, except for the name, there was nothing wrong with the place. It was, indeed, an educational institution for girls. It looked rather strict, but not like a prison; rather, it was clearly a place for children. What immediately caught my eye was the staff. They all wore pink knitted hats, although this wasn't the case for the other girls. In another couple of weeks, though, Marina would make sure none were without one of her knitted creations.

"Count Bulatov," said a woman of about forty in a pink hat with a pompom, who gave me a little bow. "Timothy Dmitrievich," she simply nodded his way, "Marina is, well...You can see for yourself."

At first I was surprised that the woman led us to the basement. I even began to wonder if I might have to aggravate her pancreatitis; keeping the girl in a dark, damp room would be harmful to the woman's health. In fact, anyone who sought to harm any of my people would automatically harm their own self. But my concerns were, in the end, unfounded.

"I'm not surprised," Timothy laughed, and I slapped myself on the forehead. And then I rested my hand briefly on the poor teacher's shoulder and relieved her of several maladies at once. "Marina! Stop it now! No more exploiting the other children!" exclaimed Timothy, causing the little girl to jump up in surprise.

Ah, yes. Apparently Marina had occupied the basement all on her own. And she'd brought almost all of the others in the school down here. Now thirty exhausted girls, instead of playing and resting, were intensively knitting pink hats. And judging by the boxes in the corner, production was in full swing.

"Grandpa!" she squealed, running to hug

him. "Uncle Misha!" she hugged me right after hugging her grandfather. Sighs of relief were heard all around. Slave labor was over..."Hey, don't stop now!" Marina turned to them and again they picked up their knitting.

I even felt sorry for them. Especially for the staff of the boarding school. What about the director? I saw her in a strict black dress. Wearing a pink hat. What was remarkable is that she bought it. Marina never forced anyone to take her hats for free; rather, she sold them.

"It suits you very well," I smiled, in response to which the woman broke into a smile.

"Now they're part of our uniforms. Marina promised to diversify production to include other colors for the hats," she said, and I saw that, although seemingly stern, she actually was quite warm with the girls under her charge. Okay, she, too, deserved free treatment.

We quickly dealt with the paperwork, but when it came to settling the bill, I had a little fight with Timothy. This place wasn't cheap, even though it was built for the children of commoners. In this case, for very wealthy commoners.

Timothy intended to pay for it himself, because, after all, he earned a good salary from me. But I flatly refused and swiftly paid the bill. After all, it was because I had been unable to ensure her safety that Marina had to live here to start with.

And thirty minutes later our motorcade had already left the boarding school, and we traveled back to the castle without incident. And then,

Timothy took his granddaughter to her room. I'd already given him an entire apartment, and he'd prepared one of the rooms for Marina. He'd done a nice job of furnishing it for his granddaughter, and even thought to pick up everything she needed for her "business." He'd built the bed and dresser, desk and so on, and all we needed to purchase was the mattress. Impressive.

After ensuring that they had everything they needed, I left them to settle in.

* * *

A few hours later
Entrance gate to the castle

"Well, what about that kidnapping?" They called me as soon as they noticed the Necromancer. He was just wandering along the road with some guy. The man was carrying his bags and trudging behind him. I sallied forth to meet him. And all I could say was that Belmore looked like he was feeling just fine.

"Ex-cel-lent!" he exclaimed. "It couldn't be better! Listen, could you have them kidnap me at least once a week?"

Right. Strangely, I wasn't even surprised. This is what I expected from him. Belmore was a highly unusual person who knew how to make the most out of whatever random situation he was in.

"Aha!" the mage smiled. "Did you know that you have a cult in your city that for seventy years already has been conducting sacrifices? My impression is the victims are animals."

"Really?" I would never have thought that there was something like that going on in this world.

"Well, there was such a cult, yes..." Belmore hesitated, and then he laughed. "And so this cult....they'd do these sacrifices because they thought that their deity would give them strength! I haven't laughed so hard in years!" And he doubled over in laughter as he remembered the somber faces of these priests in some cult.

"Okay, calm down now," I said, worried that he'd choke on his laughter.

"In short," Belmore exhaled, catching his breath. "First, I was kidnapped by some aristocrat's people."

"Right, I guessed as much," I nodded. In fact, I already knew this. "And you couldn't arrange to be ransomed?"

"Well, you yourself told me not to open my mouth, so I sat there in silence," he shrugged. "Moreover, I knew that Vika still had plenty of study materials, and you urged me to get to know this world. And that's what I did! I stayed put, and I have to say that they were smart guys, those thugs. They sold me almost immediately."

"Sold you?" I never heard of such a thing...although, why not? When I landed in this world, I found myself in a dungeon. Most likely the body I now inhabited had been sold to those evil monks.

"Aha!" nodded Belmore. "They kept trying to

assess my rank, and I summoned the weak un-
dead so as not to scare them," and he sighed sadly.
"But the morons were anyway frightened out of
their wits, screaming and shooting off their guns.
And one snuck up from behind me and slapped
some strange shackles on my hands. They got me,
in effect. These shackles suppress the Gift."

"So I'm assuming that you were playing along
with them a little right?" I chuckled, and Belmore
nodded.

"Yes, a little. Why not? I wanted to see what
they planned on doing next! But then, they
blocked my Gift, completely neutralized me, and
so they could do whatever they wanted!" Belmore
threw up his hands.

"Well, they had no idea that the Gift of Death
cannot be blocked completely, right?" I raised an
eyebrow, and the Necromancer smiled.

"I put on a good show, hissing, collapsing
onto the floor, convulsing. I saw a movie here
where the Necromancers all acted like that," he
chuckled, thinking about it. "By then, the gang of
thugs was thrilled that they'd found a strong Necromancer. They expected to fetch a considerable
sum for me."

Moreover, Belmore learned that all this was
run by a certain impoverished aristocrat. His gang
engaged primarily in petty criminal activities,
while he shielded them from the attention of the
authorities. In short, they scraped by as best as
they could.

It didn't take them long to find a buyer for the

Necromancer. Within a couple of hours, several people arrived dressed in black robes with an insignia depicting some strange purple hieroglyphs. Actually, this is where the deal ended. They handed over the money, received Belmore and took him to a vacant lot.

"Dropouts... Just dropouts..." the Necromancer shook his head, remembering the priests in that cult. "Yes, sniveling little fools"

"What made them such losers?" Really, I fully understood that this world didn't have proper mages, as such, but I wanted to know what struck the Necromancer as so bad. And I also wondered who this guy with Belmore was.

"What did you call yourself there?" the Necromancer turned and nodded to the fellow.

"The Masters of Death," he frowned.

"I'm telling you, idiots," Belmore spread his hands. "So they wanted to sacrifice me. For seventy years now they'd been slaughtering goats, and then they suddenly thought they could upgrade to a Magister of Necromancy. They thought they'd matured enough for this."

"To tell you the truth, you're overwhelming me a little," I said, shaking my head. This was a rather long story. "Why don't you write up a little report about your adventures, and I'll show up there with the guards and destroy everything there. Deal?"

"Ah, but there's nothing left there now," Belmore sighed.

Well, that was rather a surprise. It was one

thing for me, a Healer, to kill practitioners of necromancy. Plenty of people think that doing so was our reason for existence, even. And although that's not the case, I was surprised that Belmore would kill his own kind, even if tangentially so, and I told him as much.

But Belmore was offended by this. He immediately shouted that their school of magic had nothing to do with his, that they were all mediocrities and stupid, and that they had no magic at all. And the other lot was comprised of nothing but slave traders. He should have killed them right away, although they'd planned on selling Belmore to buyers abroad.

"I thought you wanted to see the world. I'm surprised you turned down the opportunity," and by this I meant that he instead killed them all.

"Yes, I do want to," he said. "Truly. But it would have been too difficult to return from there. I guess I could always create a bone dragon or a necro-wyvern, but....By the way, I wanted to ask you. Why are there no dragons here? Not even any dragon bones. It's a shame."

"So true, you can't even imagine," I sighed along with him. "But we have other options. You can buy a ticket and fly on a plane. As a last resort, you can take a train or ship; they're more reliable."

"I see...." Belmore scratched the back of his head. "But you know, I can create a bone airship or a dead horse. You see, I'm no longer used to getting around by foot. And I don't know how to buy tickets," he threw up his hands. "In fact, while they were reselling me and trying to sacrifice me, I learned a lot and came away with plenty of food for thought. And while I admit I didn't really want to conclude a contract with you, now, I'm grateful. This world is interesting, colorful, and I'm certain I'll relish the wealth of impressions that await me! I even picked up an assistant. Right, Edward?"

"Right, right, Master!" bowed the man.

"Yes, I wanted to ask. Why did you bring him here? Or have you gone completely crazy in your dotage?" I nodded at the young man, and saw then how the veins on his forehead started throbbing.

"How dare you speak like that to my master, a great and powerful lord!?" he was almost yelling as he began to throw off the bags he was lugging. He looked like he was ready to charge at me for some hand-to-hand action.

"Hey!" Belmore restrained Edward, gripping his shoulder. "Calm down, Edward. Hush, now... Down boy!" The kid was still breathing quickly and looking at me with undisguised hostility.

"But he insulted you!" he yelled, but Belmore just smiled.

"Would you like me to give you some drops? Sedatives? Or maybe hug you with necro-energy? Would you like that?" And a cloud of darkness escaped from the Necromancer's body and enveloped the guy. Right away he calmed down, and started breathing more evenly. "As your friend who is now a skeleton said, nerve cells do not regenerate. This person in front of you can restore them, and even grow new ones in the most unexpected places."

"So that makes him a Heal..." Eddie started sputtering, but again Belmore shushed him.

"This Healer could rip your head off. He could shrink it to the size of a grape, squeeze it with his fingers, and make it burst apart! Not just your head, but mine, too," Belmore chuckled.

"Hmmm....not a bad idea," I mused, while Eddie shuddered.

Just then, the two wolves bounded out onto the veranda. They'd grown fond of the Necromancer and wanted to greet him. Pouncing on him, they began licking him, and all he could do was grapple with them and treat them to clots of death energy.

"Wow....Master, your might is evident!" Eddie was ready to fall to his knees. "Your creations are beautiful!"

"What? No, this duo isn't mine," Belmore waved him off. "They belong to my student..."

* * *

Oh, how I don't like it when people wake me up. And when the sounds of explosions bring me out of a meditation, I hate it three times over. So now, right in the middle of the night, there was a roar, flashes began to flicker outside the window, after which a siren howled. Honestly, I had no idea we even had a siren. In any case, the attack came unexpectedly, and I soon understood why intelligence failed to foresee it.

Explosions rumbled outside the windows of

the castle, the floor under my feet shook and was covered in cracks, but so far nothing was caving in. But when I ran outside, I saw four machines hovering in the sky, either airplanes or helicopters. They were like that jet-like flyer Konakov sent for me when he thought that his granddaughter was getting worse. A strange chopper plane that looked like an airplane, but which could also hover in the air while firing rockets and shells at my castle!

Now four of them at once showered Willson's tower with a hail of missiles. The tower looked newer and better than the castle itself, which is why they chose to attack it. Yes, there was a reason I asked the mages to make the tower more beautiful and taller. I wanted it to be more eye-catching.

I even breathed a sigh of relief, realizing that there were idiots at the controls of the attack planes. They'd immediately started shooting at what caught their eye the most. But this particular tower was the strongest building on my estate. Simple missiles could not demolish it; and it didn't even have cracks on its edifice, and no damage whatsoever to the load-bearing parts of the structure. Meanwhile, they had yet to attack the actual castle. Just the same, all of the castle's windows were now broken. What a hassle down the road, having to buy new windows.

Quite quickly, guards poured out into the courtyard. Some began to fire at the planes with hand-held rocket launchers, others simply fired off their heavy machine guns. But no, the planes turned out to be too powerful for conventional weapons, but the Earthbenders soon woke up. One was dead drunk, while, for some reason, the other two were propping him up to keep him from falling, and the three of them commenced creating magic. They almost instantly covered all the buildings with stone shields with protuberances that neutralized the missiles by causing them to explode prematurely, before they could penetrate the shield. But this wasn't all.

Belmore ran outside in black boxer shorts adorned with white skulls. Should any of the pilots laugh at the sight, it would be futile, because the Magister of Necromancy waved his hands and a black whirlwind swirled above him, which spiraled towards one of the planes. The spell was more of a distraction, and it forced the war machines to disperse.

Then the Necromancer, having again cast some kind of spell, sent forth a whole flock of bone birds. Dead creatures crawled straight out of the ground. They assembled on the fly from the fragments of someone's bones and rushed towards the planes. There they flung themselves into the cockpit windows, rattled small knuckles on the armored body, tried to rip out all sorts of sensors, and tear off the missiles attached to the bottom. In general, they caused a lot of trouble, and most importantly, they further distracted the enemy.

Well done, of course. Well done everyone! But I felt a little put out at everyone around me doing something while I just stood there. What could I do, though? Heal the castle? Glue something over some cracks, or apply a salve? Okay, good thing I was no ordinary Healer.

I proceeded to divest myself of much of my blood, turning pale as a ghost. My head began to spin, my ears began to buzz, and sticky cold sweat broke out on my skin. I could easily pass out from such a blood loss, but I'd prepared in advance.

And then, a crystalline blood stake appeared in the red flash of a complex blood rune. It was three meters long, with a tip that shimmered from the energy overwhelming it. The bloody stake rushed into flight as if from a tank cannon. In a flash, the plane closest to me was pierced, then torn into small pieces. Yes, that's the type of Healer I am, that's right.

But that was a one-time party trick. I needed to recover now, or else find the vampire blood sphere, but I forgot where I'd left it.

One attack plane down, now, in a fiery blast, a second one shuddered from powerful blows. The Suits had entered the battle, and now, working together, they were trying to dismantle one of the planes.

But it was an impressive combat flyer, and a series of gun-barrels popped out of the hull. The pilot fired them at the Suits, forcing them to engage in maneuvering action. However, they weren't about to retreat. The Necromancer's bone birds started piling onto the gun barrels and covering the camera lenses, sabotaging the electronics. At that point, the pilots turned around and started picking up speed to fly off.

What, retreating already?

"Kooky!" I called my feathered scout, who was perched in his bird spa looking down at the combat planes with contempt.

"*Coo!*" he flew down to me.

"Take that plane down!" I pointed to one that had been seriously dented. The Suits had inflicted some damage on it. "Keep an eye on the others."

Kooky looked at me. Then he looked at the huge planes flying off. He then made a show of looking at his own frail form, and then gazed at me with a bewildered look.

"*Coo?*" he asked, waving his wing over his torso. "*Coo-coooo-coo?*"

"Oh, it's the same old story!" I didn't accept his excuses. "Just get inside it somehow and crap on everything in there." I thought he'd know what to do by now.

"*Coo-coooo-coo!*" Kooky was offended now. He said he didn't want to take a dump right now.

"Oh, that's not a problem," I smiled and stroked him on the head, giving him a shot of vital energy. "You have a minute to get it done. By then you'll have to. Do you feel it?"

"*Coo!*" he looked a little bloated now, his eyes bulging out. Then he took off, heading for the plane.

Gradually the sounds of the aircraft's engines died down, and all that remained was a red glow in the distance. That mean Kooky wasn't suffering from constipation. Well done, feathered one. Now, hopefully, he'll catch up with the two other combat aircraft.

But now that it was quiet, I could hear the groans and screams of the wounded. In the thick of the fighting I didn't have time for them, although I knew that no one's heart had stopped. But anyway, it was no problem for me to treat my wounded men.

Candidly, I'd expected action from the enemy, but I did not expect it to be so serious. Who used combat aircraft just to destroy an already damaged castle?

"Chernomor!" I called my commander of the guard. The castle got hit hard, but the barrier created by the Earthbenders had contained most of the fragments from the explosions. "Take all of the wounded to the infirmary! Report to me on the heavily wounded! I'll take care of them myself," I said, and then issued another order. "And prepare for war. Tomorrow we'll march on Snegireva."

"Do you think she was behind this?" asked Chernomor, gritting his teeth.

"No, not necessarily...She's just first in line. And after we're done with her, we'll go after the others."

CHAPTER 3

THE CASTLE, WHICH HAD BEEN in full combat readiness before, was naturally seething. We'd recently seen a significant increase in the number of guards in service to the Bulatov Family. Indeed, in addition to the recruits, we now had thirty more former fighters from the Imperial army. They weren't super star fighters, but they all had real combat experience, and that was worth a lot. We also had our fifty veterans. These guys continued to show themselves in their full glory. Among them were specialists, including snipers, sappers, reconnaissance officers, and even a group comprised of special forces and tank crews. The two pilots were of no use today, but something tells me that before too long they'd be hijacking those two combat planes that got away. And what that meant was that next time, my two ace pilots would be powering them against future enemy aircraft. Maybe we'd even pick up another one as a trophy, and then, if things really got hot, we could have Timothy fly it.

In any case, right now we had other matters to deal with.

Kooky managed to take out one of the planes and was now struggling to catch up with the other two. They'd really picked up speed, but my scout had some tricks up his sleeve. He was able to flap his wings faster than the turning of the helicopter-styled propellers on the planes.

"Report on the wounded!" a soldier shouted, pulling me out of my thoughts. He'd been addressing Chernomor, but I heard him, too. "Two killed, forty-two wounded, fifteen of them seriously. They were taken to the infirmary, and help is already being provided."

Two dead? Less than a minute had passed, why was he so sure they were already dead? Okay, not on my shift anyway.

"Lead me to the dead!" I barked at the fighter, and he swiftly led me towards the tower.

The sentries guarding it had been the first to come under massive fire. The first missile exploded near them before they could scream. Imbuing my hands with a shock dose of life-giving force, I drove the bright green flickering sphere of healing right into each of the inert forms.

Yes, they had died. But what mattered was that their brains were still intact. What that meant was that there was something remaining inside.

Cardiac arrest, respiratory arrest — none of that was the end, and it was too early to call for the Necromancer, although, theoretically one could do that. But if the Necromancer worked on a body in this state, the death energy would simply snuff out any remaining life more swiftly, in seconds.

I had to slam several more spheres of life into the two fallen sentries before one of them suddenly inhaled some air into his lungs with a loud wheeze. It took longer for me to bring the second one back. I forced his heart to beat, oxygenated his blood, but he'd suffered damage to his skull, and I had to deal with that first.

Yes, I'd rushed in treating him. But what can I say? Now the poor guy, well, he'd be a little on the slow side and also have to deal with a speech impediment, but he'd survive. Maybe later, after he felt stronger and was fully back on his feet I could fix the other stuff. Unless it slipped my mind, of course.

Chernomor was yelling something into the radio in a booming bass voice, soldiers were rushing around, equipment was roaring, and I rushed straight to the infirmary. The seriously wounded may die without my help, for Roman was still too weak. Along the way I saw a lot of blast craters. Yes, they'd fallen for it, the idiots. The tower and the fake fuel stations.

We'd stationed them not far from the wall, and the enemy wasted a lot of missiles on them. I wondered how they felt when, after firing five rockets at them, they failed to produce an explosion?

Even when the fuel tanker parked nearby was torn to pieces, all that spilled out of it was water, that, in fact, put out the fire. Yes, a clever ruse, if I do say so myself. We could do more of the same, say, plant explosives in water barrels.

As I rushed about, I noticed Vika. I hadn't neglected her, and even had Kooky assign one of the pigeons on his team to keep track of her. Should anything be amiss with the countess, the bird was to immediately report to me. But all was fine. The girl, not wanting to remain on the sidelines, had also participated in the defense of the castle. She couldn't do much, but she managed to fire a couple of shots using an attack spell she had recently learned. She also drew several protective circles, scattering some bones in them. But these were most likely to be used should the planes land.

In general, well done. She was markedly upping her skill set thanks to her hard work and focus. But Belmore did not share my views. He was, in fact, berating his student, saying that her attacks were too weak, and she'd failed to secure her persona safety. This, although Vika was wearing a powerful protective artifact that would protect her even from two direct missile hits. But I did agree with Belmore that you'd best not rely too heavily on artifacts.

I also checked on the earth mages. They'd given it their all that night, and although this was their day off, right away they set about on reconstruction work. At least Ludwig and Giovanni were up to it. Toren was another story. He'd received a serious wound, and his life was now seeping out of him. He overworked himself while fighting off attacks. Moreover, not knowing how rockets worked, he'd exposed himself to an explosion. But it wasn't easy killing a mage, and although Toren had numerous fragments in his body, he didn't lose consciousness, and, moreover, he underwent the full gamut of the most vivid sensations. Actually, I didn't bother anesthetizing him, and just injected energy into him. It was a faster fix this way, and one he'd remember better.

Yes, he now knew not to stand in the way of missiles. Of course he merited treating, though. I needed all of the mages on my staff, now more than ever.

It took me half an hour to completely treat the wounded. For cases such as this, I always kept ready-made spells in my energy pocket. In the end, ten men were immediately back on their feet, and in another couple of hours five others would be done healing. I left the rest to Roman; their lives were not in danger. Moreover, these were servants. They could wait until morning, but I needed the guards right now.

"Mikhail!" Chernomor called me over once I stepped out of the infirmary.

I learned from one of the pigeons that a meeting had been held during my absence. Kooky wasn't back yet, and I didn't expect to see him anytime soon, but he'd trained his subordinates well to carry out work in his absence.

One had flown into the dining room, and

seeing everyone gathered there, Chernomor spread out a map of adjacent territories on the table. Victoria, Chernomor, Timothy and the two mages were in a heated argument over where the aircraft had come from and the subsequent destination of the planes. They were also debating how to carry out an attack on Snegireva's lands.

"All of our men are stationed on the borders. We're ready for action. But we should wait until the backup artillery arrives," said Chernomor.

That's right. Not just our men had suffered wounds, but our equipment was also hit in the recent attack. This included armored cars that were first responders, and also our wheeled tank. The thing is, we did not yet have an underground hangar, and so our military hardware was stored here and there, for example, in nearby villages under camouflage nets in the forest. If not for the Earthbenders, we'd probably end up digging pits in gardens to stash our tanks.

Meanwhile, our fighters were ready for action, and already at the borders. We just needed to give the command, and then they'd swiftly move deep into enemy territory, rolling right over everything in their path. But not yet. The time wasn't right.

"Any theories on who it was?" I asked the others, but they just shook their heads. This included Victoria, Chernomor, Timothy, and also a couple of new commanders from the Imperial troops. We also had one of the Suits in the background monitoring what was happening.

"Until the enemy aircraft headed off in the

wrong direction I was thinking it had to be Kur-chatov," said Chernomor, pointing at a map on which they'd already drawn the flight path. "But nobody saw them fly in. However, we're in the process of reconstructing events from the cameras."

"What are your thoughts about our defense? How did we end up with so many wounded?" I asked. Indeed, not only guards had been hit, but also some of the servants.

"If we had radar, we'd have no wounded at all. But, honestly, I'm impressed at how little damage was inflicted on the tower," said Chernomor. And Timothy jumped in, saying "I was amazed, really! Those planes weren't yesterday's old aircraft. No, only Imperial troops and the very elite are privy to cutting edge technology like that. From what I could tell, those missiles launched at us belong to the Guided Hollow-Charge Shell class. In short..."

"We already know what they are called," Chernomor nodded. "What's your point?"

"What I'm saying is that a couple of such projectiles were enough to totally demolish the tower, razing it to the ground. They could melt solid rock. And then they showered us with guided bombs, but...." Timothy shook his head, "I don't understand, honestly."

'What is it you don't understand, old man?" I couldn't help but ask. Time was short for his musings.

"I don't understand why we weren't blown to hell!"

Hmm... I apologize. If the shells had hit the

castle, it would be a pile of rubble now. But the tower came out of this without a scratch. I guess this was enough to blow away Timothy. He'd thought he knew what shells could demolish a building. Now, he had no idea. And, indeed, it would take a massive amount of explosives to take down the tower. My neighbors may not have that much.

We went on discussing what needed improving, and decided that we had to install at least a rudimentary radar system so that we could get at least a five-minute alert in the event of impending attacks rather than waking up to bombs falling all over the castle. We couldn't take the risk of something like this taking us by surprise again.

Timothy knew a lot about the planes that had attacked us. He went over their specifications and capabilities, and so on. And I had to say, I so wanted one. Truly, really, yes. I couldn't say why it mattered so much, but I had to have one of those aircraft in my fleet. Even if all I did was look at it, it would make me so happy.

But the cost....No way could I buy one. For me, the only way to get my hands on something like one of those planes was to procure it in a challenging, unequal fight. Not that this was unusual; in fact, it was par for the course. The great thing was that I not only didn't have to spend money on buying one, by taking their high-end military hardware as trophies I made them weaker and poorer.

"What is that point marking?" I indicated an

"X" on the map. "Is that where the downed plane fell?" In fact, based on the flight path I assumed so.

"Yes, according to the feathered bastards, that's about right," said Chernomor.

"Then let's go pick up our trophy," I said, surprising the others.

"But..." Vika looked perplexed, first at me, then at the map. "Mikhail, that territory belongs to Valentine..."

Who was Valentine? If only she told me his last name...Oh, right, that was the baron who once tried to claim ownership over our mines.

"Well, if it strikes you as rude, we don't need to seize his lands. Not yet. We'll just take our trophy and bring it home," I shrugged. Nothing could be simpler.

"But what if they don't want us to? Have you considered this?" asked Chernomor, but I was ready for such a probability.

"Why do we have guardsmen, then?" I said with a grin.

I no longer cared about the viscountess. Let her be for now. It could be the baron's turn right now. Why not? As did many of my neighbors, he deserved it. In principle, I could attack whomever, north and south. Wherever I might lead my forces, we'd find enemies.

"Leave a guard at the castle; thirty should suffice. Let them set up in the Artifactor's tower; we know it's strong enough," I finished my orders.

We still had our usual garrison at the

fortress. And our choppers were also on standby. We could bring in reinforcements should the need arise. Meanwhile, I had the remaining troops line up in a column, and head out to the coordinates I'd indicated.

We didn't even attempt subterfuge. Anyway, the baron had to know that the aircraft had crashed on his territory and he would immediately want to scoop up whatever was left intact from it. Yes, I'd heard a crash as it went down, but according to intelligence, the plane itself was in one piece. Maybe the pilot had released his ammo before crashing. Timothy said that this was standard practice, and might have even happened automatically. It was a safeguard to protect both the crew and the hardware, itself.

Indeed, it was the kind of mechanism employed only in state-of-the-art weaponry owned by aristocrats. In contrast, the Empire wanted their damaged aircraft artillery to self-destruct to prevent the enemy from accessing its design, not to mention the data stored in the on-board computers.

While the bulk of the troops were getting ready to go, I took my strongest fighters with me in my fastest vehicles, and went ahead. Should we find ourselves in heavy fighting, the others would show up to cover the rear. Our goal was to hightail it to the crash site, clear the way for our main forces and take up defense positions there. To this end, I took all three Earthbenders with me.

I also left forces to guard the castle. And Vika

was also there to help out. Along with her teacher, who could also ensure Vika's safety, as would her two wolf wraiths. Altogether, this should suffice even if the viscountess was to attempt to seize the opportunity to attack with all of her forces. We, after all, were headed in the exact opposite direction, to the southeast.

Further on the real fun began, with one thing after another. First, we came upon a checkpoint. That's right. We could have circled around it through the forest, but that would have added half an hour to our journey. I told my guys not to hold back. I wanted to give the enemy the opportunity to surrender, but then one of their idiots opened fire without warning. So we proceeded to dismantle the checkpoint using our tank guns.

We then went onward toward the crash site. Meanwhile, Kooky told me about the battle that had unfolded there. As the survivors emerged from the downed plane the baron's forces showed up. That's when a fierce firefight ensued. The baron's forces were greater in number, but the squad of fighters on board the plan was well-trained and well-armed. The battle dragged on and we arrived just in time. Just in time to stop the baron's forces from fully surrounding the plane and putting the squeeze on the defenders of the craft. Luckily, we showed up and attacked them from the rear, hitting them with all guns at once.

Right away the Earthbenders started erecting temporary fortifications for our troops, who then dispersed in trenches and behind walls with embrasures scattered about the field. It was only after we'd secured our position that my phone rang.

"Oh, hi there!" I had to smile. "How are you?"

"Bulatov!" The baron was growling, or was that his way of shouting? At any rate, it was loud enough to blast the speakers out of the phone. "You....you!"

"Yes....I...I. So, how are you doing?" I said, barely restraining my laughter. In response the baron sputtered and screamed some incoherent nonsense.

*   *   *

A few minutes earlier
Baron Grishanov's mansion

"No, send a couple of detachments," the baron shook his head and, after listening to the rest of the reports from the commander of his guard, he hung up.

Now he sat, smiled and looked at the ceiling. What luck! Seemingly out of the blue, a fortune had befallen him! Few could afford a vertical take-off combat plane, and the baron, despite his wealth, was not among them. And according to the report he'd just heard, the aircraft was virtually undamaged. By some miracle, the pilots were able to land the combat vehicle, having first dumped fuel and ammunition into the field. Valentine had yet to determine who owned the plane, but even if some influential owner showed up to claim the prize, at the least Valentine could demand a substantial finder's fee.

Grishanov sent a couple of combat detachments to the crash site, because he was informed that the pilots, along with the fighters on board the craft were showing their teeth and refusing to play nice. He'd send the technicians in after the guards, only when it was safe.

Bz-z-z...

The phone rang and distracted his thoughts about the unexpected windfall.

"Sir!" It was one his officers, which surprised the baron. After all, only his commander was privy to his personal number, and he was only to call on matters of urgency. Officers could call in only the most extreme cases.

But then, Grishanov realized why they were calling him. He could hear the explosions, gunfire, and the roars and screams of his guardsmen. Panic and fear — that's what he heard.

"What's going on!?"

"Sir! We're under attack! I'm looking at the Bulatov coat of arms!" reported the officer, and then cried out in pain.

"You actually see the coat of arms?" Valentine was surprised. Usually that was the last thing anyone noticed.

"Well... you see," he hesitated. "It's on the side of the wall."

"What wall? I sent you to a field, idiots!" Grishanov assumed that the dumbass had misunderstood the order and gone to the wrong place, but no...

"Sir, I'm seeing it with my own eyes. The downed plane is here, but now it is blocked by a stone wall. The entire field has fortifications; this is an ambush! And the Bulatov coat of arms is on the wall!" The soldier himself didn't understand how this was possible.

Cursing, the baron dropped the call and called his commander, although the latter already knew what was up.

"Gather together all of our forces!" growled Grishanov. "All free guardsmen!"

"Sir...Should we also summon the water mages?" asked the commander, and the baron thought about it. His powerful detachment of Gifted Waterbenders were too important to waste on this venture.

The baron leaned back in his chair. For some time he nervously drummed his fingers on the table, after which his face was distorted by rage.

"Bastard..." he hissed, and grabbing his phone, he quickly dialed a number. Long beeps sounded, after which he heard the cocky, disgustingly smug voice of the enemy. "Bulatov!" Valentine growled. "You...."

He couldn't find anything to say, and his opponent's amusement only added fuel to the fire. Growling menacingly, the baron began to promise the enemy the most terrible punishments. He screamed, laughed wildly, and at the same time threw everything that caught his eye against the wall.

Some ten minutes later he calmed down, and that's when he realized that Bulatov had long ago hung up, unwilling, it seemed, to simply listen to the abuse being hurled at him.

"Summon the Waterbenders," croaked the baron, having called his commander. "All of them! Activate all of our forces!"

* * *

Why? What did I do to offend him so much? However, it didn't matter. We positioned ourselves right next to the plane, rebuilt the fortifications, and now the Earthbenders were holding back the barrage of shots from the enemy with all their might.

One good thing was that the pilots were killed by the baron's men, and therefore, when the owner made claims against me, I could say that it was Valentine's doing. And I had every right to take the plane; it was a battle trophy.

What was strange was that Grishanov's guards did, in fact, get into a fight with crew of the plane. That meant that this plane didn't belong to anyone from around here, such as Kurchatov. The baron, a vassal, would not dare raise his hand against his overlord, even if he was lusting after untold riches.

We'd dug trenches for the combat artillery to safeguard it from strikes. But even this wasn't enough to prevent injuries. All I could do was render aid to the drivers and gunners who had to flee in time to save their skins.

Indeed, we weren't facing off against simpletons. The baron's guard was well equipped, with tanks and armored personnel carriers. I didn't see any Suits yet, but I was sure they were somewhere waiting for the right moment, while mine had already entered the battle. They were attacking the rear where there were numerous reinforcements, and also dropping bombs on the heads of the attackers. The enemy was trying to get to the plane, but I noticed in time and had the mages erect a high earthen wall around it. It wasn't the kind of wall to last through the ages, but it was enough to stop anyone from randomly damaging the glistening trophy.

But despite the help provided by my Suits, the enemy's forces were only increasing in number. A triple-barreled tank crawled out of the forest, loudly growling. Aiming its turret at the nearest fortification, it belched out massive shells from its cannon, one after another, which exploded in bright flashes upon hitting the stone slab of one of the dugouts.

That's where Ludwig was. I could see the effort he was making to keep the slab together as the shells slammed into it; eventually, he was losing steam, though.

"Catch!" I said, tossing him a bag of crystals. I had added a little of my magic into this batch. I knew the crystals would come in handy. Sure, the payoff would come afterwards in the form of a serious hangover. But why tell Ludwig about this? It wasn't a need-to-know kind of thing in the heat of battle.

"Why are the crystals red?" he asked, pulling a couple of them out. Clearly Ludwig was leery about using them.

"Don't worry, they're harmless," I reassured him, shouting over the roar of shots. "Look, here comes another tank!"

* * *

Tankers are cheerful people. Why not? There they were, sitting under tens of tons of armor, calmly looking at the world around through screens and little armored windows. And there was no enemy capable of withstanding the power of three hefty cannons, capable of spitting out massive projectiles every two seconds. Shoot them rapidly yet accurately. Aim them and fire, just like that.

And so the heavy tank made its way straight through the forest. It was going to where it was told to go by the commander. And soon the iron monster, grinding and plowing its way forward, crawled onto the battlefield.

The commander easily identified the target; the gunner immediately pointed its three barrels at the stone slab that protected the enemy taking cover behind it. Machine guns were stationed there, which in short order had already managed to drink a lot of the blood of Grishanov's guard.

"One, two, three! Burn, bastards, burn!" the

gunner laughed from behind his triple-barrels.

Explosions sounded and everything around the target turned to dust, while in the tank they set their sights on another enemy fortification. But before they could move on, the smoke cleared, revealing to the surprised commander and gunner an intact and undamaged stone slab. And from it, the enemy machine guns still rumbled. The enemy mockingly fired a short burst at the triple-barreled heavy tank, after which it again switched to shooting at the infantry.

"Good job!" said the commander sarcastically. "Mitya, did you again load blanks instead of shells?! Get it right, dolt!"

"What if I drank the full bottle?" the gunner scratched the back of his head and laughed. "Commander, I'm only following your lead."

He pressed the button to load more shells, and in the span of five seconds he fired them off. He took care to ensure they'd fired off. Stone dust, smoke, and flames rose around the enemy fortifications. And after the tenth shot, the commander ordered a ceasefire. Except that this time they didn't move their sights elsewhere.

"No, enough already!" He couldn't believe his eyes as he looked at the camera screen and saw that the fortification was still standing. And where shells had hit, there were now stone flowers emerging from the stone. They were all different, yet each one was, well, lovely. Also, chunks of stone had chipped off the slab, but not just hunks of rock; rather, they were statuettes. Beautiful maidens, animals, plants, and a man flipping the bird at the tank. This stone man was larger than all of the other statues.

Before the commander could vent his feelings in colorful cursing, the tank began to shake. And a moment later it was pierced through by a stone finger that burst straight out of the ground! The multi-ton iron colossus was torn in half with a grinding sound, and a stone hand grew in its place. Its middle finger extended upwards, sundering in two the invincible metal colossus.

* * *

"Ludwig..." I had to slap the mage on the cheeks several times. "How are you?" I was a little worried. I created the crystals for myself, to be used as a last resort. And I didn't take into account the effect on the psyche.

Now Ludwig was lying on the ground, laughing quietly and evilly, and staring vacantly into space. He was able to withstand all the shots from the heavy tank, and moreover, he destroyed it.

"Mikhail...Give me more, okay?" He reached for the bag, but I grabbed it and hid it inside my shirt. But now he was offended, and crossing his arms over his chest, he turned away from me. "Then you destroy your enemies all by yourself."

"You destroyed a tank with a stone middle finger. Do you think our enemies won't wonder what's going on now?" My eyebrows went up. "Hurry up and destroy it before someone takes a photo!"

"But I won't," Ludwig muttered. I had to put him to sleep for now, and ask the other mages to destroy the evidence. Which could, perhaps, be seen from space. Yes, the crystals were great, but I wasn't going to give them to anyone else. And I wasn't going to use them myself. Better to stash them away in some safe.

In fact, the battle turned out to be difficult. Gradually all our forces gathered, but the number of the enemy army only grew with every minute. Tanks crawled out of the forest, immediately opening fire on our artillery, and armored cars showered the fortifications erected by the earth mages with a hail of bullets. But what was most interesting transpired a little later. We had a lot of combat artillery, and so we brought in new machinery to replace damaged units. What better time to employ our backup hardware? This plane we were fighting for was worth pulling out all the stops.

But then I suddenly felt my feet sinking into the ground. I looked around and saw that our vehicles and all our men were also sinking. The earth was suddenly soft and soggy, hindering the wheels of our heavy vehicles from moving over it. It was also hindering our men from moving. My legs were getting stuck in mud, and so much water was filling the trenches that to stay there the men would have to hold their breath.

Water mages....Gifted. I didn't spot them right away. They were hiding nearby and were now expending as much energy as they could to prevent our reinforcements from getting to us. Right away I indicated where to direct the mortars. They couldn't be reached with direct shots, as they were hiding in the bushes, and based on the intelligence from the pigeons, they'd erected an ice wall around themselves.

"Where do you say?" Chernomor looked at where I was pointing. "Fighters! To battle!"

Where the enemy cannot be shot, he can always be hacked to death. Or stabbed. In any case, Chernomor favored close combat. So, after the mortars fired off their shots, demonstrating it was futile, a small detachment and I slogged across the soggy soil to pay a visit to the water mages.

"Stop!" I said as we drew near the ice wall. "Okay, let's retreat," I said, upsetting the men.

Yes, I'd like to fight these mages, but I knew were I to do so, some of my men would die. I had no idea where the baron had found such strong Gifted Waterbenders; especially ten of them. But it would be suicide were we to go up against them right now. I couldn't heal my guys on the spot and still kill the mages. I'd have to choose the one or the other.

I sent my guys off to fight elsewhere while I, well, I began drawing bloody runes right on the water. Blood began to seep from the pores of my skin, and my blood sphere instantly became completely transparent. Several liters of red liquid collected in a pool, after which a trickle of crimson began to seep into the ground.

And I kept on drawing a highly complex runic

script on the water. So these bastards wanted to create a swamp, eh? They assumed that we could neither attack nor escape. And the strong Gifted were liquefying the soil more and more, with no intention of stopping there. Idiots! I'm not going to let you sink my plane just like that! And indeed, I'd finished my spell, so all would work out just fine.

* * *

"Phew..." The water mage wiped the sweat from his forehead and exhaled. "I'm sweating..."

"But we got the job done," the second one grinned. He hadn't been involved in swamping the area, rather he'd been repelling enemy attacks. "Hey, why don't we just finish off these losers? We've generated enough water to go around!"

"Yes, let's do it," nodded the senior water mage. Being the strongest among them, it had been his job to liquefy the soil. It wasn't rocket science, this tactic. The first step was immobilizing the enemy and his weaponry. And then they could travel through the water to finish them all off. "Let me have a short breather first..."

And sitting down on the ground, he closed his eyes and immersed himself in meditation. But something soon interrupted his moment of rest, and he opened one eye.

"Kirill, aren't you slacking on the job?" asked the commander of the man he'd had handling the defense.

"No, what're you worried about? They're not

shooting at us," he also sat down to rest, although he wasn't tired at all. Building an ice wall was no problem for him, even though he was the youngest member of the team.

"Why didn't you purify the water?" the commander pointed to the brown-red veins snaking through the ice crystals.

"Oh, I'll clean that up now," Kirill waved his hand and, putting his hands on the ice, he closed his eyes. He stood there for about five seconds, and then turned around in surprise. "Commander....But I can't...I don't understand it."

Meanwhile, the veins slowly spread over more and more ice. And then, the water mages banded together to purify the wall, but they could no longer control the water. Veins permeated the entire surface of the ice crystals, preventing the Waterbenders from even touching them. What they looked like was ordinary dirt, like from clay. But then, before they could figure out for sure what it was, brown ice crystals hit them all at once. Screams of pain filled the air while some managed to activate shields to contain the damage. Then, the ice melted into dirty water that flow over the feet of the water mages.

Panic ensued as they sought out their Gift, trying to control the brown liquid. But someone much more powerful was not going to let them to do that. In an instant, the entire clearing was covered with crystals that bit into the fighters' legs. Over and over again. And now it was the Waterbenders who were mired in the sticky muddy swamp while the air was filled with the smell of iron. Out of ten, only three survived, and even then, they were left with many terrible wounds to remind them of that night.

* * *

A few minutes later
Baron Grishanov's mansion

"I understand..." the baron wheezed dryly. "Retreat." There was no way they could achieve their goal. Although, perhaps they had already achieved it... Who knew when it came to these psychos?

The baron paced from side to side. In one hand he clutched an open bottle of something strong, and in the other he held his phone. From the multiple reports he'd received his guards were unable to cope with the enemy forces. They could not capture the plane. But the detachment of Waterbenders had completed the first part of their combat mission. And now there was a swamp around the fallen plane. Nobody would be able to get the plane out, and so all that remained was to wait a little... But that was the least of his worries now. There were the reports of losses — both people and hardware. And the water mages reported that a horrific Gifted mage had inflicted strange magic on them. It was as if he was some sort of earth mage, although this was hard for the baron to believe.

In any case, this wasn't the time to dwell on

it. Grishanov took a few swigs from the bottle and played the video again. It was a message to him personally. And it was beyond belief to him, the veracity of the recording. What he saw was a huge stone hand bursting out of the ground, its middle finger protruding upward to pierce one his heavy triple-barreled tanks. The tankers managed to scramble out of the tank, and were unharmed. Physically. But mentally... They wouldn't be able to return to duty.

Because what then happened was that the hand then dived back underground, leaving the people around, and the baron himself, alone with their heavy thoughts.

"But before, I thought that you were a weakling, in the throes of your death agony..." Valentine said thoughtfully, taking a couple of more swigs. "But now I realize that I was mistaken," the baron mused as he stared at nothing at all as plans germinated in his head. A weakling could not shoot down such a plane.

But Bulatov did just that, which meant he was only pretending to be weak. And therefore he'd best gather all his strength to eliminate the threat posed by such a neighbor. After all, if he didn't strike first, sooner or later the count would look his way and demand more of his property back.

* * *

Wow, I'm already sweating! To penetrate the ice wall with veins of blood and direct it against its creators was almost the easiest thing. But to make my blood look like dirt... Actually, it contained a lot of iron, and so all it took was contact with air to make it turn brown. But then I almost lost control over it. However, the enemy fell for my ruse. Now the survivors would think that an Earthbender fought against them. And I had no doubt that there would be survivors. I was able to finish off only the weakest, but left the strong ones for later. They fled in fear anyway, and were no longer a threat. In any case, they'd achieved their goal. We cannot get out of this quagmire. We'll have to abandon all our hardware here, leave the plane to the baron, and go home in disgrace.

Right, as if I'd let that happen!

Right after I finished with the water mages, I decided to finish off the remnants of the enemy troops. True, Chernomor had already had some fun there, and they retreated even faster than the frightened mages. Of course, when you're a water mage who loses control over his medium, it makes you uneasy.

Having dealt with the remnants of the enemy troops, we began evacuating our vehicles and combat artillery. Too bad I didn't bring Belmore with me. He could simply have all of these corpses drag the plane to the castle. Now we had to come up with something new. The two mages ended up creating slabs under the wheels of the heavy armored cars all the way to solid ground.

But the plane required more creativity. It plowed through the quagmire for a couple of meters, and then ran into the solid rock slab. Actually, the mages raised the plane up, but only to the limit of their capabilities. They then passed out, and I had to share my powers with them. And while we were using magic to lift the plane onto the slab, the guards were quickly cutting down trees and carrying logs. We placed them under the stone slab, and with joint efforts we dragged it.

"Why don't you just pick it up?" I asked the mages. The plane was made of metal, and could be lifted with earth magic. Seemed like that would be easier.

"Well... This is pure metal, and we can't influence it so easily," the mages explained, and I slapped myself on the forehead.

"That's right. From my past life I'm used to working with the most powerful mages," I said, shaking my head sadly. These guys were rather weak...I hoped that next time, the offworld lord might send me an Archmagister, at the very least.

Yes, the baron would be surprised. To be honest, I myself was surprised at our method of transporting the plane. But it was worth it. Let us destroy thirty armored vehicles. And forget about any other trophies, such as ammo or weapons. Let the retreating forces have it all. All that mattered was that this plane was slowly but surely crawling towards the castle. In fact, it was very slow, because we only got there at dawn. The trophy did not fit through the gate, so we placed it next to the wall. Somehow the exhausted mages cobbled together a stone and earth wall around it. Once they got enough sleep, they could finish the work, but now it would be better to let them rest.

"How are you enjoying your first day off, by the way?" I chuckled, and all three of them shot hostile looks at me. "That's it! I'm leaving!" I said, raising my hands and hurrying off to hide from their gaze.

Then I came across two strange Combat Suits. They looked intact, and they were just lying at the entrance to the castle.

"What's this?!" I turned my gaze to Belmore, who, along with Vika, came out to meet us.

"What? They showed up and started shooting. I went a little crazy..." shrugged the Necromancer.

There is no escaping the most powerful wave of death energy. Strong armor and energy won't help; the release of the pure force of death was very powerful. Belmore did not invent anything new, and simply lashed out with the full force of his power, without using any connections or spells for this. And it worked! Now it was even scary to imagine what was left of the operators imprisoned inside. But I wasn't the one who'd have to wash them out.

Yes, Baron Grishanov's plan was clear. He deliberately delayed and did not retreat until the very end, although after Ludwig's attack it was obvious that we could not be defeated on the battlefield. The Suits showed up here for a reason. The Baron thought that Victoria and I were here, and wanted to eliminate us while the main forces were engaged in battle. Pretty mean, to say the least.

"Just think, sending as many as two Suits to storm a dilapidated castle," I shook my head, but the Necromancer corrected me.

"Actually, three..." he pointed somewhere to the side, and only now did I see a pile of smoking ash, from which melted and broken parts of a Suit were visible.

"Ah, well. We can't salvage that particular suit," I sighed sadly, but my attention was immediately attracted by a crazy scream.

"Bastards!" squealed Willson. "Filth! Why so few? I'll tear everyone apart! Give me more flying enemies! Woohoo! Let's go!"

The Artifactor had suffered a lot lately. Apparently, he'd gone off the deep end when they started firing rockets at his tower. His psyche could not handle it. He walked out of his gate and looked around at us all. His eye twitched and he was swaying on his feet. Of course, now he looked like a Christmas tree. He had all kinds of artifacts hanging off him, enough to replace the need for clothes, even.

"And this, apparently, cannot be cured..." Chernomor muttered, looking at the distraught Artifactor.

"More! Give me more enemies!" Willson continued dashing about, pointing his lethal attacking artifacts in different directions. I got the impression that with the right motivation, he could create some truly powerful weapons.

CHAPTER 4

"JUST TELL ME! What possessed you? Did you have to go there?" asked a middle-aged man in a formal suit holding a glass of sparkling wine as he frowned at a short, rather stout old man, who was also attired in a severe suit.

"What do you mean?" asked the older man. "Those were my lands! They've always been mine!"

"When were they yours?" asked the first guy incredulously. "Okay..." he sighed. "We've been fighting for a year now, and we haven't seen any gains. I propose we resolve our differences through peaceful means. Let the village of Silovka go to you, and Kipushino to me. Deal?"

"Now you're talking!" said the other, extending his hand. The two then shook to confirm the agreement. "We have concluded a peace treaty in front of witnesses!" he said loudly enough for the others.

There were, in fact, quite a few people around. About thirty in number, including all of the aristocrats in the city of Arkhangelsk. The meeting was held in a luxurious mansion in the very center of the city, and, in fact, it was the innermost circle of the elite in attendance. About half were aristocrats, and these were only the most influential.

They held such meetings every six months, in part to settle any disputes that arose over the year between any of them. It was not a ball, and there wasn't any entertainment. Just some light music playing in the background, and a table with all sorts of delicacies in the middle of the room. There was also a stage, and several tables with comfortable chairs in the corner of the room.

The guests were primarily chatting with each other, displaying whatever new acquisitions they'd picked up, and simply catching up on things. But there were also conversations of substance. For example, the mayor of the city again raised the issue of the increasing numbers of Interface portals.

"Gentlemen, let us not stand aside anymore!" he said, addressing the room, his manner reproachful. "Allocate more funds to fight the Interface world. If we don't, we'll have to face the consequences later."

"That's what I've been saying for a long time now. Innocent people are suffering," sounded a deep bass voice from the back. Everyone turned to look at the speaker. He was a tall, beefy man standing near the table with food. "Now, we're forced to compensate the victims. At present, only Konakov and I are stepping up to the plate."

Duke Konakov hadn't come to the meeting as he had too much going on. Also, he saw no reason to attend, having no matters to negotiate with anyone here. He'd long ago given up on these meetings. Almost everyone present here would have devoured his Family long ago if they had been strong enough to do so.

"Ha, compensation," one of the attendees grinned. "We should give them knuckle sandwiches, not money! And tell them to get back to work!"

"Shut up already. You spew nonsense," said Verzilin, the beefy man. "You risk getting drunk on power and sounding like a jerk. Or have you forgotten that our power rests on the shoulders of ordinary people?"

"Right, the common people," the other sneered, and Verzilin sighed and said "I see why you have financial difficulties."

"In any event," he went on, "we aristocrats long ago decided unanimously to increase the funding for services to counter the Interface portals. We must pay for soldiers, military hardware, detection equipment. We all know that if the situation was to get out of control, we'd all suffer serious losses."

"I beg your pardon, gentlemen!" Baron Grishanov raised his hand, attracting everyone's attention. "But I wanted to ask, how long will this chaos last?"

"Valentine, are you inebriated?" laughed Mayor Gushin, although he suddenly recalled the recent theft of his geese. It was a total mystery what had happened to them. Indeed, the best sleuths in the region simply threw up their hands. The geese had vanished into thin air, plain and simple. Apparently they were migratory geese. "What chaos do you speak of? What are you talking about? Our city is calm and orderly!"

"That being said, there is one aristocrat who does whatever he wants," said the baron. "With all due respect, Mayor, I don't see how it is you have failed to take note."

"Who are you talking about?" asked the mayor, puzzled, although some present were clearly in the know.

"Count Bulatov. He showed up out of nowhere, and his behavior is downright confounding. He took the mines away from me, although I was intending to use the proceeds from them to help meet the needs of the city and the Empire," Valentine was now jubilant, seeing that he could at least present his case to the powerful people gathered here. "And he attacked the Snegirevs just like that. Only because of some infighting between them."

And the baron went on and on, complaining about Count Bulatov's transgressions. The gist of what he said portrayed the count as randomly attacking everyone for no good reason. Killing innocent guards that strayed on his territory, wantonly attacking lands that belonged to his neighbors. What he left out was that these lands had been the property of the Bulatovs for hundreds of years and were stolen from them in surprise attacks.

Of course, it's not like those present at the gathering didn't know about this already.

"Also, there's something going on in Arkhangelsk. Warehouses burning down, attacks on our retail enterprises," said the baron. "And somehow, Bulatov manages to equip himself, and find weaponry somewhere. He's renovating his dilapidated castle, and he recently erected a hideous chimney."

"I believe you're referring to a tower," chuckled someone, an aristocrat who'd seen photos of the new construction. "Konakov is helping him, and it seems that his team built either a tower or a wall..."

"Yes, but where is he getting the money for this?" the baron asked. "The bastard must be playing a dirty game."

"Why are you so upset by the guy?" laughed Verzilin. "Are you afraid of him?"

"Why would you say that?" Grishanov made a show of being shocked, but the beefy guy wasn't buying it.

"But what do you know about it?" Grishanov then waved dismissively. "Butt out, already."

"Okay, let's calm down," said Kurchatov, who was also present at this meeting. "Don't kick someone when they're down. Bulatov already has problems, why finish off an already almost extinct Family?"

"Count, I have always been impressed by your

mercy and kindness, but Bulatov is a wild beast that needs to be put to sleep. He's a freak who attacks everyone!" Valentine wanted to portray Bulatov as a villain of the worst sort, and he succeeded, although he didn't think it was going as well as he wanted it to.

"Valentine, we only have your opinion; Snegireva, unfortunately, is not here," Kurchatov said, taking a sip of wine and smiling genially. "And secondly, we have no evidence. If we did, I personally would put a stop to him," he shrugged. "Let's not jump to conclusions. We're all neighbors, and need to treat each other with respect."

"But how can we tolerate the scum!?" shouted the baron, but then, seeing the look on the count's face, he shut up. But after a pause, he suddenly smirked. "You want evidence?"

And he pulled out his phone, and started playing a video. First, the plane crash, which suddenly ended.

"So that's where it is!" exclaimed one of those present, a man of about fifty, tall and thin, his whole face was covered in wrinkles, and his eyes were tenacious and cunning.

"Count Vodonaev?" Gushin was surprised. "Is there something wrong?"

"That's my plane!" he pointed at the screen. "Yes, it is mine! My men lost contact with it yesterday, and weren't able to locate the crash site. Baron Grishanov, let's discuss compensation with you. I would like to get my plane back. I think we can agree on a sum that suits both of us."

"I would be happy to provide it to you for free," the baron shrugged. "But Bulatov...The bastard invaded my lands and shot the crew of your plane. My people tried to protect them, but they themselves incurred losses. And the plane is now in his possession."

Vodonaev stood, shook his head, groaned and sweated profusely. The thing was, he'd had no idea where his planes had flown that night. He'd let his idiot son take the four new toys out for a spin, and the dolt had taken them to bomb a random weak aristocrat, just for kicks. The count assumed his son would simply have some fun bombing some mountain in the wilderness, just to check out how the planes flew, and have fun testing what they could do. But in the end, only two planes had returned.

Of course, Valentine failed to mention that it was his own men who'd killed the crew of the downed plane. After all, if Bulatov had not taken the plane, the video of its crash would never have surfaced anywhere.

"And now I urge you all to watch another video," the baron turned on a recording that he'd watched endlessly already.

"Wow..." the aristocrats exhaled at once, surprised at what they saw.

They reviewed the recording several times, after which they all agreed that this count should be eliminated. Indeed, he was a dangerous, nefarious person who posed a threat to them all. As such, he warranted swift, harsh treatment. He had no right to exist.

All present assumed the count had powerful artifacts. How else could he have created a stone hand with a protruding middle finger capable of sundering in half a heavy triple-barreled tank?

"I think that he's colluding with offworlders..." concluded Gushin. "Well, we need to think about what to do about him."

*   *   *

"*Coooo....*" Kooky plopped down on the table right in front of me exuding pathos as he feigned passing out.

In fact, he did look rather worse for wear. Poor creature...maybe I erred in tinkering with him.

Until recently, he looked like a healthy ordinary pigeon, well-fed, with glistening, smooth feathers. Now, I could see his bones under his thin skin, his feathers were falling out and they looked a mess. I didn't know how he made it back alive, but he'd definitely lost massive amounts of weight. I needed to be careful with the laxative spell, as it was clearly more lethal than you'd think. However, my feathered fiend had sullied the interior of the plane so much that it could not continue on its way.

"Okay," I said, sending a wave of vital energy through the pigeon. "Tell Timothy that I'm giving you an entire granary for your needs."

"*Cooo?*" Kooky immediately jumped up at that, tears welling up in his eyes. Hmm... Do pigeons really know how to cry? Not that it mattered. I had never before seen him so happy. "*Coooo-coo-coo?*" he asked, ensuring that he'd heard me right.

"Yes, one granary. You can peck at whatever you find there. Only don't forget where to poop out the digested food."

"*Coooo-coo-coo!*" he saluted me with his wing, informing me that all the grain would be processed and delivered to our enemies.

And he already looked better. I dismissed him then, and off he went to inspect his new storehouse of grain. Just then my phone began vibrating very insistently.

"Good afternoon, Duke!"

"Bulatov..." Konakov said calmly. "I have no idea what happened, but you again have big problems. How do you make so many enemies?"

"It's not like I'm doing anything special..." I said, replaying recent events in my head. "Sure, I beat up the baron a little...."

I then found out that the aristocrats of Arkhangelsk sometimes get together to discuss the latest issues. And this last time, I was the biggest topic of conversation. In fact, they all saw me as someone who needed to be eliminated.

"This time I skipped this gathering," said Konakov, clearly regretting it. "And now we see the result..." he sighed heavily. "I know that the baron is a nitwit, but this isn't a joke."

"Well, what's got them so riled up? I didn't even know whose planes I shot down, if that's what this is about," I threw up my hands. "But if it's someone important, let him send new planes, I'll shoot them down too."

"This isn't about the planes! There's a video of your forces employing a powerful attack artifact!" exclaimed the duke. "And now, you might well see forces from other cities coming for you. You can't reveal you have things like that. Others will all want artifacts like that for themselves."

The duke paused as he turned over various options. I said nothing in the meanwhile. It's not like things had changed much at my end.

"You know, I could purchase these artifacts from you. We could conclude everything officially, and nobody would dare attack me. They'd be too scared." And then he said, "Although…that might not work, actually," he sighed. "It all depends on what kind of artifacts you have. On the other hand, what difference does it make? These vultures will come up with anything to justify their actions."

"Thank you, duke. I really appreciate it, but I'll work things out myself." I said, having considered his offer. "The only thing I'd like, if it's not too much, is more deliveries of stone."

"How much more?"

"Twenty time as much, at least. And if you can deliver more, I'd be grateful," I said, as the duke, hearing me, started coughing in surprise.

"I'll try to give you quadruple the amount. You can count on that," said Konakov after collecting himself. "But do take care of yourself. If necessary,

I can provide shelter to your Family. Most of all, take no unnecessary risks; you haven't completely cured my granddaughter."

But of course his main concern was for his granddaughter. That being said, I got the impression he wasn't wholly indifferent to my fate, either. And for me, this was something of an opportunity.

"Duke, I'm not the kind to run away from problems, and so I'll face this matter straight on."

"Just don't do anything foolish, Bulatov. Just don't!" said the duke in a deep voice. "All of Arkhangelsk has lined up against you. Just remember that."

"I understand, but fail to see how things have changed; they've always been lined up against me. An economic blockade is also a kind of war. If only I had access to stores and auctions."

"Tell me what you need to buy," Konakov sighed, realizing what I was getting at.

Not that I was trying to drop any hints. Anyway, I proceeded to list what I needed to wage a normal full-scale war. Electronics, spare parts, fuel, ammunition. Right now I had to get all of this from other cities, and it was difficult and costly to get it all delivered here.

"I can't buy ammunition for you; the controls over purchases are too strict," Konakov said. "But I have every right to share what I have from my reserves. So that's not going to be a problem. As for spare parts...for what?"

"Well, a plane, for one," and the duke again started coughing.

"So you really did haul it to your castle? I know that you managed to shoot it down, but how did you get it to your castle?" And then he realized that he was asking too many questions. No, I couldn't tell him everything. "Never mind. Give me a list, I'll help you in any way I can."

But my needs were great. For example, I needed radar. It might not help when Suits attacked, but it would alert us to heavy aircraft. We also needed weapons. I realized now how acute our shortage was. We also needed a lot of cable, because now we needed cameras at all of the borders. It was, in short, a long, long list, and I briefly discussed it with the duke. I'd have Timothy draw up a spreadsheet to send to the duke's people, and then we'd settle on the final cost.

As I thought about all of this, Chernomor walked into my study. He wanted to know what to do about the viscountess. I just waved dismissively, saying that I had no time. The baron, after all, had jumped in front of her in line. In fact, according to pigeon intelligence his troops were approaching our borders.

"By the way..." Chernomor froze in the doorway. "Snegirev is permanently out of the picture! He died in prison. An accident."

I was expecting something like this. I only wondered if the investigators managed to properly interrogate him? Find out what the real story was with him and Kurchatov. I doubted if they'd succeeded in finding anything out...

CHAPTER 5

THE NEWS OF THE VISCOUNT'S DEATH changed my plans a little. It was unexpected, but not critical. What did I care about the viscount? My hands were full already. We needed to review our defense, make some changes, strengthen the borders.

I rested a bit, did some meditating, and then went to give some orders to the mages. I promised them two days off, and the first of them just ended yesterday. I'd give them the next one sometime later, when the opportunity arose. Right now was not the time. Unfortunately. But they understood the situation we were in. It was far too dangerous for them to be idle now, and their lives, too, depended on the quality of our fortifications.

I wanted a series of small bunkers with passages for infantry, and also subterranean storage for our hardware on the borders. This kind of infrastructure was, in any case, very useful. We could station a lot of guardsmen ready for battle, all unbeknownst to the enemy, and when they least expected it, we'd roll out guns onto the battlefield. Of course, the mages proposed erecting a wall along all of the borders of our territory. This would cut us off from our enemies, and we could install security cameras, maybe plant mines all around us, and have flocks of feathered scouts to prevent any bad actors from taking us by surprise. But I nixed that plan. In any case, to me boundaries were fickle. In no time, I might well expand them.

After I was finished with the mages, I went off to pick up Victoria and her teacher for a little excursion via horseback to visit the baron. I didn't want him to get bored. It wouldn't be very neighborly of us, would it? We should do our part to bring some pizzazz to his otherwise drab existence.

First, we headed through the dense forest riddled with potholes and ruts. No way was there any surveillance here; this place was so remote and unkempt. But while the horses were making their way through the thickets, Kooky showed up with a report that enemy forces had been spotted heading this way.

Like me, the baron wanted to surprise his neighbor, and his troops were now assembling in this very forest. However, I wasn't terribly upset, if at all. I'd wanted to penetrate deep into the baron's lands and make some noise, but this was even better. My victims were coming to me at my border, so I didn't even have to bother seeking them out.

"This place looks perfect," I said after scanning the area. I'd even remembered the long-forgotten chain of Sonar Runes. And, of course, I tuned into the heartbeats. Thus, I knew that the nearest enemy post was about five hundred meters away, while their central camp was eight hundred meters away. As luck would have it, this was ideal.

"And you," I turned to Corgi, "make sure the other two beasts don't make any noise," I nodded toward the offworld horses.

"Neigh!" responded the horse, looking sternly at his subordinates, both of whom did their best to look invisible.

Looking good, all in all. My Corgi ruled over any other creature with hooves. I'd have to see if this included, say, cows, actually. After all, why should I stop at poultry? We could always use some cattle. Expansion was good. Conveniently, the baron had herds of cows, and pig pens, too.

As I was pondering his, Belmore had Vika draw a good circle for summoning hounds, and then he imbued it with power. Now he and his student unfastened the rattling bags of bones carried by the horses and dumped them into the center of the magic circle. In two minutes, two hounds stood before us. They had empty eye sockets with flickering eye lights, powerful bones, long sharp claws and fangs. These were what I would call real bone hounds, not like what Vika had conjured up in those ruins of the dead. These bone hounds could fetch their own bones to chew on by ripping them right out of living flesh.

With the creation of the hounds, we were almost ready for action. While Belmore was busy with the final fine tuning of the necrotic creatures, illustrating to Vika any room for improvement, I pumped energy into the feathered scout.

"Did you eat well?" I asked the glowing green pigeon. Vital energy was now overflowing in him, and he was visibly ready to show what he was made of. "Don't worry. I'm not going to use a laxative spell on you."

"*Cooo...*" he wiped a bead of sweat from his brow. "*Coo-cooo!*"

"Alright, my feathered friend," I patted him "Fly away! You know what to do."

And with a brief nod, the well-fed pigeon soared into the sky while I took off my saddlebag, checked the charge of the bolts, and ensured the spare magazines were loaded, and...

And thus began the hunt. These people thought they could invade Bulatov lands and take over my castle, kill my guards, and maybe even our servants. All of these guys played dirty, never counting their losses, so why would they show mercy to my people?

"Well, let's go," I smiled, turning to the Necromancers. Belmore smiled back, while Vika shuddered slightly when she saw me.

She'd wrapped a bandana around her face while I put on my plague doctor mask, and then I aimed the crossbow towards the nearest post and fired three bolts off. Three clicks echoed through the night forest, and then the charged bolts found their targets. They hit their targets in the heart, instantly killing the sentinels.

The hounds shot off then, and swiftly returned, dragging bodies into the circle. Belmore waved his hand, and his necrotic powers immediately separated the flesh from the bones.

"I don't like dirt and stench," he shrugged in response to my silent question. Right, though it be a waste of energy, let Belmore be comfortable.

To my surprise, Belmore did not raise zombies, but forced the hounds to quickly clear the bones before creating two more to help them. As I trusted him to know best how to wield his powers, I just moved on, and under the cover of the two Necromancers I continued shooting the baron's men, one after another. I shot until I was out of bolts, then slammed in a new magazine and shot some more. Kooky did his job well, retrieving the bolts from the bodies of the dead.

* * *

"Gosha, what are your plans once we're done here?" Several guards were sitting around the fire. The camp had not yet slept, because the detachment had only recently settled in. And the plan was not to sleep that night, but simply wait for reinforcements.

"I plan to get drunk," shrugged Gosha. "What else?"

"Me too," sighed the other, tired. "But they promised us so much money if we capture the countess alive that I'm afraid my liver might not be able to handle it."

"Yeah, the countess's Healer is a tool. We'll capture him alive too, and you'll be doubly happy!" laughed another fighter.

"Uh-huh, you know what we've been told to do to the count," said the other chatty fellow.

For a few seconds there was silence near the fire, but soon another fighter spoke, albeit in a strange muffled voice, as if he was wearing a gas mask.

"What's that we're supposed to do with him?"

"Hey, were you sleeping during the briefing? We're supposed to cut off his hands and put them...."

"But who are you?" asked Gosha, realizing he didn't know. He'd interrupted his comrade and stared into the darkness from whence came the voice.

"It doesn't matter," said the voice as a black figure in a cloak separated from the darkness of the forest. "But why does everybody want my hands? That's just strange..." he said thoughtfully, and before the soldiers could move, a bright red flash lit up the darkness of the night.

The red ball soared past the men, landing in the fire, producing a powerful explosion of minia-ture red crystals that spun and whistled all around the camp. They pierced every single one of the twenty trained fighters sitting around the campfire. As soon as the bodies fell to the damp ground, a pack of bone creatures flew at them.

Then a siren wailed, lights turned on, and there were men running about all over the place. Several flashes lit up the darkness again, and the bloody spikes whirled about, again overtaking their targets, over and over again.

* * *

Could I have quietly wrought destruction upon at least part of this camp? Yes, of course! Which is what we did over the first hour when we eliminated sentry posts, and sleeping soldiers. But my goal today wasn't to be quiet. Indeed, I'd blown up deadly clots of blood on purpose, to create a stir. I wanted to be as loud and splashy as possible!

I wanted to compel the baron to send as many reinforcements as possible to ensure they all ended up mired in the impenetrable wilds of the dense forest. This would also divert his attention from attacking elsewhere, giving the Earthbenders time to build fortifications. In short, it made a lot more sense to create a show right here.

I slung my crossbow over my shoulder onto my back, pulled out my sword, and carried my staff in my left hand. I'd been engaged in healing people a lot lately. My vital energy was beginning to overpower my blood energy, and I'd correct this situation today. And thus, I held a staff with a blood sphere from the vampires, and it was filled to the limit.

Runes lit up, one after another, and a cloud of blood rose above me, surrounding me for meters. No one understood yet the source of the danger, and so they were firing indiscriminately, while cries of pain filled the air.

The hounds, of course, where attacking from all around. Some were dragging corpses to the Necromancers to replenish their numbers, and others simply attacked, sinking their teeth into flesh and then jumping back. I made my way to the center of the chaos. Gradually, energy discharges began snaking through the bloody mist. And anyone touched by this viscous fog passed out, collapsing onto the ground. Only those who had strong Gifts could hold out, if only for a minute, but these I impaled on blood stakes that burst out of the ground here and there.

This was complicated, intricate magic, and very expensive. But it was for this that I saved my blood, after all, was it not? And not only my own. Each person killed shared their blood, making the spell even more deadly. And if not for the strain on my weak body, I could further develop the spell such that it would cover the entire camp! As it was, I had to limit my range to thirty meters. The cloud completely protected me from enemy shots. They simply could not see me and fired at random, and the rare bullets that were on target got stuck in my bloody dome.

From time to time, I launched other attack spells that suited the situation. The blood in the sphere quickly ran out, but then I simply made use of the blood from fallen enemies, creating all kinds of runes with my staff to launch one surprises after another at the enemies hiding around me.

Whoosh! A man with the Wind Gift burst into my cloud. He blew apart the red fog and moved swiftly toward me. But I dodged his blow, and I plunged my sword into his stomach, sending a wave of vital energy through the blade.

He was no longer among the living. I took note of the hounds dashing about. Necromancers do not have endless powers, and even from here I could feel Victoria going through her last grains of energy. In contrast, Belmore was using his supplies judiciously, making sure to hold some reserves back, just in case. Smart, and that was how any competent mage would approach a battle. That's the way to make sure the job got done.

For the next twenty minutes I made my way about the enemy camp, creating a splash wherever I went, always on the attack, and making use of many long-forgotten blood runes. I wasn't trying to be efficient here. I wanted to instill fear in the hearts of the enemies, compel them to call for reinforcements and forget about any lingering thoughts about invading the Bulatov lands. And yes, I got the feeling I'd succeeded.

I left behind me the mutilated bodies of the baron's guards scattered all about, and trees covered with a thin layer of blood. Desiccated mummies, piles of broken bloody bones, necrotic bone creatures broken into many pieces. We did not clear the entire camp, as we did have to eventually retreat. I'd left a message, though, so mission accomplished, and finally, when I sensed a powerful detachment of three dozen strong Gifted soldiers moving our way, I activated the last rune.

The Bloody Flame. Flashing with a red light, the rune was absorbed into the ground, and the energy and blood I had to expend on this made me turn pale. I did my best to keep intravascular pressure at a minimum so as not to lose consciousness right then and there, and calmly hobbled towards my horse. A second passed, then a second, and a third... And then, a powerful heat burned my back. No, this wasn't fire magic, but the power of blood, and thus, I could generate a blaze from the magical flame. Which is what I did.

The clearing behind me was engulfed in a roaring raging fire, burning abandoned equipment and surviving soldiers, as well as the entire squad that was sent after me. It didn't kill them. More precisely, not everyone was killed, but they gave up thoughts of catching up with me right then.

Belmore and Vika were already astride their horses. Vika looked extremely tired, but judging by their happy faces, she'd learned another lesson that night and was now a little stronger. This was very good because soon she'd be a full-fledged novice mage, and I'd no longer have to worry so much about her. Although, who was I kidding? I'd always worry, and do whatever it took to ensure her safety.

We returned to the castle, and an hour later I

was standing in the courtyard sending Gerg and his Combat Doves to the viscountess's lands. No, I wasn't going to take her out yet, but no one could stop me from keeping her on her toes. So my detachment of offworlders would just harass her forces scattered about the countryside, divest them of their artillery, and so forth. However, they wouldn't be able to steal any vehicles. They still needed to learn how to drive. Theoretically, they didn't know how already, although I wouldn't be surprised if they actually knew something about it.

Now, all I had to do was sit tight and wait. What would be the baron's next move? I expected him to either go on the offensive, or else regroup with more forces in the depths of the forest.

But to my surprise, Valentine didn't do anything. The troops he'd stationed on the borders were simply standing by, as if waiting for a good time to make a move.

However, where I didn't expect it is where something happened. According to the pigeons, it was in the viscountess's lands that the troops were all convening into a single strike force, a "hammer". From all over her estate, fighters and combat artillery were coming together around the mansion, which seemed to be going through a rebirth of sorts. And she was behaving strangely. That's why I dispatched Kooky to take a look. If anything was up, I'd be on it.

"So, the plan is to attack us from two sides at once," I laughed as Kooky shrugged. Yes indeed. I knew full well what the baron was waiting for. Too bad for him that he'd be waiting in vain. I could bury myself underground and wait for them all to invade, or I could strike first! Nobody would expect me to just show up.

"Chernomor!" I summoned my guard commander. "As I recall, you were ready to drop in on the viscountess, yes? Well, it looks like she's issuing us an invitation. Are the troops ready?"

Chernomor smiled, and with a quick nod, he slipped out the door and starting barking orders and instructions into his portable radio. Right way, I heard the roar of engines firing up as military vehicles began lining up in columns while our troops piled into trucks, ready to rumble, so to speak.

I brought with me only my sword and my crossbow. We moved swiftly along the road, not even aiming for stealth. In any case, we'd be surprising them. But halfway there my phone rang. Against the backdrop of the hysterical roar of the powerful engine of the armored car I was in, I picked up the call. This was an unfamiliar number, and it had been some time that I'd been bothered by someone I didn't yet know.

"You're wasting your time, Bulatov," said a mocking voice. "You'd do well to turn around, and get off my land!" This clearly wasn't the viscountess, as the voice was masculine. "No doubt you're surprised, but Snegireva no longer lives here. Now these lands belong to Duke Khorkov! So I'm giving you one last opportunity to turn tail and dive back down your rotten hole. And, by the way, I'll be waiting for you to return the lands I've purchased. According to the documents... Yes, according to them, almost all the lands, right up to the castle itself, belonged to the Snegirevs, and now they belong to me."

Wow. I wasn't about to quibble with this guy over the rights to my land. Moreover, it wasn't like I had many people around to vouch for me in any dispute. Of course, I could appeal to the Imperials for proof of my legal rights, but this would take a lot of time.

Then I received an email confirming my suspicions. In fact, almost right up to my castle, our lands were now as if owned by some Khorkov. Okay, Konakov warned me. I had to expect something like this.

Too bad for Khorkov, because he'd be finding out that his acquisition of these lands was clearly not the most profitable business move.

*   *   *

Somewhere in the sky above the endless forests of the Tver Principality
A comfortable private jet

Snegireva sat in a luxurious armchair with a glass of red wine in her hands. As she gazed out the window, she sipped the exquisite beverage, and smiled.

How to feel anything but pleased when, even

in the most hopeless situation, she'd found the best possible solution for herself? Her son had settled in to his boarding school and was not in any danger. His education was paid for until he came of age, he had a place to live, and there was no reason to worry about him. And she'd sold all her lands which, in any event, would have passed on to her enemies. Now, she was off to conquer the capital. With her beauty, finding a new husband will not be difficult. Her only concern was her hairy back. And that mustache, yes, she could feel it sprouting even now. But other than that, all was well. And these cosmetic issues, well, she could deal with them, even without magic.

Kurchatov, of course, had been a fool to not jump at the chance to share her bed. At least, that was the viscountess's view. But this no longer mattered. What awaited her was a small, charming estate, and a sparkling life in the capital among the real elite. What a shame that Bulatov was still alive and well, but now he was Duke Khorkov's headache, not hers. The duke was a serious man, who had no mercy when it came to his enemies. And if he couldn't cope with Bulatov, she could always revisit the issue.

"Hello?" the viscountess picked up a call with a smug smile. How funny that just as she was thinking about him, he'd called. How very humiliated he must feel. "How are you?" she asked mockingly, reveling in being the one on top now.

"Not bad. But, seriously, you shouldn't have done that," his words made her smile even more as she imagined how desperate he must be feeling. And then he went on, "You know, I let you live only because those lands were legally yours."

"What are you saying," the viscountess laughed. "This isn't because your Family is doomed and you can't do anything about it? No? Well, let me warn you that Khorkov knows his stuff. You're wholly unequipped to deal with him."

"Well, we'll see," Mikhail smirked. "Why am I calling... What are you doing there?"

"Well, I'm drinking wine, flying off to a new life..." Snegireva exuded.

"Ah, wine. Is it good?"

"Very!" she assured him. "It tastes like victory!" she was downright jubilant, but couldn't stop some doubts from creeping in deep down. And so she activated her food testing artifact, which revealed that, in fact, the wine was poisoned. "Nice try, but you didn't know that I have the Gift of Poison. It is impossible to poison me!"

"Wow," Mikhail said, openly feigning surprise. "You sure had me fooled." Silence reigned for a couple of seconds. "By the way, does the pilot, like you, have the Gift of Poison? Because we wouldn't want the poison to work on him, right?"

*　*　*

Yes, the wine is tasty. I wasn't sure how good the viscountess's bottle was, really, but I certainly appreciated my own sample of the fruit of the vine. I kept this bottle just for such an occasion. After all,

I now had one less enemy. Ha! I'd had Kooky poison only the water, because it was unlikely that a pilot would be drinking wine. But the bird had been extra careful it seems, poisoning all of the beverages. Kooky also took the time to shit all over the instrument panels in the cockpit, shorting out all of the electronics with his acid.

But although I had eliminated one problem, another had surfaced. Amazingly, the viscountess had succeeded in ruining my plans. She up and sold all her ancestral lands! I never would have thought that an aristocrat could renounce their heritage so easily. But she loved status and money much more than land, subordinates and the memory of the merits of her ancestors. So for her, it meant more to settle closer to the capital, and live a life of leisure there.

By the way, I got it. Sadly, the only reason I had not killed her long ago was that, in the event of her death, her property would all have gone to Kurchatov, the overlord of the Snegirev Family. In selling it all, she untied my hands, but...I had to wonder how Kurchatov, who'd been thrown under the bus, felt about all this?

Thinking about it, I couldn't help but chuckle. What did it matter to me that now I had to deal with this rather slick duke? They all acted like I was supposed to flee in terror or seek refuge somewhere. This duke, after all was of the second rank, a seasoned warrior and the patriarch of a rich ancient Family which he managed well. But these lands weren't anywhere near the forefront of his concerns, and so in all likelihood he'd be appointing a manager to deal with the inconvenient neighbor, that being me. And I could most definitely turn this situation to my advantage.

* * *

Meanwhile....
Kurchatov's study

"Find her!" the count yelled in an inhuman voice. "Find the b*tch right now! Kill her!" Hearing him, the guard commander stood rooted to the spot, afraid to move. He'd rarely seen his master in such a state. Perhaps he'd never ever seen him so incensed, screaming, choking on his rage, lashing out. "No! Don't kill her! Bring her back alive!"

Someone spoke into the commander's earpiece, and he sighed with relief. But still his skin was pale, and sticky cold sweat trickled down his forehead.

"Sir, she's already dead," he said calmly, and the count froze in amazement for a couple of seconds.

"Well, that's was fast acting on your part," he muttered, confused.

"It wasn't us," shrugged the commander as the tension subsided.

"Who was it, then?" asked the count, plopping into a chair and straightening his jacket.

"I don't know," the commander shrugged. "What are your orders in light of this?"

"We do nothing," Kurchatov inhaled several times through his nose and exhaled through his mouth. "Let Khorkov's son fight Bulatov, and we'll just watch. And once the count is dead, we'll show up and kill Khorkov's son. That's the plan! We can then just say that they killed each other."

* * *

"Willson, how are you? I see that you've settled in, right?" Without searching by heartbeat I might have never found him. Cunning man, he'd arranged his workplace such that no one could disturb him.

Except me. And that's why he was disgruntled now as he looked up from his work bench at me, waiting for me to tell him what I needed from him.

"What do you want" he finally asked.

"Are you done?" I asked. "You fulfilled my order, right?"

"Orders, orders..." Willson sighed. "That all anybody ever wants. What about me? I make orders, and that's all..."

"Willie, quit whining!" I cut in. "Did you do what I asked?"

"Yes, but of course, don't worry." And opening a desk drawer, he extracted a bag.

"Why are you so miserable?" I asked, looking inside. Everything looked great. It's just that there weren't enough artifacts in there.

"There's just one thing I don't get. Why, in a

world where there are bombs, mines, shells, dyna-mite, explosives, etc., order explosive amulets?" Willson was puzzled.

"Because we don't have enough mines, explo-sives, shells or dynamite," I opened the desk drawer wider. "But we do have you. Give me eve-rything you have here."

I didn't bother telling him that the explosives here didn't produce as big of a bang as did a well-crafted artifact. Sure, you could blow up whatever, but you'd have to use a lot more explosives. Which take up a lot of space, and is also heavy stuff to lug around. Right now what I needed were com-pact explosives. So after getting whatever I could from Willson, I went to my study where my faithful combat veteran was waiting for me.

"Ready?" I asked, and Kooky, perched on my desk, thrust out his chest.

"*Cooo!*" he sounded menacing, and saluted me with his wing.

"Who are you?"

"*Cooo!*"

"Why are you here?"

"*Coo-cooo!*"

"You are a war machine!"

"*Coooooo!*" My feathered warrior was pumped up and ready for action now.

"You're glorious!" I smiled and put a special strap around his chest.

This was a camera mount that enabled me to remotely monitor what he did. Also, I handed him two bundles of artifacts, one for each of his clawed feet.

"Now, off to battle!" I growled, and Kooky, cooing passionately, rushed right at the wall. And then he disappeared and reappeared outside, soaring up into the heavens.

For the next two hours, I, Vika and Chernomor were glued to the screen. The servants kept us well-supplied with snacks galore, and we couldn't tear our eyes away from the fascinating footage.

Kooky flew directly over enemy lands, but he did not attack anyone, and was invisible to both radar and enemy eyes. No one would notice a bird in the sky at night, and so my new weapon was safe.

"How is it we didn't think of doing this before," Vika said, munching on potato chips.

"To my shame, it didn't occur to me. It's Willson who asked me why we didn't use Kooky this way," I sighed. Yes, it could have made our life a lot easier. "Oh, he arrived!" I pointed at the screen. "This is going to be fun!"

Yes, just then Kooky was flying over an airfield where two vertical take-off combat aircraft were parked. The steel monsters were spending the night in the open air, ready in a flash to take to the skies and rain down a hail of deadly projectiles on the enemy. But no, this was not to be. No one should be firing rockets off at my castle.

And thanks to Konakov for the tip. Kooky hadn't been able to catch up with these deadly planes to track them, but I got a call from the duke with some interesting information about Count Vodonaev. Indeed, since these planes lacked emblems or any other signs of ownership, it would have been hard for me to find them on my own. But once I found out whose they were, I sent off a flock of pigeons to Vodonaev's domain and they found the airfield with the planes.

"Aaahhhh!" sighed Vika, when the screen turned orange. The artifacts found their target and the first plane burst into flames, after which the explosive artifacts landed on the second plane.

"I need a drink," Chernomor said. "I'm off to pour myself something stronger."

"Chernomor, but you don't drink!" exclaimed Vika.

"I just saw a pigeon destroy two pieces of equipment worth sixty million each. I have to drink. I have to," he snapped and headed out. But I stopped him.

"Wait," I grinned. "I would like to present my work, which took a whole week to prepare! *Coo-Coo!*" I shouted the code word, and we heard a response behind the open door.

"*Cooo! Cooooo! Coo-coo-coo!*" and a couple of seconds later, several pigeons filed into the room. They were, in fact, marching like little feathered soldiers. "*Cooo.....coo!*" their commander cooed, and once the last pigeon had passed through the door, the squadron stood at attention, saluting with their wings.

Each of the pigeons had a belt with a camera across its chest, and many of the birds were adorned in different colors. Blue, yellow, white.

"This squadron is the crown of my creation!" I crowed. "Combat pigeon scouts!"

"What...?" Vika was choking on her chips. "So now we have pigeon warriors?"

"This is just the beginning!" I said with a cunning smile.

"Cooo....cooo!" the commander of the pigeon squadron sounded threatening, and Chernomor, cursing, stalked off after that bottle.

Little did he know that I'd made some improvements to each one of these pigeons. Now, they were stronger, faster, and each of them had a modified digestive system, along with enhanced endurance and carrying capacity. Yes, there was a lot we could do with a formidable force such as this.

CHAPTER 6

WILLSON HAD COME UP with a great idea, which I significantly refined and improved. You see, Willson assumed the pigeons could only drop explosives. True, he'd been influenced by what he'd seen hand grenades do at the time. He was chagrined, actually, at seeing the damage non-magical "balls" like that could inflict. Then, he'd tinkered around with them, seeing what would come of melding such explosives with his magic. In so doing, he roped himself into producing explosive artifacts on an industrial scale. Along with the other orders I placed on him, of course.

And while it was Willson's brilliant idea to have the pigeons drop the explosive artifacts, it was I who came up with the plan to mount cameras on the feathered ones. Why not? We had the technology. That being said, the range of the cameras wasn't great, and so we used our less trained pigeons to serve as translator stations along the way. As the size of our flock increased, all of the skies around my county would be filled with flying relay stations. Our deadly feathered bombers would force our enemies to flee and hide underground. All good stuff, even if it was only part of the solution.

In fact, when Kooky destroyed the two planes, that was just a test run. I wanted to simply see how it went. After all, this was far different from Kooky's usual method of dropping bombs, and it's also not like the pigeon had a gun sight.

And along with testing the artifact bombs out, I also relished the opportunity to punish Count Vodonaev for his perfidy. I had Duke Konakov to thank for providing me with the intelligence. If not for that, I wouldn't have even known that Vodonaev was the chief villain. He was my most powerful enemy, because his people actually manufacture those planes, and other combat machines.

And he was also one of the bastards blockading my Family, meaning he'd ranked among our enemies for some time now. And although I'd only inflicted minor damage on him, at the least I'd diverted his attention away from me so that, at least for the time being he'd be too busy to bother me.

Of course he was no doubt targeting me now because we'd captured his plane. Our earth mages hid it underground in our new subterranean hangar next to the castle, and now my mechanics and engineers were checking it over and making any necessary repairs. We'd have to find some dedicated specialists at some point, though, because Timothy, for example, had rarely flown anything like these aircraft. My current staff only had a rough idea of how such cutting edge technology worked.

And Vodonaev might also attack to stop me from complaining about the attack. With whom might I lodge a complaint? With the Imperials, of course. To the best of my knowledge it was against the law to rain missiles down on a castle in the dead of the night unless a declaration of war has been made. He could be fined, and forced to pay me compensation, and he'd lose a lot of reputation points.

In any event, I resolved the issue my own way, and was extremely pleased with the result. Now that I was sure of how useful my feathered squadron promised to be, I asked Chernomor to provide me with twenty operators to oversee the pigeons.

They would monitor the cameras, collect the data, transmit orders to the birds and report to me about what they saw on the screens.

* * *

Later
Vodanaev's test site

The count settled into a comfortable room at the top of a small tower at the edge of a large concrete pad. This was where Vodonaev tested a lot of his artillery aircraft and more, and he personally monitored the progress of the tests. It might be a powerful new bomber, or a combat motorcycle. No matter what it was, monitoring the developmental process, including the testing, was important.

Now, the testing was about to begin on a modified prototype of a vertical take-off combat plane. This was Vodonaev's pride! These aircraft opened up huge prospects for his Family, because they could soon be sold to the Imperial forces, or even to other countries.

But a recent incident highlighted flaws in these formidable flying weapons. Of course the count suspected who'd been behind the blasts a week ago that had taken out two of his planes. There was no way they'd spontaneously exploded whilst parked on the airfield.

Clearly, this was all due to his slow-witted son who'd decided to test the planes when this was uncalled for. At the same time, who would've thought that there was someone capable of downing such a marvel of technology and engineering?

But all these musings vanished from his mind as soon as the two latest versions of the combat planes started their engines. First, a deep rumble, then the howl of the turbines sounded as the massive, powerful propellers started spinning, faster and faster.

The mechanics and engineers scurried about their instrument panels, carefully monitoring the readings, and measuring this and that as they squabbled with each other. Of course, that was the way of engineers, to argue over every little thing.

It all seemed to be going well. His mechanical "birds" were better than ever, virtually invincible. They were just about to ascend into the air to show him what they were made of. The count couldn't help but smile as he thought about where the next test would take place. He had no doubt whose castle he'd be sending the special missiles, the latest deadly projectiles in his arsenal. These were designed to destroy bunkers.

But then, it seemed that something was amiss with the ongoing test flight. First, one of the guards pointed up at the sky. He even fired off a couple of shots, but to no avail. This was because one of the propellers on one of the planes exploded just as it was lifting off. And then the other propeller burst into pieces. Worse still, the other flying battleship followed suit. Both planes came crashing down, creating a powerful explosion, followed by a fiery mushroom cloud.

A few seconds later, a shot rang out behind Vodonaev. Right away, the count realized that no, this wasn't an attempt on his life. It was simply that his chief engineer, who'd been sitting behind him to observe the test flight, had shot himself in the temple.

* * *

I wonder how long someone can exist on edge unable to relax for at least a few hours? Actually, I had only one way of finding out.

I'd been checking out this kind of thing lately. Time flew by unnoticed, days flew by, one after another, and my fighters, having gathered into sabotage detachments, brought fear and terror to the enemy. In addition to terrorizing the enemy, we were causing them great financial stress, to boot.

The pigeon squadron showed itself in all its glory. Not long ago I hired several electronics experts and computer scientists to help set up a system for tracking, and even dropping artifact bombs on the enemy's heads. It greatly facilitated the process, except that Willson simply didn't have the time to make us enough artifacts. We had to keep some in reserve in case of a major battle, and we swiftly ran through the rest.

And so under Belmore's guidance, Vika was tirelessly honing her skills in summoning various dead creatures. In fact, she'd recently created some bone birds on which we mounted explosive amulets, and used them to single-handedly take out an entire column of light vehicles. The trucks were carrying supplies to a large detachment that had taken up residence in one of the forests on the border.

However, our enemy wasn't sleeping on the job, either. The baron made several attempts to storm us, but these were actually exploratory attacks. Unlike us, he didn't have any pigeon reconnaissance. He'd used up his three Combat Suits, and planes were for those wealthier and more influential than him.

And so he tried it the old-fashioned way,

sending infantry and armored vehicles to our lands. I had no idea what he was even hoping for. Our earth mages had created numerous simple, yet extremely effective fortifications. And reconnaissance from the air always allowed us to direct our forces to the scene of any budding conflict in time, and the invaders were simply shot by my guards, who didn't even have to leave their cover. And so none of this was of particular interest.

At the same time, I had to keep in mind our other enemies. Several pigeons were always monitoring Khorkovs' lands, which previously belonged to the Snegirev Family. However, all was quiet there as the new inhabitants settled into the place and finished dismantling the dome around the mansion. No doubt they were impressed by how stripped down the estate was. Ha! We'd even taken the time to ravage the wallpaper. It's not that I needed it, but why leave it behind? And the same held true for the wiring, actually.

But the baron and the Khorkovs weren't my only enemies. I had Kooky himself overseeing the operation to distract Vodonaev. The feathered warrior somehow found out that the count was going to test new combat aircraft and, so Kooky, along with several assistants, dropped several explosive amulets on them. Right onto the propellers during takeoff. Now, we could expect one of two scenarios. Either Vodonaev would be consumed with fretting over his technological issues, or else, suspecting who destroyed his planes, he'd head my way.

But, seeing that he had yet to show up, that

meant that he was unsure about who had been responsible, and so I didn't have to worry about opening a second front quite yet. Ha! As if it would be a "second" front. I'd lost track of how many fronts I had to manage now.

"Mikhail, you have to see this..." Chernomor distracted me from my thoughts and memories. I could tell by his expression that he was surprised by something.

I followed him to the surveillance room used by the men monitoring what the pigeons were up to. Pigeon managers. We hadn't yet decided on their official title. They referred to themselves as the Feathered Aerial Attack Squadron, but there was another unofficial name applied to them. No, they weren't called "peckers," if that's what you're thinking, even though pigeons "peck" their food. They were called, jocularly, something else related to pigeon anatomy.

"What is that?" I asked, approaching a screen. I saw what they were talking about.

"Look," said one of the men, pointing to a stockpile of equipment "At first we thought it was enemy combatants, but then feathered fighter number seven descended, and allowed us to take a closer look.

"Yes, now I see..." I shook my head. "I wonder what they did with the horses?"

"The second bird shows the horses," reported another operator. And indeed, a herd of thirty horses was galloping through the forest towards the castle. I was avidly interested in what Gerg would have to say once he got back to the castle.

"Good job!" I praised the guys. They truly did work hard day and night, and thus far not a single enemy detachment had made it past them. Both these guys and the pigeons they managed never got more than three hours of sleep a day. The rest of the time they survived solely on my nourishment.

"Sir, please don't take this as impudence, but may I ask you a favor?" asked the commander of the operators, and I nodded. But of course. "Ummmm..." he cleared his throat and began to speak hesitantly. "We would like you to forbid everyone from calling us 'wingnuts'."

"Well, I can't prohibit the impossible," I said, shaking my head. "So, sorry. Anyway, would you like me to give you a shot of energy?"

They just shook their heads and stared at their screens as if totally immersed in their work. Well, okay then. No need to talk them into it. As regards the nickname, it was too widely used now to do anything about it. I could issue an order, but it would be impossible to enforce.

Soon the captured equipment entered the castle grounds, where I greeted it with open arms.

"Sir, just don't swear," Gerg immediately raised his hands. "But when we saw these machines, we simply couldn't help ourselves. It was beyond our powers."

Thirty motorcycles drove into the yard. More precisely, twenty-nine, one of which had a sidecar. When I said I wanted to see the offworlders assimilate in this world, I meant something else. Anything but this.

Now, thirty brave fighters, freed by me in another world, decided to switch to this world's transport, and their choice fell on motorcycles. And according to the law of the Bulatov Family's pilots, these cyclists had obtained their own equipment. And they'd all made their own personal choice, evidently. Yes, all of these "iron horses" were different. Only Arnold, the old runologist, didn't sit astride one, but there was a place for him, too. He was in the sidecar, happy as a clam. He wore a helmet, and was holding a machine gun and his smile stretched from ear to ear.

However, this wasn't a bad thing. Motorcycles weren't likely to be picked up by radar, and so Gerg and his Combat Doves were now far more mobile. This is because these motorcycles were faster than horses.

I left Gerg and his team to deal with their new "toys," having given them access to the repair shops and mechanics, and then I went to review some reports. Specially trained guards regularly provided me with brief updates on recent events.

In addition to several serious attacks, Valentine was tirelessly sending small reconnaissance detachments into our lands. In this regards, the pigeons again were helping out. They would take note of any border violations and pass the information on straight to Chernomor. What happened next would vary. Either he'd send out the Combat Suits, or else Chernomor himself would take a few strong fighters to deal with the threat.

And the pigeons were wonderful. But they'd been working so much that exhaustion was beginning to set in. Now all we had to do was keep an eye on the baron. As for the others, we couldn't fully keep tabs on them. I did make a point of keeping the key figures in enemy territories under surveillance, but that was all.

And solutions to our inadequacies were always manifesting. As happened just now. Duke Konakov just recently sent me several vehicles loaded with all kinds of equipment. Even though such expenses hit my pocketbook, I still had some funds in reserve, and if necessary, I could start selling the most common, cheap artifacts. I dared not sell anything truly valuable or rare, but my selling commonplace artifacts wouldn't raise any eyebrows. Moreover, I had already publicly participated in repelling Interfaces several times, which meant I could have easily obtained such artifacts in battle.

The equipment sent by the duke included tens of kilometers of cable, repeaters and transformers, a couple of generators, and, most importantly, cameras. Within a day my people had them hung on almost every tree on the border with the baron, and these cameras included motion and noise sensors, and much more. So now all I had to do was download a special program to the central computer, and press the power button. In fact, now was the time.

"Sir, we have checked everything, and now we

turned off the system, and we suggest that you start it up yourself," the chief technician said with a smile. Or was he a computer scientist? I couldn't tell the difference. Simply put, he was the guy who'd installed all this stuff in the room next to my study.

Now I just had to press a button, and images from multiple cameras would be displayed on numerous screens. But that's not all, as the sensors placed throughout the forests would also be displayed on a map that spanned an entire wall. If any sensor was triggered, then my operators would know exactly where the intrusion occurred.

I really loved this kind of high tech stuff. Yes, something like this could be constructed using magic, but that would consume energy. This way was simple, fast, and cheap.

Except for one thing. As soon as I pressed the button, the computers all around us began to come to life and make noise, but then all of a sudden the sounds died down and all of the lights went out.

"What's going on?" I asked. My vision immediately switched over to accommodate the pitch black and I saw a puzzled computer guy who was trying to figure out by touch what happened. "Kooky!" I called my main informant after stepping out into the corridor.

In fact, all of the lights were out, all over the castle.

"*Cooo!*" my scout responded. "*Coo-cooo!*"

"What do you mean, everywhere? Fly higher,

look." According to the bird, it was not only the castle that was without power.

At first I thought the computers were malfunctioning. Or, as electricians say, "the fuses blew." But no, they were fine. Moreover, it wasn't only us who'd lost power. Kooky ascended high into the heavens and said that, wherever he looked, he could only make out individual lights. In our fortress, which was powered solely by generators, there was light.

But Arkhangelsk, which used to blaze with lights all night, now looked like a black hole. I went straight to the operators' room. Previously, they watched the pigeons through screens, but as soon as the screens went out, the operators switched to special tablets. A field option, in case of special missions.

And so from them I managed to find out more. First, the lights were off everywhere. In some places, generators were firing up, as would be the case here at the castle any minute now. But the most interesting thing was now happening in the area of the power plant that supplied the entire city of Arkhangelsk.

"Do you hear?" one of the operators said in fear. I also strained my ears and heard sirens wailing in the distance. "Code red...

I know very well what this red code of theirs is. When you hear such sirens, whether you are an aristocrat or a commoner, wielding a weapon or a Gift, even if at such a moment you are fighting an enemy, you must immediately stop everything and move towards the sound. It signaled an emergency situation that required all hands to resolve.

And thus, at the main power station the fun was in full swing, it seemed. We could see flashes of magic sparkle as one portal after another opened up releasing an ocean of offworld warriors, mages, knights and catchers. They all set about destroying everything around them, meaning that now the power lines and stations providing electricity were all down as the dense wave of invaders streamed toward the city in an attempt to conquer it in one fell swoop.

This was the most serious attack by the Interface world I'd seen yet. And we all had to throw whatever we had into dealing with the threat. My only question is what would the baron do? Could I expect him to join everyone else in fighting the offworld threat?

Um, no, I don't think so. In about ten minutes the servants started the generators. They simply hadn't been ready for something like this, so they swiftly filled up the tanks to the generators, and then started working on the castle's electrical system... In the meantime we were left without our new surveillance system for tracking what was going on across our borderlands. So yet again I had to dispatch our poor pigeons.

They soon they transmitted a video showing how a host of Grishanov's detachments were approaching our borders. As I expected, this scoundrel didn't even think of helping out in the common cause. Perhaps he'd sent a couple of troops to signal that 'Hey, I'm a good guy." And all of the rest he'd dispatched to seize my lands.

Right, as if I'd let that happen! Chernomor immediately mobilized his fighters, and a column of equipment headed to the borders, where the incursion was planned. The mobile group occupied the fortifications, and when the first enemies appeared, my guards opened heavy fire on them. So they had to regroup and wait for reinforcements.

I went with Chernomor, taking the earth mages with me just in case. The battle promised to be hot, and I'd need all my strength. But I left Victoria behind. She'd already spent a lot of her energy with Belmore.

Flashes of gunfire and explosions were already visible from afar, and when we approached, a fierce battle was unfolding. The baron was pulling out all the stops, probably assuming that he might never get another chance like this. First he sent in the heavy tanks to try to take out our border fortifications. The artillery started firing, each shell kicking tons of smoking earth into the air.

Infantry poured out of the forest thickets with menacing cries. And judging by intelligence data, even under heavy machine gun fire, the number of enemy troops was only growing. This was going to be complicated, but I only smiled at it all.

"Gerg," I called the lead biker over. "Circle around and hit them from behind. They have a lot of equipment there for supplies, so burn it!" He nodded, and his detachment roared their engines and sped down the road. "And you, Chernomor, get ready. We're going to have some fun..." I said, my sword shining with a barely noticeable greenish light. The energy discharged over the crossbow slung over my back and fed the energy supply in the bolts.

And a complex blood rune manifested in the air before me. I'd been creating all sorts of supplies for generating interesting very colorful spells this past week just for something like this.

Bz-z-z...

"Well, as usual..." I cursed and interrupted the casting of the spell, quickly placing a securing seal on the rune. This way I wouldn't have to generate it all over again.

Sometimes such a seal was called a "dinner seal." You can get tired creating complex spells and runes. And so you might want to check out for a bite to eat. As for me, I was simply picking up a call.

How timely. The enemy just started another attack, and hundreds of enemy fighters were already visible from here. There were also a few more tanks, a couple dozen armored vehicles, and much more...

"Hello," I sighed. "Who is this?" I didn't recognize the number. Not that this was unusual.

"Count Bulatov?" I heard an irritated voice. "Why aren't you there?"

"I didn't arrange a meeting with anyone," I shrugged. "So, excuse me, but who is this?"

"I am Colonel Borvin! We've sent you some wounded!"

"I'm dealing with my own wounded now," I sighed. "Baron Grishanov is attacking me. That is why I am unable to help you," I said, pretending I was about to hang up.

"Stop! Forget about the war, head to your infirmary immediately! I'll take care of everything else."

And, in fact, a minute later the baron's troops suddenly stopped, and swiftly retreated. The tanks stopped firing, the artillery fell silent, and they all went back to their lands at once. All I could do was shrug. I completely forgot how I managed to avoid the war. I was a registered Healer now, and so I was no longer expected to help repel the Interface. I was supposed to fulfill my medical duties.

By the time I got back to the castle the baron had pulled his army back all the way to his mansion. I don't know what the colonel said to him, but I suspected that he hadn't pulled any punches. Even through the phone I heard how riled up he was when he learned that during a red code and a general mobilization, someone was attacking his neighbor instead of stepping forward with everyone else to defend the city and the world.

It was total chaos in my infirmary. Roman was doing his best. He'd recruited several maids to serve as nurses and was dashing about the infirmary from one patient to another. And he was simultaneously tinkering with medical equipment and using his energy whilst trying to apply his new knowledge. All the while, his eyes were sparkling. He was in his element, as it were. Of course, at the same time, he was clearly exhausted, as evidenced by the black bags under his sparkling eyes. We had at present only ten wounded soldiers. Half were seriously injured, and half were dying. There'd been more, but Roman had already cured them, and kicked them out of the infirmary. Well done, although I wouldn't waste so much energy on minor injuries.

"Stabilize the patient in bed five!" I ordered Roman, who ran over there and started pouring vital energy in him. Okay, now he'll live to see me, and then we'll figure it out. In the meanwhile, I began treating another patient. He'd lost a lot of blood, but my vampire sphere helped me. I could have restored his loss without it, but it would have required too much extra effort. I was sure that this wouldn't be the only batch of wounded we'd be dealing with.

Right I was! Just as I had stabilized the condition of two patients, the doors to the infirmary burst open and twenty men ran in. Without further ado, they unloaded a few more dying people and then disappeared, leaving me alone with the wounded. Okay, then...

Making sure no one could see me, I threw a cloud of life energy into the air. A green haze stretched across the room, a barely perceptible mist. This would make things easier, and hardly anyone would notice. And if they did, I'd just show them an artifact and say that I'd used it. The main thing was that I didn't want anyone to die in my infirmary.

"Mikhail! How can I help?" Victoria had rested up after her last difficult sortie in which she'd created a putrefactive golem, which took all her strength. But she'd awoken from all of the hubbub, and I saw in her eyes a burning desire to be of some kind of assistance.

Commendable. A Necromancer could always be of use.

"Come here," I waved her over, and as I made my way to one patient, I stabilized four more along the way. "Send these ones off because they can now self-heal," I said, indicating who I meant. They still had wounds, but all internal damage was repaired. And their bleeding had also stopped. "Do you see?" I showed the countess the curse imbedded in the fighter. "You inject some necrotic energy in that spot, and I'll clean up after you."

This would make it easy and also save me energy. Which mattered, because I could see headlights outside the window, which meant that the influx of patients wasn't about to stop.

"Am I doing it right?" Victoria was surprised that she could heal people. And yes, she was doing great; exactly what we needed. When she'd finished, the wounded man's chest was covered in blisters and his skin began to turn black. But with one flash of green it was all just fine. So then, next one...

* * *

One night flew by, and so did the following day. I sometimes had to draw strength from my servants, along with whoever delivered me more and more wounded. And gradually I noticed that among the crippled fighters there were more and more guardsmen from influential Families.

Perhaps I was hasty in my statement that only the living would emerge from the walls of the infirmary. And indeed, only one was carried out feet first, but he asked for it himself. And I didn't kill him, I just dealt him a couple of powerful blows in the heat of the moment, breaking his jaw and knocking out his teeth. There was no need to be impudent in my infirmary. No one is allowed to do this, be you an emperor or a divine being.

At some point, in addition to the guards, aristocrats were being brought here. But only those who were not from these parts. The local aristocrats figured they wouldn't leave here alive — that was my guess.

"Ooh... sweet," a young man in fashionable, tattered clothes broke into a smile as soon as he opened his eyes. "Honey, wouldn't you like to take a ride to the capital? I could show you around and then we could go to my place...." he said, his greasy gaze wandering over Victoria. The girl was tired, and therefore she didn't even have the desire to immediately hit him with necrotics. As for me, I always had a reserve shot for something like this.

Hands off, punk.

"This is the countess," I said to give him the opportunity to make amends. "And I am Count Bulatov"

"I am Duke Bobrov, I rushed straight from the capital to save your village," the guy laughed nervously.

"Careful, Evgeny. He just saved your life," hissed the large man who accompanied the kid everywhere. Apparently this was some kind of mentor.

"Oh, Uncle Pavel, what's wrong? You know I'm a chick magnet, don't you?" Bobrov guffawed, but not for long. After all, it's not so funny to simply pass out.

"I have to ask you to leave, Pavel," I said seriously to the idiot's mentor. "I guarantee that he won't die. I just need to talk to him alone."

"Well, okay," said the uncle looking distrustfully first at me and then at Victoria before stepping away.

So what did I do? I waited five minutes and performed several manipulations on the guy's body. His wounds were all healed, as well as his broken arm, but there were now a couple of surprises for the future. Since he was resting anyway, and there were no dying people in the infirmary yet, I took a walk around the castle, and only after that brought Bobrov back to his senses.

"Oh! That was some blackout!" he said, jumping to his feet and looking himself over. "What, am I healthy? In just five minutes? Count, you are a wizard, of course. But my offer still stands," and he winked at Victoria.

"You were out for two weeks..." I sighed. "It wasn't easy, but I almost succeeded. But I couldn't quite manage..." I took something out of my pocket and showed it to the duke. Seeing it, he again passed out, back to dream land. And then we talked...I assume that in future he'll be more careful. What he didn't realize was that I'd showed him ram's balls.

Why did we have them in the refrigerator? Well, for some time Kooky wanted, well, an enhancement to his gonads, actually, but I hadn't gotten around to it.

The carnage in the city lasted for quite a long time. For four days, explosions roared, the clatter of machine guns could be heard, and even from here I could feel the swaying of the magical aura from the power of the spells of the offworld mages. The Emperor himself was behind the masses of wounded sent to me. The fact is that the hospitals filled up in the first hours of the invasion, and after that, there was simply nowhere to take the wounded. And so they activated all of the Healers in the area.

I agree that this had to be done. But now what? The fourth day passed, and the influx of wounded stopped. Now the Interface was closed, and all that remained was to finish off the individual detachments of offworlders scattered about. So many troops had been called to Arkhangelsk that clearly this wouldn't be a problem, and there was no need to worry about security.

What was a hassle was the mess created by crowds of patients and their loved ones. The snow had just melted and the damp ground had been plowed up by all kinds of wheels, so now there was nothing but mud all around. And they'd also strewn garbage all about. So much for gratitude for saving their lives.

Diling!

That was an incoming message on my phone.

"Three hundred and fifty thousand credited..." as I read this another message appeared. "You have made a significant contribution to repelling the attack from the Interface world and are hereby invited to the spring ball at the Emperor's palace. Please RSVP your attendance."

But now I had to apologize to the Emperor. I was in the midst of a war and had no time at present for balls. And so I had to refuse the invitation. I was sure that this was an automatic invitation to all the aristocrats who took part in all this. And so nobody would notice my refusal. And if I was wrong and they did notice, I didn't care. I had too much on my plate right now. By the way, how was the baron doing?

"Kooky!" I summoned my feathered scout. "Remember that we talked about new balls for you? Perhaps you've changed your mind?"

* * *

Meanwhile
The Emperor's Palace

In a luxurious, spacious hall, members of the Emperor's family had gathered for dinner. They discussed the recent offworld attack, which had caused a stir throughout the country. It was a rare event for one to occur on such a massive scale, and never before had it transpired near a large city.

"I can't wait for the ball..." one of the Emperor's daughters said lazily. "Judging by the number of guests, you're going for a grand event this year, right?" she asked, looking at her father. The Emperor sat, frowning, and silently devoured his food. The recent events made him nervous and also left him very tired, both mentally and physically.

And although the Emperor thought of himself as young, in reality he was already eighty years old. But as he had the best Healers in the country looking after him, he felt like he was fifty.

The man was quite tall and strong, and his powerful Gift allowed him to keep himself in good shape. But the downside to this was that Healers couldn't do nearly as much to influence the health of those with strong Gifts. They could not break through his natural defenses. He personally managed the dispatching of troops, and it had been hard work ensuring that, in the process, the borders remained secure. Should he give their enemies a reason, they'd jump at the opportunity to attack his empire.

"I invited anyone who distinguished himself," he shrugged. "Just the deserving."

"Oh, and one turned us down," said the youngest daughter in surprise, looking at her tablet. "It's that Healer!" she said, even more surprised. "Remember? They told us about him. No one could understand why such a Gifted Healer was languishing in the hinterlands."

"A Healer?" The Emperor raised an eyebrow, then picked up his tablet and looked at the screen. "Why did he refuse? Is there a reason?"

The entire Imperial Family was suddenly interested in the strange count. It was highly unusual for anyone to turn down an invitation from the Emperor. In fact, it had never before occurred. Everyone wanted to be closer to the ruler, to show off, or somehow attract attention.

"How odd. He says that his Family is at war. Refuse the Emperor's invitation because of some war? Is he crazy?" the middle daughter was indignant. "I see this as a sign of disrespect!" she frowned. "Or perhaps there is no war, and he simply wants an excuse to not attend the ball! What kind of war can a Healer be in?"

"So let's check," the youngest daughter, Victoria Romanova, began poking at her tablet. "By the way, Fedot was treated by him, I think!" she exclaimed, and they immediately call this Fedot to the dining room of the Imperial Family.

The old man came in and stood at the table, and the Emperor, nodding, allowed him to sit down. After all, Fedot wasn't a "nobody" here at the palace.

"Well, tell me!" frowned the Emperor. "You were in his infirmary. What do you think of him?"

"Well..." Fedot hesitated. "Bulatov said that he was seventh rank, and according to the documents it is so. But he struck me as being fourth rank, no less," he spread his hands.

"I see..." the Emperor scratched his beard. "Interesting... Come on Vik, look up his background. What kind of war would compel him to refuse my invitation? Vik, what is it?" He looked at the girl who was staring at the screen with wide eyes.

"Um...Papa, his Family's forces consist of a hundred men."

"So what? They're weak. It happens," he shrugged.

"It does? For twelve years now they've been engaged in war against twenty-one Families! And those Families, well, they each definitely have forces that exceed a hundred!" the girl handed the tablet to her father, who, still scratching his beard, immersed himself in deep thought.

"Is he really a Healer?"

CHAPTER 7

"EHHH...."

"What's wrong?" asked Vika in response to my sad sigh.

We were in the drawing room about to enjoy some tea over a little chat. I, though, was staring into the fire, thinking about the problems that had befallen me.

"What's wrong?" I echoed, sighing again. "I got a message from your emperor."

"Our emperor," she corrected me, and I simply nodded.

"Okay, from ours....In any case, he's being pushy...He won't let me refuse his invitation," I said, showing Vika my phone screen. "What's ironic is that I had no trouble getting out of the summons to war, but this invitation to the ball, it seems, is mandatory. I tried to turn it down, but they sent me a message urging my attendance. To me, this is unfair."

"Really, how are we supposed to manage here without you?" Vika understood the full depth of the problem.

"Well, we've got our bases covered here," I reassured her. "First, I'll let you in on something, in case you didn't know. We have living here three earth mages. They are in and of themselves a formidable force, especially against the local misfits. And second, in the apartment next to yours lives a Magister of Death Magic and Necromancy. Not to mention two unique, well-honed wolf wraiths."

"That's true, but what if our enemies all attack at once...?" Victoria shook her head.

"We have the pigeon squadron," I reminded her.

"Okay, I give up," said the countess raising her hands. She knew I was right. "Although I have to wonder why we haven't yet killed all our enemies."

"We could have dealt with everyone by now," I shrugged. "But the thing is, we shouldn't do it too swiftly. I was too hasty and impulsive once, and lo and behold, I've now captured the attention of the government," I said, indicating the invitation on my phone screen.

"Well, you drew their notice by your miracle cures. You could always allege that you used stockpiles of artifacts held by the Family," responded Vika.

"I see. So in your opinion, should a struggling Family suddenly ascend to power in Arkhangelsk by killing half of the aristocrats, nobody would have any questions!?" I laughed, taking a sip of hot, sweet tea. Actually, by now it wasn't so hot. "Of course, I'm exaggerating a little. It would take a little while to kill all our enemies, but what I'm saying is that, if we were to bring all of our might down on them, we'd most certainly draw the notice of the truly powerful Families. This is why I've remained inside the sandbox thus far."

"In principle, I agree," the countess nodded. "I can hold the fort down here. You don't have to worry."

"But of course you could handle it, but I need you to go with me," I shrugged. Really, there was no question about it.

"That would complicate things," she said.

"True, but read the letter," I said, handing her my phone.

"On behalf of the Emperor, for your invaluable assistance in the fight against the offworlders...Hah!" she couldn't help but laugh at that. "Right, that's you! Holding back the offworld infection! Fighting them with all your might! No time even to sober up!"

"Okay, so I've had a drink with them a couple of times, what's the big deal? They're really a lot like us," I said, waving off her snark. "But you're right. We have to give Belmore a vacation."

"Oh, I think I comprehend!" she skipped ahead as she read the message. "Wow, so they want to give you an award? I mean, well...you really cannot refuse this invitation. But look, it says that they'll provide us with immunity for two weeks. We won't have to worry about attacks from our enemy Families," she indicated the invitation.

"Anyway, that's what it says here. For two weeks the Emperor himself will be our patron, and if someone attacks during this time, he will suffer greatly. Moreover, the disputed lands are also factored in here, so military actions are also prohibited there."

"Okay, so....go ahead and respond," I said to Vika, who still held my phone. "List the Families with whom we have the worst relations. Let's ensure they all know about the consequences should they attack us."

"And, as luck would have it, our construction work is in full swing. It's a good time to have a break," said Vika happily as she set about formulating a reply. I was impressed, watching her fingers fly over the little keyboard.

"Yeah, that's right, construction work," I sighed heavily. "As they say, you can ask for the best, but you can't always get what you want." Vika glanced up from the screen to shoot me a questioning look. "I had plans set to act decisively. Ultimately, checking out for two weeks will give the advantage to our enemies, to our detriment."

"Well, it's not like we'll be sitting around doing nothing," she smiled. "How many mages can you get drunk in that amount of time?"

"So many that we'll need to replenish our

wine cellar," I chuckled. "But, sadly, I won't be here. I'll be off to the capital. Ehh..." I sighed, yet again.

But that fact is, since I couldn't refuse the invitation, I had to somehow turn this trip to my advantage. I didn't yet know how, but I'd figure something out. And Vika was happy. She's needed a break, and a change of scenery would do her good. Me, I get to take jaunts to cities in the Interface world. She, in contrast, has been stuck inside this castle. A few years back she'd been studying in the capital, but then, things suddenly took a turn for the worse at the castle, and she'd had to return home.

We had three whole days to prepare for the ball. Still, we had to work day and night until our departure to ensure the castle had enough protection in our absence. I was pretty sure that, despite the Emperor's protection, someone would try to take advantage of the situation. They could hire mercenaries, say, who wouldn't know who their employer was, and that was just one possible scenario.

I dispatched Kooky to swiftly recruit more feathered fighters. To this end, I had four large lodges built for feathered creatures, and assigned servants to each one of them. Kooky insisted on this, saying that his fighters should have humane living conditions.

Now, the servants would add grain to the feeders, ensure fresh water for the bird baths and for drinking, clean the nests out inside the lodges, and lay down bedding. Kooky was also closely monitoring his diet. And it was gratifying to see how proud he was at his increasingly prominent role in our defense structure.

With so many new feathered warriors, I had to devote time to enhancing their capabilities. On the good side, I didn't have to worry about displaying my powers when I worked with the birds. That being said, it was a surprise to me to see what appeared to be stupid "birdbrains" making demands of me. One wanted green feathers, and another wanted blue ones. Four out of eight pigeons wanted bigger eggs. And that was just the start! The female pigeons wanted so many changes to their appearance that I had to introduce a uniform dress code.

At first I considered dividing them by color. Field aerial reconnaissance — blue feathers, forest spies — green. But I had to abandon that idea. If I were to do that, then the birds would be locked into a narrow specialization. And I had to put them all through a lot of training, as well. This required me to torture a lizard a little — I'd stolen it from the zoo. It wasn't hard to steal it, actually. My guys were professionals now, having learned how to steal geese.

What I needed the lizard for was a certain gene that enabled it to change its skin color at will. It wasn't easy, using it to make it possible for the pigeons to use this chameleon gene. But I was pleased with the result. Now, all of the pigeons but Kooky could change their color.

He refused, and instead asked me to share his "ghost" gene. But that wasn't something I could do. My pigeon is one of a kind, and it would take me years to replicate his abilities and pass them on to others. It's not even a given that it would work out that way. It could be that any pigeon I gave the gift of invisibility to would simply end up flying into walls even though invisible. Or else they might end up flying straight through the gates to the aviary afterlife!

In these three precious days, I also gave a "to-do" list to the fighters. I had Chernomor here in charge, and he could independently render decisions, but it made sense to discuss everything in advance. We established border patrols, had the Combat Suits inspect enemy lands around the clock, and had the pigeons doing their eavesdropping. We needed to get a handle on what they were planning for a couple of weeks from now. I expected we were in for a good time, at the very least. Also, while I had immunity, many of my enemies didn't. So Kooky could have some fun with them, disrupt surveillance systems, take dumps on their heads, although not the acid piss, but good times, just the same. After all, we had to keep the bad guys on their toes.

"I'll go with you," Belmore said firmly. "I need to look after my student, it's in the contract."

"I take responsibility for the student," I said. "You sit tight, guard the castle and study this world. It's not up for discussion. In the capital they'll figure you out right away and it wouldn't be easy getting you out of there."

"It's a different story out here," I went on. "We don't have anyone with truly strong Gifts to worry about. And even those with good sources lack the knowledge to use their Gifts to the full extent. However, in the capital, you might well encounter someone who is truly formidable. In any event, right now we cannot justify the risk of taking you. Why seek out trouble when trouble has no problem coming right to us?"

Willson also got his share of work. I had no plans on giving him days off, and I originally intended to make sure that our Artifactor was always busy. He, of course, whined to no end, calling me a tyrant and an exploiter. He was right of course. But deep down, I knew that Willson enjoyed his work.

After all, he had everything he needed, including great tools, fabulous accommodations, servants, and a charming masseuse with a comely figure. She got that from me, literally, and I'd worked hard to please my Artifactor so that he'd be inspired to work.

My one regret was that we weren't ready to launch the surveillance system in full. Electricity was still out throughout the region, and there was no way to purchase new generators, not even in neighboring cities They were sold out everywhere, as it was unknown when the power plant would be up and running again.

It got hit pretty hard, judging from the news reports. As did half the city, it seems. Once the portals opened, fires broke out all over Arkhan-gelsk. The news was full of wild speculations, and theories abounded. But I knew full well what caused that kind of instant destruction. What could take out all those power plants, and net-works feeding apartments and businesses all over the city? It had to be a powerful lightning mage to make all that instantly go up in flames. He struck with lightning speed, overloading the line, and his lightning bolts spread along the wires towards the city.

Yes, to me electricity itself was a kind of magic, even if the most ordinary kind. Although, in fact, what was mined at power plants is strik-ingly different from what is controlled by lightning mages. However, I had yet to delve into a serious study of this topic. In fact, lately I had precious little time to reread the rich library at the castle. For now, all I could do was acquire as many books as possible, and someday I'd find the opportunity to immerse myself in studying them. Ah, dreams.

One way or another, I had no doubt that this attack was planned jointly with persons from this world. It was all thought out to the smallest detail. The offworlders could not know all the intricacies of the electrical grid, and without hints, even a Lightning Archmagister could not have achieved such destruction.

Speaking of.... For some time I've wanted to enjoy some wine with one such. A lightning mage would definitely be useful on my team. There were wires everywhere, and with one such mage I could simply disconnect from the network while he started fires throughout Baron Grishanov's lands. Or throughout Kurchatov's county, should that suit our aims. Whatever the case, a lot of instruments and machinery relied on electricity, and without it, all that stuff was useless.

The day before leaving for the capital, I allocated a little... okay, a lot of money to Vika. I made her so happy, though. She used it all to buy new clothes. She even bought me a couple of new suits. I trusted her judgment in this regard. I do have good fashion sense, but I lacked the time to devote to shopping. Moreover, we could also make purchases in the capital, so I wasn't worried about it.

Vika tried on her new outfits all day long, sometimes showing me particularly chic dresses and glowing with happiness, and closer to night, she came to my room in a short, light dress. Actually, it looked more like lingerie, it was that revealing.

"I'm ready..." She said breathlessly, drawing near, and I snorted, sending apple juice through my nose.

Ahem... I cleared my throat. "I'm afraid to ask what you're ready for."

"Please, I'm ready for you to get rid of these scars."

Phew! I was thinking of all sorts of things. Although I have to say that Victoria was extremely attractive to me. Her face was lovely, her figure — perfect, and on top of this she was a woman of character. I could go on and on singing her praises, but I would come smack up against the fact that I was unlikely to be interesting to her as a man. And I wasn't the kind to coerce anyone into sleeping with me. Not that, as a Healer, this would be a problem. Even without using my Gift, I've never had any problems in that respect. All I had to do was secrete the right substances through my skin. I could fill any girl with the desire to throw herself at me....

Not that I ever needed to. Healers were always loaded with money, and that's all it really took. But Vika, I'm sure, would share my bed only to save her Family. That is why I never made moves on her. I didn't want to take advantage of the girl.

"So what influenced your decision?" I said, no longer interested in my glass of apple juice. "Lie down, then," I said, indicating the bed.

"Well, we're going to the capital, and it's been a long time since I've been there. And I have girl-friends there. I don't want them to see me with scars." Victoria blushed deeply and lay down on my bed, looking away, embarrassed.

In fact, there really were a lot of scars on her body. I'd removed them from her face, but her body...Had she deliberately exposed herself to damage? I couldn't think of how else she could in-cur so many wounds.

"And what about your lust for vengeance?" After all, she'd wanted to keep her scars as a re-minder of her enemies.

"Now I have you to help me wreak vengeance," she shrugged.

"True enough," I had to smile. "As they used to say in my world: if you want to upend the world, anger a Healer," the continuation of this proverb immediately came to mind. "And if you want to destroy the Universe, anger a Hunter. Right...." I muttered the last part under my breath, but Victoria heard it.

"What kind of Hunter?" she asked.

"Let's not worry about that now."

I removed the scars, and that was all. Victoria was naturally beautiful, so were I to alter anything else, that would only do her a disservice.

And the next morning, we set off. We could have waited another day, but since the castle was ready for anything, we decided to take the time to explore the capital, and see what we could buy there. I had some savings, and besides, the Empire itself recently transferred three hundred and fifty thousand to my account, so we had something to party with.

I brought Kooky along with me. Initially, I planned to leave him here, but over the last few days he managed to train his fighters, and the castle would be left in the reliable talons of his squad until our return. Chernomor, of course, thought that he was in charge, but the fact was that everything would be under the close supervision and control of the feathered bastards.

We arrived at the capital in a matter of hours, although we had to land to refuel along the way. However, the pilot warned me about this in advance and chose a completely safe stop belonging to a neutral and rather powerful Family. We only conducted business with major players now, as smaller Families could be bribed by my enemies.

The capital... How should this be understood? Helicopters were not allowed within the city, and we had to travel all the way from the airfield. Which was itself the size of Arkhangelsk, perhaps. And if the flight took a little over three hours, then the journey to the capital took another four. There was too much traffic here, and despite the width of the roads, the lines of cars were all stuck in numerous traffic jams throughout the city.

The first thing we did was rent a couple of armored cars and went straight to the hotel. It wasn't cheap, either. Victoria even recommended choosing something simpler and further from the city center, because such accommodations were beyond our means. But I just waved my hand at this. I'd spent enough time in cheap taverns, and didn't need to go back to that way of life. I didn't come to this world to sleep with bedbugs.

We chose a hotel that was conveniently close to the emperor's palace. We had to show up there tomorrow, and this greatly simplified getting there. We could simply walk from our hotel, and be there in five minutes. Plus, this hotel featured a nice restaurant, which I planned to enjoy with Victoria this evening.

The hotel itself occupied a twenty-story building with sharp spires on the roof. The rooms were all very comfortable and, yes, expensive, the service most accommodating, and the decor tasteful.

Tall, gilded columns and a marble floor polished to a mirror-like shine. The walls were full of paintings, and the halls featured lustrous chandeliers. Ludwig would have liked it here, but no, places like this were off limits to him. He would want to further enhance the interior decor, completely ignoring the people all over the place. No, we couldn't bring him to the city at all, even. It was crammed with architectural marvels — they were particularly evident in the city center.

Even my head was spinning. And that was me. I couldn't even imagine how Vika was feeling. Right after we settled in, I withdrew some funds and we went shopping. Near us was a large shopping center for aristocrats, and she would have never forgiven me if we were to pass it by.

The day flew by. Before I knew it, evening set in. First we walked around the fashion boutiques. I had to proffer my opinion on countless handbags, then we moved on to dresses, and then we ended with hats. The total cost was around forty thousand rubles. But it was worth it to see how happy Victoria was. She was glowing, and I was glad, knowing the hardships she suffered in recent years. We also walked around several artifact shops. And without a doubt, they were far more interesting than our provincial shops, primarily because no one tried to deceive me. Not to mention, no sidelong glances; the service was extremely respectful.

Each of my requests was fulfilled without fail, they showed me a variety of different items, and after being subjected to the magic of the sellers, I almost bought a couple of artifacts that were useless to me. Fifty thousand apiece, I must say. But all the shelves in my study were filled with this stuff.

Small protective medallions cost an average of sixteen thousand here. But medicinal crystals or something more complex had much higher price tags. And forget about average protective artifacts that could protect against both bullets and enemy magic. Vika had one such, and when she saw the price, she stashed the figurine into the depths of her new handbag. It would still work, and why show the world that she was carrying an artifact worth almost a hundred thousand?

What wasn't here were standard household artifacts. All they had were pictures of them, as these were single use items kept in a warehouse. Refrigeration artifacts, artifact furnaces, rock climbing artifacts. That sort of thing cost a lot, while all kinds of flints that worked on magic could be bought for just a couple of thousand. That is why the offworlders would use them on hikes.

At a couple of places, I cautiously asked what I might get were I to offer artifacts for sale, and it was just as I expected. Shops here were willing to buy whatever for half the market price. However, if I chose to sell wholesale, they offered more. I immediately backed away, joking that I, being from the wilds, couldn't possible have that many artifacts.

My impression was that they believed me.

"Can I go look at more bags, pretty please?"
Victoria had a pleading look in her eyes as we
walked into a gun shop. She could tell that I was
planning on being here for a while.

"Don't step away from me," I shook my head.
"As long as we're here in the big city, we should
stay together."

"I understand," Vika sighed.

In fact, we'd even booked a suite for two. Although this included two rooms, and we could
sleep separately.

Anyway, the countess understood my concerns. After all, this city was a paradise for those
who loved weapons. Yes, I am more into magic, but
that doesn't take away from my delight at seeing
what was on display here.

This store was housed in an underground
hangar. In addition to machine guns, grenade
launchers, pistols and other firearms, there was
all sorts of military gear, as well as the latest Combat Suits. Some models were viewable in three-D
models, with consultants hovering nearby who
could discuss any weapon with you in detail.

"Good thing Chernomor isn't here," Vika
chuckled. "His heart couldn't stand this," she said
looking at the room with machine guns. This entire room was dedicated to them. The old commander had a special love for automatics. I even
considered buying him one as a gift.

Take the six-barreled beauty weighing almost
one hundred and fifty kilograms capable of releasing a week's budget in a small urban-type

settlement per second in the form of massive bullets on the enemy's heads. Right in front of us, one aristocrat played with this toy, instantly shredding the dummy target into a pile of shrapnel.

Yes, I had to buy it. If not for the two hundred thousand price tag, I'd buy a couple more for myself. But this was just the initial investment. Next, I'd have to buy wagons of cartridges, which also commanded an indecent price, to put it mildly. So all I could do was look and drool. And also plan on how I might in future transport merchandise from here. I mean, the selection here in the capital greatly surpassed what could be found in Arkhangelsk, no doubt about it.

"So what's up with you?" Leaving the shopping center I encountered Kooky. He was perched on the back of a bench with downcast eyes, pondering something. "Are you sick or something?" I touched his forehead, but he turned away.

"No, his madam turned him down," smirked Vika, who had witnessed the pigeon's love drama. It seems that while I was absorbed in studying the display cases with weapons, the girl was more interested in watching the pigeon outside the window. And he also complained to her that the lady bird said something like "Leave me alone, you country bumpkin."

That's the capital for you. Even the pigeons here put on airs.

"Don't worry, Kooky. At home you have a Jacuzzi and hordes of lady pigeons!" I said, trying to cheer him up, and I succeeded

"Coo-coooo," he uttered thoughtfully, and having reached some kind of decision, he took off. Perhaps he was going to brag about his bird spa in the hopes of winning her over. However, I could use some spies in the capital, so I wished him well.

Next, Victoria and I want to the restaurant. It was quite noisy, as if they were preparing for some kind of celebration, but we took a table away from everyone else just to have a bite to eat.

It would take at least a week to try everything on the menu. And I'd have to sit in the restaurant and order one dish after another.

As usual, I elected something meaty to eat, but to my mystification Vika chose a couple of light salads. This wasn't like her at all. Usually she ate more than me. Although, I soon realized that she was just looking at what others were ordering and did not see any ladies choosing baked wild boar or grilled elk leg for themselves. Too bad, too, because they were missing out on the best items, at least in my opinion.

"Do you remember how we threw you through the window of the women's residence hall that night? Hahahaha!" some young aristocrat shouted at a table not far from us.

His two friends obviously remembered, because they, too, burst out laughing. But they didn't stop there and continued to reminisce about their student years, washing it all down with liters of alcohol. And gradually the noise from this table rose to a crescendo.

"Young men, I ask you to keep it down," a

man reprimanded them, after which it became a little quieter. But over time, the alcohol fueled brains couldn't be contained, and the young aristocrats lost all sense of decorum.

I didn't care as I could simply turn my hearing down. They weren't attacking anyone, just sitting there having fun with each other. But I could tell how unpleasant this was for Vika. She came to have dinner with me in an expensive, gourmet restaurant, but ended up in the equivalent of a port tavern with drunken riffraff.

"Excuse me, but could you shut these young people up?" I asked the waiter loudly.

"Listen to the bumpkin!" one of the rowdy lads guffawed, without giving the waiter a chance to answer. "Is it too much trouble to say that to my face?"

"Okay," I shrugged and approached the three aggressive punks.

Three punches later, their bodies fell to the floor. And who did they think they were? Did they really think that their personal shields would protect them from a shot of vital energy? I guess that for whatever reason, they, along with everyone else, was deluded when it came to Healers.

All the sounds around me died down, and I calmly went back to my table to finish my still hot steak. There was a commotion at the door, but I didn't even turn towards the sound. After all, I checked in advance what kind of security there was here. And I must say that it was quite worthy. I would never have thought that a Gifted of the second rank would work as a doorman, no matter how posh the place. And from all appearances he was such a modest little man.

Now he, along with several other guards, was holding back attempts by several guardsmen, those careless and harsh guys, to break into the establishment.

"Look at the young people we have," a woman of about forty-five quietly addressed her husband. "They jump right into a fight at the littlest little thing."Ehhh…"

"I can hear everything if you have something to say," I turned toward them, ending their conversation. And that was great, because it was the only way we could eat in peace.

Gradually the incident was forgotten, and the restaurant filled with familiar sounds. Calm, soothing music again filled the air, we finished our meal, and I asked the waiter to bring us some wine. We were very comfortable at that point. All the more so because some kind of event was starting up here. There were several tables in the center of the hall now, laden with a variety of delicacies. The tables around the center were left as they were.

Soon the place was full of people, the music was now louder, and new faces began approaching our table. Or, rather, they approached Victoria with the aim of becoming acquainted or inviting her to dance. How slow-witted they were, though. I politely informed the first man that I was sitting right here and that the girl was with me. The second man, well, I was a little less polite with him. The third approach forced me to raise my voice. And then I simply lost count. Each new guest considered it his duty to approach the countess and try his luck with her, ignoring the fact that she was not alone.

"I was blinded by your beauty, and I..." some slicked-back skinny turkey approached, but I didn't let him finish. I stood up and loudly, ensuring that everyone present could hear me, I issued him a warning. It was meant for him and everyone else ogling Victoria.

"The next man who draws near us will end up in a coma. And he will also lose his ability to reproduce. In other words, I'll rip his balls out. Guaranteed!" That was probably harsh sounding, but oh, well. "If you haven't noticed, the girl is not alone here, she's with me," and the turkey vanished like the wind, and there were no more men angling to meet Victoria anytime soon.

"Excuse me..." about twenty minutes later another man approached us. He was around twenty years old, of average height, with light hair and blue eyes. It would be a shame to have to castrate someone like that. But since I promised... I stood up and looked at him.

"Since you began with an apology, I'm giving you a choice. I can strip you of your dignity and then send you into a coma. Or I could first ensure you've passed out before freeing you of what you're better off without, that being your balls," I said.

In response, the young man's eyebrows shot

up and he laughed. "I'm afraid that if you deprive me of the opportunity to continue the family line, my father will be upset. Not much, perhaps, but still... It would be an irreparable loss," he said, and then he hesitated. "But actually, you are the one I came to meet," he smiled at me.

Vika immediately burst out laughing, and I rolled my eyes and landed back in my chair.

"Sorry, but I'm not of that persuasion," I waved him off. And that's when I noticed that absolutely everyone present was looking in our direction. And the stranger had no intention of leaving. Hmm... "And the inability to continue the Family line would be a loss for whom?"

"For the Empire, of course," he shrugged and sat down opposite us at the table. "Allow me to introduce myself....Alexander Romanov!"

But of course. Who else could this be? None other than the emperor's son, that's right.

"Actually, I had two questions for you, but one of them disappeared all on its own. How and why is it that you are waging war against twenty-odd Families, I already get that, but... Satisfy my curiosity, because my sister and I argued about this all evening."

I raised an eyebrow, and the emperor's son leaned in a little closer so that no one else would hear. "What rank are you as a Healer?"

"Oh, I'm nothing special," I waved dismissively. "I'm weak. Why are you interested? Is someone feeling ill?"

"Intriguing..." Alexander said thoughtfully.

"Is it only you who live in Arkhangelsk who have weak Healers who can treat four hundred wounded at once? The Imperial Healer, for example, would have died after treating a mere two hundred."

That is when I realized that they'd been not entirely forthright about the Healers in this world.

CHAPTER 8

VIKA WAS SURPRISED that the emperor's son had sat down at our table. Well, me too, but only slightly. In the old world this was a common occurrence because, after all, my brother was the emperor. He and I often dined together, had some drinks, and swapped stories. Right, the memories came flooding back, and now they were unpleasant to recall.

"Please forgive me, Alexander, but we were about to leave. I hope to see you at the ball," I stood up and bowed politely to him, then offered my hand to Victoria.

She looked slightly aghast and even paled, but she took my hand and also got up from the table. Alexander's eyebrows rose in surprise. He'd just been abandoned, after all. I'd been unerringly polite, but it was as if the first time something like that had happened to him. He had no verbal response, in fact. He simply nodded and called the waiter over. Apparently, he decided to eat away his surprise.

"To be honest, I didn't expect to meet him here," I said quietly as soon as we were outside.

"Why not? The Romanov family doesn't eat from a golden spoon. It's not strange for them to frequent such places," Vika shrugged, and now it was my turn to be surprised.

It turned out that this was part of their way of being here, and it compared favorably with other rulers. For example, a member of the royal family might step outside to talk with protesters. People might gather in the square to demand lower taxes, and then the eldest daughter would come out to discuss the issue. Afterwards, the discontent would dissipate. There had been a couple of assassination attempts, but there was a reason that the Romanovs were the ruling dynasty. It wasn't at all easy to kill one of them, even if they were for whatever reasons without guards. Which didn't often happen.

"I'm truly amazed," I nodded approvingly.

"What did you think? That they'd bring out the guns as soon as the people stirred?" chuckled the countess, and I just gestured as if to say, sure, why not?

"Sounds to me like you hail from a cruel world," she said.

"Yeah, said the one whose Family was almost destroyed by its neighbors," I quipped.

"Um, it's not just my Family anymore. You are also a Bulatov, so your Family, too, was almost destroyed by your neighbors," Vika frowned, cocking her head. "But really, why didn't you want to talk to the emperor's son? It's an opportunity not given to just anybody."

"I couldn't figure out exactly on whose behalf he wanted to speak. Although now I think that, most likely, it was on his own," I said thoughtfully. "In any case, it makes more sense to talk to him after the award ceremony, and avoid any unnecessary gossip. For example, rumors that I was given the award only because I know Alexander."

It's wasn't like I even needed this award. I wasn't going to throw it away, but I would be tossing it, say, under the bed once I got home. To me, it was nothing more than a worthless trinket.

"Do you think that Alexander Romanov doesn't have the intelligence to realize this?" asked Victoria. Right, she herself only now realized it. But I didn't voice that thought. Instead I said,

"I don't think Alexander Romanov gives a damn about it." And smiling wryly, I added, "After all he is the emperor's son. But in fact there's another reason why I wanted to leave as soon as possible."

"What's that?" she asked, curious. "Tell me!"

"Did you see his guards? The weakest of them is of the second rank. And all of them were staring at me. After all, I'm the guy who just knocked out three aristocrats in the presence of the heir to the throne. Were I to sneeze, they'd have riddled me with bullets!" Indeed, Alexander's security was strong, and also on edge. Each of them had been ready to release all their power at me at the drop of a hat.

"Yes, you're probably right about that," sighed the countess.

"Of course I am," I shrugged. "I was a little hasty once, and now we are forced to hang out here in this capital."

"That's a good thing!" Victoria exclaimed, and I just sighed. It was good for her, of course.

By now we'd reached our suite. She went into the far room, while I occupied a spacious bed. As soon as my head touched the pillow, I plunged into a deep, dark slumber. I needed sleep, that's for sure. I'd worked myself to the point of exhaustion over the last few days, and now my body was demanding payback.

I woke up in the morning from a certain bird pecking me on the forehead. I peeled one eye open, and was immediately bereft of sleep. This was because before me was Kooky's swollen, beat up face.

"Kooky, what happened to you?" I quickly examined his wounded carcass. At least half of his feathers were missing. His body was covered in scratches and wounds, and one eye was swollen shut.

"Coo-cooo," he intoned, tired, and waved a wing as if to say "just do it."

All I could do was shrug. One green flash, and a newly invigorated Kooky, fresh and bright, stood before me. It might take a couple of hours for all of

171

his feathers to grow back, but my feathered fighter was again ready for action. Nodding at me, he flew off somewhere through the wall. Ungrateful creature didn't even thank me!

*   *   *

Some time later
Mansion on the outskirts of the capital

"Okay, scumbag, will you or won't you tell me?" The man in a formal suit dealt a stinging slap to a servant tied to a chair. The pathetic man uttered a short cry and started trembling all over. "Tell me! What happened? Why do I need this incompetence? I charged you with one simple task! Look after my aviary, that was it!" The aristocrat was so incensed that saliva sprayed out of his mouth right into his servant's face.

"I swear, sir!" sputtered the servant. "It was just like I said! I'm telling you the truth!" Another blow ensued at this as the aristocrat howled in impotent rage.

Of course, just yesterday he had expected to reap considerable riches from what had now resulted in a huge loss. Baron Volodaev had had to tap a lot of connections, spend a tidy sum, and take risks by breaking a couple of laws in order to acquire six offworld hawks.

These were real super-predators, aerial monsters several times stronger than regular hawks, although outwardly they looked just like them. He had to pay for them in gold, and then wait several long months, not to mention invest in constructing a special aviary and hiring experts in caring for raptors such as this.

He'd been anticipating participating in competitions with them, as well as using them for hunting, and simply enjoying owning them. They'd be his trophy birds, and he'd show them off. And Volodaev had no doubt that these were indeed offworld hawks. He saw with his own eyes how strong they were.

But less than two weeks later, five of the six hawks had died. And then, on his way home from work, he learned that the sixth one, too, had perished. It had happened in the morning, right in the aviary, even though he'd posted a guard there, and no outsider could enter. Alarms, cameras, strong loyal fighters, all of this turned out to be useless.

"Now then, again tell me! And think about what you say," said Volodaev through clenched teeth. The servant was in charge of guarding the birds, no matter what it took.

"Sir, I swear!" By now he was crying. "A pigeon flew into the aviary. The birds were out flying about. You yourself said that whatever the hawks killed was fair prey! So I issued the command to catch and tear the pigeon apart!"

"Well, my hawks weren't poisoned! They were torn to pieces! Who did this, I ask you for the hundredth time!?" The baron's composure began to crumble again. He had heard this story more than once.

How the pigeon had eluded the swift attack of the first and fastest of the six hawks. And then the common little bird, the pigeon, had grabbed the hawk by the neck, breaking a couple of vertebrae. Then this unknown pigeon struck the other hawks with its wings a couple of times, and so, gradually, one after another, simply tore them to shreds. That being said, the dastardly pigeon had suffered damage in the process, as well.

"The last hawk could have killed the bastard. But no, the pigeon returned in the morning, alive and well, and finished the fight," the servant sighed, and the baron's face twisted in rage.

"Tell it to the executioner, you sorry son of a...." he waved his hand and left the torture chamber. "Half a million..." Volodaev shook his head in amazement. "They were supposed to live for a hundred years and grow ever stronger, but they were dead in a week."

* * *

Surprisingly, I find that in this world, I often have to do things that I absolutely do not want to do. But it is necessary....which is a word I've never liked.

The morning and afternoon flew by. Vika and I had a quick breakfast, and then walked around the center of the capital. For fun, I looked at real estate prices, and when I saw them, I immediately lost my sense of humor. Why would anyone buy apartments and houses here? What would be the point? Okay, if you worked here, perhaps in the emperor's court, you could justify it. But to opt to live here just for the sake of it would be extremely stupid. I, for one, enjoyed living outside of Arkhangelsk. There were beautiful places if you wanted to hike, or just enjoy nature, and there were plenty of Interface portals opening, and all sorts of fun, interesting events.

Anyway, before I knew it, it was evening. Vika and I, along with a couple of guards as a driver and a spare driver, headed for the palace. The place was full of people. That was a good thing, though. With a crowd like that, they might not even notice me, and that would save me the trouble of spinning tales about myself. Although I'd managed to invent a good background story, so that even if I happen to be put on the spot, I'll manage.

The palace was far from abundant in over-the-top luxury. We walked into the main entrance, and beheld a spacious hall. Paintings and other art adorned the walls, and gilding glinted in the lights, but none of it was excessive. It wasn't like the "in your face" luxury found in the former Snegirev mansion. This was tasteful.

The Imperial Palace was not like a single edifice; rather, it was like a network of interconnected buildings. The emperor himself and his family lived in one of them. Another housed the administrative offices and meeting rooms, where the council met, and his advisors worked. It was from there that the country was governed.

And here I was, in the center of Imperial power. A couple of spacious floors, and numerous rooms, and all them created specifically for major receptions and balls. It was like the Imperial Party Center.

We arrived at the start of the event, and had to wait for all of the other guests to show up. And then the awards ceremony began. Suddenly the music stopped, and a big shot general ascended a stage in the center of the main hall and began handing out all sorts of awards as the names of the recipients were called out.

"Evgeny Romanovich Kurdin!" yelled the general, the cluster of medals jingling as he clutched them. "For your exceptional contribution to the defense of Arkhangelsk, I award you the Order of Courage, 3rd degree!" Everyone applauded as a soldier in a dress uniform, his hand swathed in bandages, clambered onto the stage. He also had a bandage over his right eye.

And then, one after another, military men and aristocrats who had made a contribution to the defense came up. And also, fallen heroes were remembered. Their loved ones accepted their awards on their behalf. I didn't understand what the point was. Why invite relatives of the dead to this ceremony? But Vika explained that this award meant that the families who were deprived of their breadwinner would be provided for from now on.

"Oh, look," I nodded at another important aristocrat who, at the general's invitation, came out into the center of the hall. "A freeloader."

"What do you mean?" Vika was taken aback. And not just Vika, several people turned around to glare at me.

"Look at his hands. There's not a single callus there," I chuckled. "His award is for the bravery he exhibited in rushing up to the portal and taking upon himself a massive attack of offworld magic."

"But he was also wounded...He's got that bandage around his head, and he's also limping," protested Victoria. "It does look like he was injured when he busted into the portal."

"He broke into the dining room to help himself to leftover pie," I laughed. "That is what most likely injured him."

No, this guy was no warrior, that was obvious. Sure, he had a high rank, but he was an armchair warrior who'd never seen real fighting. Genuine warriors had a hardened look that this guy lacked, and I am never wrong about this kind of thing.

Despite this guy, though, most of the awards were given to real heroes. I saw many worthy and strong people go up to the stage. Brave warriors, who risked their lives to selflessly bridge the gaps in the defense, saving the city from hordes of alien invaders.

"Wine?" A waiter distracted me from my thoughts. He had several glasses on a tray, but by the time I turned around, all of them had been snatched up by others. "Sorry, I'll be right back with more!" he said, paling at my expression, and dashing off. And in a flash he was back with more, including a glass just for me. Actually, two glasses. However, Cherepanov wasn't here, so I could drink in moderation, meaning, I didn't have to imbibe to the point of unconsciousness.

I'd almost been depleted of energy in our last drinking session. I'd had to activate blood magic to purge alcohol from my body. I had too little vital energy for that amount of alcohol.

A pretty, older woman walked up. But she wasn't seeking me out; rather she wanted to speak to Victoria. She asked her what she was wearing around her neck, and the countess blushed and smiled as she said it was a Family heirloom. In fact, I hadn't even noticed the jet-black beads that absorbed the light.

What a shame that this obviously expensive trinket was devoid of magic. But I could fix that! I just had to remember to give them to Willson. He could buff them up. If, of course, Victoria allowed it.

"Oh, that on is strong..." I nodded approvingly. "He's gone through some serious trials."

"What do you mean?" Vika asked, training her gaze on a stern man who was receiving two awards. She saw nothing remarkable about him.

"He has several marks on his energy canvas," I said, having carefully scanned him. "He's the real deal, yes. This was someone who has more than once pushed himself to the limit."

The general awarded a couple dozen more people, and then he left. But before I could breathe a sigh of relief, Alexander Romanov came up on stage. I'd been hoping that they overlooked me.

"And now, I shall award those who have displayed exceptional feats in distinguishing themselves," he said, and a hush fell over the throng of people in the large hall.

The first awards went to two soldiers guarding an apartment building who'd faced down a massive attack of offworlders over the course of several hours. They'd been riddled with wounds, and I remembered one of them. We treated him in my infirmary. They'd written him off, but now here he was, almost totally pain free. Of course, I deliberately made a point of not being the only one to treat him, or the others lest I arouse suspicions. As for this guy, he'd be good as new before too long. In, say, two months the fractures and damage to his internal organs would be fully healed.

After the awards for the fighters had been passed out, the emperor honored the chief physician of the hospital. He turned out to be some poor aristocrat who'd ensured that the network of hospitals was fully prepared to receive the injured even before they were wounded. He'd also paid for several generators out of his own pocket, and had them up and running when the power went out. His flawless organizational skills had helped save countless lives, and for this, Alexander Romanov was now presenting him with an award. It was, I believe, well-deserved. And moreover, this man was a Healer. A weak Healer, but still, he'd given all his energy to the wounded, and to this day he was still exhausted.

Alexander presented awards to a wide variety of people. Not all of them were warriors or aristocrats. For example, there was a truck driver. He was terribly nervous at appearing before the emperor's son, and when Alexander himself pinned the medal to his chest he was shaking all over. But really, why? The worst was behind him. What he'd done was drive a multi-ton dump truck loaded to the brim right into a large detachment of offworld cavalrymen. He'd rammed them over and over again, until his truck was destroyed. How he survived was anybody's guess.

"The next award goes to one who used his healing Gift unsparingly, at cost to his health!" Alexander smiled and looked at me. Ahhh....just the same, I was up.

I walked out of the crowd, climbed the steps, and the emperor's son began to pin an award to my chest. It was strange looking, but somehow familiar.

"The Star of the Hierophant," he announced, and I was damn near flabbergasted.

"Star of what? Excuse me?" I wanted to make sure I'd heard him right.

"The Star of the Hierophant marking the Third Rank," Alexander repeated. "Don't feign ignorance, Mikhail. Thanks to you, many good warriors and honest people were able to live to see this day," he patted me on the shoulder.

I simply nodded curtly, and returned to stand by Victoria. But now the sounds around seemed to have died down, because... Hierophant? I looked at the star again and noticed something familiar about it. From my past world, where I had been a member of the Order of the Hierophant. Initially, I was thinking of just throwing away this useless trinket, but now that was out of the question. I would study this star inside and out once I got home, because I needed to understand what exactly was so familiar to me. I mean, besides the name.

Vika quickly realized that it was futile to talk to me now. She wanted to chat about this and that, but I was so immersed in my thoughts that I didn't hear her. How did they know about my Order here? I don't recall any of my subordinates coming here. Or... No, I, personally, performed the ritual to transfer my consciousness after the Order was destroyed. And it was completely destroyed right before my eyes. In short....this was all too, too mystifying. There's no such thing as coincidences...

I was distracted from my thoughts by a distant noise coming from the other end of the hall. Vika and I were now in a room where refreshments were laid out on tables. Vika mentioned that she wouldn't mind having a bite to eat, and headed for a table laden with delicacies. Suddenly, a woman approached her and almost accosted her, saying, "Ha! My fiancé wasn't awarded a medal like yours was, but he's a real hero, not a fake one!" The woman went on, sounding mean. "There's no way any Healer could save so many lives! It has to be connections, that's what! What rank is he, even?

Seventh? He's a weak coward, and a scoundrel."

"You're a narrow-minded fool, and you don't even understand what you're saying," Vika retorted. Why bother arguing with someone so twisted?

"What?" the other woman gasped. "How....how dare you! I challenge you to a duel!"

"Fine," Vika responded.

Well then, should I do something to sort this out? Although, why? Vika was a grownup, and, like me, she had every right to manage her own affairs. Time for me to step back and let her shine. Anyway, the unpleasant woman harassing her had a weak Gift of Flame, and I didn't see her as a serious threat. Moreover, the duel was only to first blood, and also, since I was there, Vika would come to no harm.

The duel between the ladies turned out to be anything but short and sweet. With men, it's always simpler. We unsheathe our swords and go at it. But this wasn't the case with women. For one, before fighting, they had to change their clothes. Guards had to be sent out to fetch the appropriate attire, which, it seemed, the ladies had brought with them. In fact, I liked Vika's dueling outfit more than her dress. Not that I dared voice that thought.

It took an hour, and then the girls were in the dueling circle. They then drew their swords, and the judge, this being the general who'd handed out awards earlier, announced the start of the duel.

Vika's opponent exploded in flames and

launched a ragged stream of fire at Victoria. But Vika didn't even flinch. She fired a bolt of death towards the fire, which exploded into a black cloud in the path of the Flame spell. Then, as the cloud began to disperse, Vika emerged from it swinging her sword. The ensuing battle was quite interesting. Vika didn't use all her powers, because, after all, being a Necromancer, she required corpses for that. That's why she attacked only with spells from the school of death, and even then, the weakest and simplest of the lot. If she used anything from the serious arsenal that Belmore had only just begun to teach her, it would raise too many questions. Therefore, the battle unfolded with the two ladies employing the pure force of the two elements, and sometimes the ringing silence of the banquet hall was cut by the clanging of steel.

The fight ended unexpectedly. Vika leveled a short swing at the impudent aristocrat, inflicting a deep scratch on her cheek. But Vika's death force penetrated the wound, so that just a few seconds later black veins began to spread from the wound while the girl's skin blistered. It was disgusting to look at and the girl could forget about her former beauty. It would take a powerful Healer to restore her looks.

"I..." a guy in his early twenties jumped out of the crowd and grabbed the girl who held her face in her hands. "I... challenge you to a duel!" he roared, seeing what Vika had done to the woman's face.

"You're a daredevil," the countess grinned.

"What rank are you?"

"Sixth," he hissed. "I'm strong enough to roll over you, village scum...What right did you have to attack my bride?"

"She's the one who provoked me by maligning my fiancé," Vika said, throwing up her hands. "She got what she deserved."

"What she said was true. All manner of idiots are making up legends about themselves!" growled the guy, grabbing the hilt of his sword. "Draw your weapon and prepare for a duel, carrion!"

"Better that I fight you," I said, stepping out of the crowd. "I challenge you to a duel."

At first he was surprised, but then a predatory grin appeared on his face. But of course, no seventh-rank Healer could face off against a Firebender, even if he was unranked. Although this guy was pretty strong, I had to admit. And he knew how to wield his Gift. True, he knew nothing about enhancing his Gift with magic, so no, I wasn't scared.

"Well, since you're challenging me to a duel, that means I can choose the weapon," he thought. "We'll fight with rapiers," he said, and a whisper went through the crowd of onlookers. But I just shrugged. Weird choice, but okay, let it be rapiers. Small matter that it had been a century and a half since I'd last used one. But I had a good teacher back then, and I trained hard for a couple of decades, and so I still commanded the skill set.

Of course, we had to wait around for them to find a rapier for me. I didn't have one, because I didn't need one, and so I was given a weapon from the emperor's own armory. The palace kept weapons on hand for when disagreements broke out that could be resolved by a duel right away rather than an extended war later.

My rapier was so-so, but the tip was sharp, so it would do just fine, even if the balance was mediocre, and the grip was awkward. Meanwhile, my adversary had a costly weapon made from offworld alloys that were excellent at conducting energy.

"Ready?" asked the general and we both nodded. "Then begin," he waved his hand and took a few steps back.

My opponent immediately released his power and skillfully concentrated it at the very tip of his weapon. I understood why he'd chosen the rapier, It was perfect for breaking through his adversary's personal shield, and then sending flames under his skin. He could do serious damage even to someone with a strong Gift, not to mention what he could do to a seventh-rank Healer.

But try as he might, I deftly dodged his attempts to stab me and I parried his blows. I dared not use my blood magic here, and so I simply made do with vital energy. In this way I didn't reveal all my powers to everyone here.

What I did was increase my muscular contractility, strengthen my tendons, ligaments and bones, and I slightly accelerated my reactions. Sometimes I deflected the flames with my diamond armor. One of the enemy's hands was free, and with it he launched fireballs, streams of flame and whirlwinds of fire at me. I guess that was all he had in his bag of tricks. Several times my sword scraped against his strong energy layer. I could have broken through it with the first blow, but that would have aroused suspicion. So I decided to harass the man a little.

True, I also allowed him a few points. Our duel was to the death, and so I allowed him a little taste of my blood. I permitted a couple of deep cuts on my arm, although I swiftly stopped the bleeding, and I also let him jab me in the stomach. You should have seen his surprised face when he tried to launch a concentrated flame at me, but instead the fire flared up onto the hilt of his sword. I wasn't about to let in someone else's energy, so I redirected it back at him. Seeing his confusion, I swiftly plunged my rapier into his chest, and he fell on his back, his eyes rolling.

"Doctor! Medic! Healer!" screamed his girlfriend, rushing forward to her man's side. The crowd stirred, and many in it stared at me.

"Well, I'm a Healer," I said, grinning. "Oh, right, I'm a charlatan," I said with a wave, "I forgot."

"Why am I still alive?" my opponent opened an eye. The sword that had pierced his chest right through to the heart was still sticking out of the wound.

"You have to know where to pierce someone. For example, I know anatomy quite well. Now you have time to apologize, but if you pull out the sword, you will die," I pointed at the thin blade, causing it to sway from side to side. "For now, though, you can still drink wine and spread your stupid rumors."

Then I stood up and looked at the girl, his bride, frozen in horror.

"And you," I ran my hand over her cheek, removing the ugly blisters and healing the wound. But not completely, so that a neat scar remained there, as a reminder of today, "From now on, watch your language."

Then I nodded to Vika, signaling that it was time for us to prepare to leave. I had already received the award, participated in the fight, and I had something to think about that warranted I find some peace and quiet. So, taking Vika by the elbow, we headed towards the exit.

"I demand that the rank determination procedure be carried out!" yelled the idiot with the rapier sticking out of his chest. "He is a liar and is hiding his strength!"

"You don't appreciate my kindness, little boy?" I growled at him, but he wouldn't shut up.

"I am Count Larionov!"

"You're a sniveling punk!" Several in the crowd gasped at this. But why? I was simply stating the obvious. And he'd started it, so there. "And I'm not opposed to an examination. If it would make everyone feel better, of course," I looked around at those gathered. None of them believed that I was only a seventh rank Healer.

And what was funny was that it was against

the law here to hide your strength, but forcing someone weaker than you into a duel, well, that was just fine. As if that made sense.

"What's going on here?" said someone who was obviously angry, and turning, I saw it was Alexander. He'd walked into the banquet hall and stared in surprise at the guy lying on the floor. With a sword sticking out of his chest, of course.

Then he slowly turned his gaze to me, but I could only shrug. It happens, doesn't it? Don't pretend you've never seen a man with a sword extending from his chest.

"Mikhail, please satisfy my idle curiosity," he said, approaching me. We moved away a little and sat down at one of the tables that stood along the walls. "You certainly know anatomy, so I wanted to ask why this young man did not die, although you pierced his heart?"

"Not the heart, but the pericardium," I smiled. "I guess he was just lucky."

Clearly Alexander didn't believe me, but he didn't press the issue. We chatted a little on unrelated topics. I told him how the attack of the offworlders went down in our neck of the woods, and I didn't forget to mention Roman, my student, who also diligently helped me with the wounded. Meanwhile, Firebender with the sword in his chest wouldn't let up. He didn't notice that I was talking to the emperor's son, and so he continued to grumble that I would definitely be punished and that I had lied about my rank. It cannot be that he, though rank six, had been defeated by me, rank seven. Worse still, I, a Healer, had defeated him, a Firebender.

"You'll answer for this, you bastard! You'll answer for it!" he said with a sneer. "Do you know what's gonna happen when the truth comes out?"

"Of course I know," I chuckled. "After they find out you're wasting everyone's time I'll again call you a sniveling punk. You and your girlfriend deserve each other."

"You...you...I'm going to..." he hissed and I just laughed.

"Yeah, get that rapier out of your chest, and then we'll talk."

All this time Vika was standing not far off smiling sweetly. I could see she was pleased at how it had all gone. She'd stood up for the honor of her family, and showed them all that it was better to not mess around with the Bulatovs.

And then, fifteen minutes later the court Healer arrived. It took him that long because, as it turned out, in another hall another couple of aristocrats had ended up fighting, and the court Healer had to treat both of them at once. He had to spend a lot of his energy working at the palace, poor guy.

"Oh, young man," exclaimed the hunched, thin old man. This was indeed the Imperial Healer, one of the best in the country. "A millimeter over and you'd be a dead man!" he exclaimed, carefully pulling out the sword and immediately pouring vital energy into the wound. "I would say that whoever inflicted this wound was at the least a first-rank sword master. Wherever did he come from? There are only two such masters in the entire Empire."

In the end, everyone wrote it all off as exceptional luck, while I just stood there and smiled. While the treatment was taking place, a team of examiners came to the hall. They asked me to sit down and began to lay out their instruments. A few artifacts and a bunch of electronics, you can't fool such technology. At least they didn't think so. And in reality I had to work hard, because this equipment was much more precise than what they used to torture me in Arkhangelsk. After all, this was the capital. And we were in the Imperial Palace.

The artifact began to literally suck energy out of me, but I held back most of it. The artifact didn't like this, so it sent out a reverse impulse, but it passed through me, because all the energy was reliably hidden in my peripheral magical channels. In simple terms, I argued with the equipment for about ten minutes, and sometimes even fought. But in the end the device started beeping, and some piece of paper was ejected from a slot, and the examiners nodded with satisfied faces.

"It's all in order! Count Bulatov is a sixth-rank Healer," said the head examiner, turning to Alexander.

"Ha! I told you so!" said the Firebender. "A liar, a cheat and a shameless deceiver! So what do you say now, huh?" he said, pointing at me. "You gonna admit that you're an impostor?"

"I really do have something to say," I sighed heavily. "First, you're a sniveling punk, but everyone already knows that," I said. He started sputtering, but I raised my finger and continued, "And secondly... Let's listen to the experts. I think they're not done talking yet."

"That's true..." the chief examiner was glued to the screen and spent some time comparing the data to something in his book. "It seems that you evolved into rank six between four and seven days ago."

"That is when the big Interface took place..." said Alexander, who was closely following all this. "When Mikhail healed four hundred wounded people!" The Imperial Healer, an old man who had saved the worthless life of the Firebender, approached me, along with Alexander. Both men were elated.

"I've heard of this happening....As one rises to a new rank, this can be accompanied by a powerful surge of power. This is what allowed you to heal so many people; now everything makes sense. I'd been racking my brains, trying to figure out how it was even possible!" he said with a sad little laugh. "Young man, I both congratulate you and sympathize with you. You knew you had a surge, right?"

I nodded in response. What was the point of making excuses when things were panning out even better than I planned? The old man came up, sighed heavily again, and put his hand on my shoulder.

"You truly do deserve this medal! The Empire

can be proud of you."

"But why do you sympathize with him?" Alexander asked, finding the old man's words to be enigmatic.

"He could have strengthened himself with this surge. But Mikhail sacrificed this opportunity and his own wellbeing, choosing instead to save people," the old man looked at me. "You have the makings of a true Healer. Study, young man, and someday you may well be exceptional."

"I promise that once I'm stronger, I'll heal your knees. I will clean out the stones from your kidneys and gall bladder, I will deal with the pancreatitis issues that started not long ago and remove the varicose veins, and also cleanse the plaque from your vessels..." As the old man was already at an advanced age, it took me ten minutes to list all his maladies.. Nothing critical, but all together this had long been poisoning the life of the old Healer. And the only thing that kept him going was his Gift. I enjoyed the surprise on his wizened face.

"How do you know all this?" he exclaimed, and again I smiled and shrugged. "I'm a serious student, that's all..."

"A student? You just named my entire disease map! Moreover, I knew only about a third of everything you listed! Much of it is news to me!"

Oops... The show-off went too far. Yes, we need to be more restrained. I see that not only was the old Healer surprised, but so, too, was the emperor's son.

"Just because I said it doesn't make it a fact," I said, but no way was this going to shut the old man up.

"It is true. You guessed correctly about what I already found in my self-diagnosis. And that means the rest is true..." he sighed, trying to recall all of the ailments I'd listed.

"Okay, old man, get treated for them then," I grinned, and, lost in thought, the Imperial Healer walked towards the exit, thinking about how to seek treatment.

Gradually people began to disperse, and Vika, Alexander and I sat down at the table again, still chatting. Yes, I had been planning on leaving, but then they brought so much delicious food. And the wine they served was excellent. And the emperor's son turned out to be an interesting person, with whom there was always something to talk about.

"If you don't mind, I'd like to see what's on that table over there," Victoria was already a little tipsy, her cheeks were flushed, and the girl was high on life right then. "I'll get some of those amazing pies."

The girl left, and I felt someone standing behind me.

"Can you diagnose me, as well? And cure me of my ailments?" I heard a deep bass voice behind me.

"But of course, although Healers, you know, usually expect compensation for their work," I said jestingly, and went back to the conversation with Alexander, but the man joined us, and smiled.

"Would a million suffice?" asked the potential client with the booming voice, and I laughed.

"For a million, I'll not only diagnose you, I'll also cure whatever ails you! What's more, I can make you look twenty years younger... Ahem... "— I turned toward the man, and realized that this was the emperor himself speaking to me.

And turning to my right, I saw Kooky having a soak in the fountain, clasping his head in his wings. Then I looked to my left, and there I saw Victoria hugging a bucket of popcorn and eating it by the fistful, as if watching a movie.

Ehh....what was up with me? Why was I such a braggart tonight? Did I really have to throw in that bit about rejuvenation? What gave me such loose lips, anyway? But that being said, a million, well, that wasn't something to argue about!

CHAPTER 9

"HAH!" LAUGHED THE EMPEROR. "I appreciate a doctor with a solid sense of humor!" And then he slapped me on the shoulder, but I dared not risk carrying out diagnostics. Although I would have liked to actually. But what if he wasn't as transparent as he seemed to be, and might actually notice my injection of energy into his body?

So instead of diagnosing him, I breathed a sigh of relief. And also chuckled a little, as if to say 'yes, I was just joking. I'm a funny guy, yes.' But as he was silently looking at me, a way out of this was forming in my head. I could slip out of the Imperial palace and dive through the nearest portal, and from there move to another country.

But no, this was not to be. And actually, I was joking about my willingness to rejuvenate him. Something like that would cost far more than a million.

"But all jesting aside, Mikhail, I want to personally express my gratitude to you for saving so many of my loyal subjects," he said with a brief nod. "And I would like to add that I admire the way you handle a rapier. I never would have thought that a Healer could also be such a fine melee fighter."

Yes, yes....I'd heard that a hundred times already. I had no idea how it came to be such a widespread belief, but in this world Healers were supposedly peaceniks against using force to resolve conflicts. In everyone's eyes, it was against their principles to take up arms; thus, they would employ other methods. For example, they might use proxies to fight for them.

Okay, I, too, have used others to fight my causes, and more than once. But that being said, I knew how to wield both weaponry and magic, and the only time I used anyone to help me resolve issues was when I was too lazy to get the job done myself.

"Usually Healers are loathe to kill."

"Right, well, I didn't kill anyone," I said with a smile and a shrug.

"Yes, you employed an intra-cardiac injection of wisdom," chuckled the emperor, patting me on the shoulder again, and then he left to chat with other guests.

Finally, I could breathe a sigh of relief. After all, he'd joked about my diagnosing him. Indeed, why should he spend money on some young

Healer when he had the royal Healer, who possessed a wealth of experience? As for me, what I
didn't need was the emperor's seasoned Healer
looking over my shoulder as I conducted diagnostics on 'His Highness'. Were that to happen, he'd
end up was a lot of questions.

And while before I was going to leave the ball
early, now I decided to wait until the very end. Vika
drew near once the emperor melted into the crowd.
She'd managed to consume a bucket of popcorn
while he and I had been talking, and now she was
looking at me strangely. Of course, she waited until Alexander was gone to talk to me. And soon she
calmed down. realizing that we weren't in any danger of my being exposed.

Thus, the rest of the evening was uneventful
and calm. We mingled, and other aristocrats came
up to exchange pleasantries and ask how our
Family was doing. After greeting Victoria, they
would then introduce themselves to me

These were apparently old acquaintances of
the Bulatovs. Some had known Vika from the cra-
dle, others had studied with her at the academy. I
had little interest in these people, so I just sat and
enjoyed the food and wine, not making the slight-
est effort to participate in these conversations.

But there was someone who caught my attention there. It happened after Alexander left, and
there was a lull in those flitting around us. That's
when I noticed a middle-aged man who kept looking in our direction, clearly puzzled about something. Finally, he looked intently at me, and then

he broke into a smile as he strode over to our table.

"Mikhail!" he smiled and extended his hand. "To be honest, I didn't recognize you right away!"

Okay. To be honest, I didn't know recognize him off the get-go, either. But now as I looked at him up close, I recalled who he was. This was the entrepreneur who'd given me a lift after I left the evil monastery. And I must say that he didn't take a penny for it; he helped me out of the kindness of his heart. So I extended my hand to him and quickly went through first the diagnostics and then the treatment. I tweaked the blood vessels in the brain, putting them in order, thus reducing the risk of stroke. He was not strongly Gifted, so I spent virtually no energy on this, and he noticed nothing.

I did recall that he'd never introduced himself when we met. But seeing that I was at a bit of a loss, the entrepreneur said, "Everyone here is talking about you," he chuckled. "Yes, I know your name, but failed to introduce myself when first we met. Vladimir Andreevich Smorodinov. I would list all my titles, but it would take too much time, but I am nothing more than a supplier to the Imperial Forces."

Smorodinov, then. Vladimir. Well, in any case, he'd always been a nice person, and I had no regrets at all that I helped him. He asked if he could sit at our table, and right away I motioned toward a chair.

"I just wanted to say," Vladimir said, now more quietly. "I am forever in your debt. I have no idea how you did it, but I'll remember you until the end of my days."

"Ah, yes. So how is she doing now?" I recalled how weak I was when I cured his then-pregnant wife. I lacked the energy to do all that was required right away, and so I'd launched a long-term treatment. This was the type of thing where, ideally, the Healer should keep an eye on the patient, and make adjustments as needed.

"Excellent! Our son is a beautiful baby, and my lovely wife is glowing with happiness and health!" he said, with a wide smile.

Vika sat there sipping her wine, looking first at me, and then at Vladimir. He, incidentally, said nothing about how we'd met. Commendable, I must say. He understood the importance of keeping some matters confidential. As for myself, I completely forgot to share with Vika the details of my journey from the monastery to Arkhangelsk, although I'd shared with her my interactions with her father, and assured her of how I'd avenged those who'd captured and killed him. I might not have destroyed them all, but I'd taken out most of them.

"Don't worry about the debt," I waved it off. "You paid it in full, and I only did what I do best. What I'm saying is that you owe me nothing."

"I disagree," he said. "And so I do hope that someday, you'll allow me to pay you back through my services."

"So do you sell your products in Arkhangelsk?" asked Vika casually, and I looked first at her and then at him.

Actually, right away I'd realized how very useful this man could be to us. But I wasn't into engaging with the aristocrats here in the capital to any great extent. They were all close to the emperor, and I didn't need to draw attention to myself. I could handle the aristocrats of Arkhangelsk on my own, but the capital crowd could cause me a lot of headaches. Let them have the big city lights while we kept to ourselves in the backwaters. Someday, I might feel the need to expand to the capital, but at present, that time was in the remote future. It would be better for me to take my time.

"Why is it that you don't already have suppliers lined up in Arkhangelsk?" asked Vladimir, surprised, and Victoria sighed, saying "Our Family is in an economic blockade. There is only one Family that will trade with us. He sells us stone, and that's all," she shrugged, and Vladimir's eyebrows rose.

Here we go. I didn't want to tell him, but now it looked like it couldn't be avoided.

"Can you provide me with a little more detail? A complete economic blockade is an extremely rare phenomenon," he said, intrigued. By then, I could see no reason to hide anything. He could find out the full story if he wanted, but it could well be a distorted version, so better for him to hear me tell him the truth.

"Not long ago I became the head of the Bulatov family," I began.

And I launched into it. Even Victoria hadn't

heard it all. I told him about all of the attacks on my Family, and how our enemies were joining forces to crush us, all the while trying to hide their tracks. Of course, I didn't reveal any secrets to him, and I only depicted events in general, but in the end, he came to understand the full extent of the trial and tribulations that had for some time now been plaguing the Bulatovs. And after all, he'd asked, and so I told him.

"Ah, so now I finally understand the circumstances behind our meeting," said Vladimir with a sad smile. He then explained that in this country, when a young man was preparing to become the head of a Family, it wasn't uncommon for ill-wishers to kidnap him. So Vladimir assumed that's what happened to me, and that I'd simply managed to escape. And, in fact, this was almost true, except that I wasn't readying to assume the role of head of the Bulatov Family. It's just how things had turned out. But why correct him?

"By the way, an economic blockade is impossible in the capital," he said, for some reason. "It's the kind of thing that only happens in the provinces when there are so many Families that they're always squabbling over this and that."

"Interesting," I said, "but I'm not planning on moving to the capital. What would you advise me to do?" Vladimir was a smart guy, so why not hear his thoughts on the matter.

"At the very least, destroy the industries of those participating in the blockade," he said with a mock serious face, and I nodded. It was a solid idea, actually. "Then, as there'd be a shortage of goods in the city, and an absence of competitors, a stream of aristocrats from other cities would take their place. They'd seek to take advantage of newly opened markets."

"Right, that's a good idea..." I said, and at first Vladimir laughed, but then he realized I wasn't ribbing him, and then he fell into thought.

"Um...Actually, I was joking."

"But I wasn't!" I said, smiling. "I've put a lot of thought into this. And thank you very much for the great advice." In fact, I hadn't thought of that exact approach. I thought I could just destroy their goods and such, but to what end? They could just start up production again, given time, and it wouldn't make any difference. But should they lose their entire market, that would be serious. I knew from personal experience that mining ore wasn't a problem for me, but selling it...

"Oh, I didn't help you at all," Vladimir waved his hand. "Chances are that you simply cannot succeed. Don't be offended, but your Family is small now, and to destroy factories you need aircraft capable of dropping bombs," he added, causing Vika to choke on her wine and end up coughing. I'm thinking that she understood now why I've been fussing around so much with the pigeons.

"We'll definitely think of something," I said with a smile.

"That'll be interesting," said Vladimir with a speculative look. He apparently knew I had some kind of plan in the works. But no, I wasn't about to share it with him. "In any case, I'd like to be of help in one way or another."

We talked a little more, and then exchanged contact info. Right here and now, Vladimir could not give any guarantees or answers. He had some connections and a network of his own, but first he needed to speak with his suppliers.

"At the very least, you need weaponry, that's my understanding. This is at one and the same time both an easy matter and a problematic one," he said. True enough. A Family at war with his neighbors needed just that. And great weapons made everything easier. "I'm a licensed supplier to the Imperial Forces, so that means I can easily negotiate for you. The issue would be with delivering your orders."

What it all came down to was that any weapons and ammunition sent to me could be considered a legitimate target for my enemies. They could simply intercept the delivery process and take possession of the ammunition and weapons that I was in desperate need of.

"The transfer needs to be set up far away, and for each convoy we'd need to arrange serious security. Preferably from one of the capital Families, and their prices, well...." he said thoughtfully, and started to calculate something. He even drummed his fingers on the table, and then he shook his head. "Really, I don't understand how you've managed to stay alive."

"Well, I usually get my weapons for free," I shrugged, "but the problem with the cartridges is that they run out too quickly."

We were already in the weeds with our discussion by now, so why not throw something else out? Might hit the jackpot, or something. "By the way, I have excess weapons and such for sale. Interested in used weapons?"

"Candidly, no, I'm not. It's not what I'm into," he shrugged. "But I can find you some buyers. Just tell me what it is you've got to unload. What models?"

I took out my phone and started scrolling through the photos, showing Vladimir what I could sell. For some items we were out of ammo, and others were awkward to use. Not to mention we didn't have the right mechanics for all of this. Half of our armored vehicles were simply gathering dust, of no use to us. Okay, I gave some of the trucks we didn't need to the peasants. But what would they need armored vehicles for? It's not like they could plow a field with a wheeled tank.

"Listen, why do you need ten tanks of various models?" asked Vladimir as he perused the list of seemingly random military hardware. "This one, by the way, is interesting," he stopped me, pointing to one of the images. "It's unique, homemade almost, made for personal use. How did you get it? And what for? You can't use any standard shells in it!?"

I continued to show him everything I wanted to sell, and with each item Vladimir had more and more questions.

"Okay, enough already!" he stopped me. "I

can't understand how you can wage battle or mount a defense with all of this stuff!"

"That's why I want to sell it," I laughed.

"So why did you buy it all to start with?" Vladimir looked like he wanted to clutch his head in his hand as he imagined all of the money I'd wasted.

"Well, I didn't buy it..."

"But..." he opened his mouth to say something, but the words got stuck in his throat. "Ah-ah-ah..." he drawled, "Got it, I have no more questions."

"I have one more question," I began, feeling like I could trust him with this matter. "Might you be interested in more, shall I say, extravagant goods?"

"For example?" he asked, leaning in closer.

"Artifacts," I said with a shrug. I didn't plan on showing him all I had, but I could send him something interesting. If in Arkhangelsk, my artifacts would raise eyebrows, then I think the capital could take them in stride.

"Perhaps," he nodded.

"I sometimes come across interesting specimens. You know yourself, it's not a city, but a hotbed of portals," I chuckled, because that was the reason for the ball in the palace. "So I sometimes show up and close them. And then I might collect artifacts from fallen enemies."

"Well, let's see, then," he sent me a message with an email address. "This mailbox is just for business such as this. Just upload photos;

descriptions are optional. And if the goods are worth more than one hundred thousand, we will personally fly in and pick them up in our own transport."

"How convenient, however..." I calculated how often he would have to fly out if I were to sell in limited quantities. Something like a hundred thousand trips.

"Oh, and I hope that you wouldn't feel badly if I, say, bought something from you for a hundred thousand, and then put it up for sale for twice that amount or more.. I must apologize, but I cannot in any way violate my principles when it comes to business. Of course, I provide the best terms out there. I'll pay you top price. Deal?" I didn't follow him, even. How could I take offense? We were both on the level here. I had no intention of selling him artifacts with the expectation of special treatment.

All the more so as he had numerous clients. Among them were members of the most ancient Families. If any one of them were to find out that he provided better terms to anyone, he'd be facing a lot of disgruntled buyers.

In any event, the evening ended before we knew it. For a while we ironed out details, and then we moved on to other topics, and when we noticed that the throng of guests was dispersing, we decided not to linger, returning then to our hotel.

"Well, shall we stay around in the capital a little longer?" I asked, looking at Vika. She started to smile, but then sighed.

"I'd love to see my girlfriends from the

academy. But I do know that we need to take advantage of the truce and prepare for warfare." Smart girl indeed. She realized that this wasn't the time for distractions. And when having a good time, the best approach was to do it in such a way as to make your enemies fume.

"Okay, then you pack while I..." I picked up my phone and called the pilot. "Warm up the helicopter; we'll soon be there."

Hearing the pilot's affirmation that my order was received, I hung up and quickly got my things together. But Vika...well, I know that she knew how to get it all done in short order. But for some reason, she didn't always opt to use this particular skill. Thus, it was only some forty minutes later that we made our way to the elevator and slowly climbed upward to the roof of the hotel. There, our helicopter was ready to go.

Incidentally, the hotel's elevator had glass walls — an interesting feature. From inside, the occupants were treated to a wonderful view of the city. Spread out below us were streams of cars crawling about the networks of streets, with people hustling to and fro, trams leisurely gliding along the avenues, and some helicopter engulfed in flames falling from the roof of the hotel. Hmmm....

"That...that..." Vika froze as she looked at the falling flaming chopper. "That isn't ours, is it?"

I, too, watched in fascination as the debris from our transport fell, and I sighed sadly.

"It's ours, Vika....Ours."

And then the elevator thudded to a stop and

there was a commotion outside, and I found myself standing there, watching, and also thinking about what to do next. After all, someone had just attempted to assassinate us. But the bastards had missed us by literally a minute.

And what was funniest of all is that the helicopter hadn't been parked on the roof for long. Except for the emperor's guests, it was against the law to spontaneously fly over the city. It was only with official authorization that anyone could land a chopper on the roof of the hotel. I'd been happy about not having to sit in traffic jams.

"It's a shame about the helicopter," I sighed again. Fortunately, it didn't fall on any pedestrians down there, having instead landed on the roof of a neighboring building, causing no real damage there.

"But the pilot..."

"I don't feel sorry for the pilot," I said, and for some reason Vika glared at me. Well, why feel sorry for him? The bastard was standing on the roof, safe and sound, unharmed by the explosion. How did I know this? I could feel his elevated heartbeat a few dozen meters above us. "What I didn't understand is why the elevator stopped. Could this also be part of the attack?"

"No, that's a security measure. True, it looks suspicious now. Like, what if a fire suddenly started..." mused the countess. Meanwhile, I was doing my damnest to summon Kooky. It was only five minutes later that the cheeky bird showed up, for which I scolded him.

"*Coo-cooo!*" he protested and tried to explain, but I was hearing none of it.

"Let's go, do what I taught you to do. Find the panel and unlock it; we need to get to the roof," I told him, and right away he did his disappearing act. Victoria was looking questioningly at me, waiting for an explanation. "Well, what of it? I spent four nights on his training. But now he knows the basics of hacking."

And a minute later, Kooky confirmed this. He finished his hack, and the elevator glided smoothly upward.

"So he knows how to operate equipment? Did I understand you correctly?" Vika was having trouble grasping the notion. It's a little bit of a downer knowing that a bird comprehends electronics better than you do.

"I've buffed up his brain so much that he could probably complete a master's degree and land a prestigious job," I laughed. "Or else perish from the overload on his psyche. That, too, might come to be."

We exited onto the roof and met the pilot. It was the younger of the Gavrilov brothers, Maxim, as I recall. He was clutching his head and looking over the edge of the roof, watching his burning chopper. Clearly he was grieving as if over a lost friend. With good reason, assuming he knew the first rule of the Bulatov Family pilots.

"Well, what gives, then? In theory, you should be burning with the helicopter right now, not sunbathing on the roof."

"Sir..." he responded in an empty, lost voice, as if life had lost all meaning. "You took forty minutes, and I had to go to the toilet."

"Yes, someone had to pack their things," I looked at Vika, and she shrugged. "By the way, why didn't you go earlier? After all, the flight lasts several hours" That being said, who would risk dropping bombs in the capital?!

For a while we all silently mourned, looking at what was left of the helicopter and our things. Most of our luggage had already been transported to the helicopter. In particular, my backpack with all my belongings had been lying inside.

Soon the door leading to the stairs swung open and numerous hotel guards burst onto the roof, as well as two of my guards who were supposed to bring the last of our bags with some of Vika's things. They were all clearly surprised at the sight of the aftermath of the assassination attempt. The helipad was demolished, essentially. Where the helicopter should be was now a crater with little fires burning here and there. Of course, the helicopter itself was no more.

I saw no reason to linger on the roof, and as we could not fly home that day, we headed back to our room. I entrusted the investigation to the hotel staff, and of course, to Kooky. The pigeon was sent out on reconnaissance as soon as he'd finished hacking the elevator, and was now carefully studying both this and the neighboring buildings, looking for suspicious people or devices capable of carrying out a remote detonation.

I had no idea who was behind this attack. While the assassination attempt had failed, who was desperate enough to take me out here when I'd just received an award from the emperor, and, in theory, was under his protection? All of this was strange. Stranger still was that Kooky uncovered nothing at all. He flew about for several hours, peering into various rooms, examining the roofs and windows of neighboring buildings. Then, hotel security showed me footage from cameras that clearly revealed from whence came the projectile that hit my helicopter. As it turned out, the explosion was caused not by a bomb, but by a missile. The air defense system was hacked and therefore, without orders, someone fired a projectile at my helicopter. This building belonged to a well-known large corporation and there was no reason for them to involve themselves in my elimination, especially in this way. So yes, they'd been hacked.

Early the next morning, I heard a knock on the door, and an entire delegation of men in formal suits appeared on the threshold.

"Mr. Bulatov, I represent a certain organization," he said crisply.

"What is it?" I asked.

"The Corporation for Reimagining Aviation Perfection: We are C.R.A.P!" he announced proudly. "And right away I can assure you that this unfortunate incident was no fault of our own. Those who attacked you hacked our security system and we, too, have been victimized here."

"CRAP. Hmmm....Your company is aptly

named," I said, understanding what this pale, thin little man in a jacket was getting at.

"What?" he asked, puzzled, but I just gestured for him to go on. "Yes, what was I saying? Ah! On behalf of our company, we are ready to offer you compensation for the damage inflicted on you. This sum should suffice," he said, scribbling something on a piece of paper and handing it to me.

"Hmm..." I turned the paper over, trying to understand whether it was a joke or a mistake. But judging by the confident look of the impudent fellow, he seriously thought that these kopeks would be enough to buy me off. "Vika, look at what they're offering us..."

"Oh, Mikhail, it must be a mistake" she waved dismissively. "He must be a little confused; he left off a zero. It happens, right?"

"That is the full amount we can offer you, unfortunately. You cannot expect any more. We have already assessed the value of your helicopter, and this amount is completely consistent with its condition before the tragedy," the idiot stated firmly.

Hearing this I was rather angry. Just a little...True, I barely restrained myself from sending the representative of the company with the telling name flying straight out the window.

"What you're saying then is that all that I had in that helicopter, and which also went down with it, wasn't worth anything?" I asked, settling into my chair more comfortably and smiling.

"Those are associated costs. But I can talk to

the management and maybe they will allow me to add another ten thousand to the compensation amount."

"How generous, really, how very magnanimous of you," it was hard not to laugh, looking at how pretentiously arrogant this peon was. There was nothing new about his attitude. People have looked at me like that more than once, thinking that I was just a poor, beggarly count, the head of a dying, weak Family. Why were they all convinced I couldn't do a thing to them for their snide disregard? After all, by their logic, what did I have to lose?

"Okay, good. Incidental expenses... Vika, make an appointment with the emperor tomorrow. I must personally convey that the Order of the Hierophant, Third Class, awarded to me wasn't worth much."

"Excuse me," the functionary interrupted me, turning suddenly pale. "But..."

"Yes, and one more thing..." I didn't let him get a word in. "In the message to the emperor, we must make sure he knows that the royal order stating that I be provided two weeks of full protection under the auspices of the Imperial Family has been violated."

"Excuse me, please!" the peon wheezed, again trying to say something to me and Victoria. "It's just that..."

"By the way, this is a pretty good photo. Show him, Vika," and she showed the company representative the photo on her phone. There I was with a medal on my chest and a wide smile, and behind me stood the emperor.

"The offer must immediately be amended!" shouted the company peon, "I apologize, but we were misinformed! I must upgrade your compensation. Mr. Bulatov, can we offer you something from our corporation? It is not difficult to understand what we manufacture --- it's evident from our name."

"Oh, I'm afraid to imagine, to be honest," I read again the acronym for their company, which was fixed in large letters on the roof of one of the tallest buildings in the capital.

"Here, look, Mr. Bulatov," he fished a tablet out of his bag and began quickly running his fingers across the screen. "Will this satisfy you? If so, let's sign the paperwork right away stating that there are no claims.

"That works," I nodded, and the pathetic fool, now bathed in cold sweat and pale as a ghost could finally exhale.

I could have pressed for something else but...Yes, I was willing to fly back on the aircraft that they were offering me. I was played out, and didn't want to haggle over this anymore.

It was called a Pathfinder, although who knows why? Four turbines, massive wings, a long body. It was something like the vertical takeoff plane that I had buried near my castle, but this one clearly looked far better. According to the pale negotiator, it cost around fifty million.

I signed a paper that would save his company

from further claims, but at the same time the document clearly stated that they were obligated to find the guilty parties. And if it turned out to be one of their employees or even a big shot, they would be held responsible.

By the way, the Pathfinder had special anti-missile devices, so now transportation would not only be more comfortable and faster, but also safer. Not to mention the cargo that we could fit on board...

"Congratulations on your new acquisition!" Vika said, punching me lightly in the shoulder once we were alone. "We'll be traveling in comfort now, right?"

"I expect that for fifty million the Pathfinder should feature a massage chair," I chuckled.

"What about a big closet?" asked Vika hopefully, which worried me.

"Don't even go there...The load-bearing capacity might be high, but just the same, it isn't infinite."

* * *

C.R.A.P. Headquarters
General Director's office

"What do you have to say for yourself?! Enlighten me, moron! Speak!" said a bald, rather short man resting his hands on the table and incinerating his subordinates with his glaring eyes.

"What, me?" asked a ghostly pale young man,

part of the delegation.

"Yes, you!" barked the boss. "What do you have to say for yourself?! How did six hundred thousand in compensation morph into fifty million? What do you think you are? Financial geniuses? Idiots, idiots..." howled the General Director.

"We had no choice, Vyacheslav Mitrofanovich," said the man in charge, the peon who had spoken to the victim.

"There is always a choice! Surely you know that there are other ways to strike a deal? The goal is to benefit your employers, not a half-dead Family. What were they even doing in the capital?" growled the General Director. He was truly at a loss as to what had transpired. The power wielded by his corporation was such that they could have paid nothing, and the count would be helpless to do anything about it.

"Sir, I was faced with a choice: pay compensation and save the company's reputation, or..." and the delegation head pulled out his phone to show his boss the photo. "This is the count with the emperor. Here's a photo of the protection order."

"Ah! I see...I see..." said the General Director, calmer now. Then he sat back in his chair and picked up his own phone. "Hello...No need to find out who wanted to kill Count Bulatov. It wasn't an attack on him; it was aimed at us. Yes, someone wanted to set us up," he said, hanging up and sinking into thought. "What bastards... They know full well that the Imperial Family stands behind its word, and that they come down on anyone who crosses the line," he shook his head.

"Okay, so what next?" asked the underling, and the boss just waved his hand.

"Do whatever we promised."

"I completely forgot that the Imperial Award was also destroyed," added the thin underling.

"What the hell!?" howled the boss. "What god-damn award?"

"I don't remember. The third order of some kind of combat healer....Hierophant?...." he said hesitantly.

"What?" The General Director turned his screen, and the underling saw the very star that Count Bulatov had shown him. "Well, what to say? This is bad. Very bad. I just hope that the count is happy with the Pathfinder. They don't hand out awards like that to just anybody, no. Throughout the country there are no more than five of them."

"So now what?" asked the underling help-lessly.

"Make sure the Healer is satisfied with the plane. We want him out of here and gone. Can you do that much?"

"Shall I install massage chairs on board, then?" he dared to chuckle, but his boss frowned.

"If you have to, install a big closest for his countess!"

CHAPTER 10

"I HAVE NO IDEA who it was," Vika sighed. For a full hour now she'd been running through our list of enemies, and still was at a loss as to who had the power and resources to pull off something like that attack on us. "And who would want to be behind it? I mean, the emperor himself made it crystal clear that we were under his personal protection," Vika said, and then after a couple of minutes added thoughtfully, "You know, my impression is that this attack was not aimed at us at all, really. This wasn't the doing of our enemies."

"So you think they were setting CRAP corporation up, then?" I smiled. Finally she'd figured it out. I was wondering when she'd get there. "Impressive! You grow in intellect with every new day!" I said by way of a compliment, although for some reason it made her mad.

She frowned and released her death aura, lightly touching me with a black cloud. But it dissipated right away, and I raised my finger in a threat.

"Uh-huh, don't even try. It'll take you another century to even get near me, trust me."

But anyway she tried. I simply brushed aside her ridiculous attempts to use her simple spells to get to me, and, taking out my phone, I called home.

First I talked to the earth mages. I could tell that they'd been enjoying some time off. But I wasn't upset at all, thanks to the video to which I had access. Sure, they'd tied it on a little and had noticeably relaxed in my absence, but they were still meeting deadlines. The underground hangar was ready, fuel tanks were well-protected, and now, finally, some of the rooms in the castle itself had been luxuriously renovated in such a way as to make even the emperor envious. They'd also finished filling the lake and they'd completed a lot of other smaller tasks. While I had them on the phone, I assigned a few more little jobbies to them. These were tasks with which they could easily cope even if inebriated. Anyway, they might as well enjoy a break now, because once I got back, they'd have their hands full, and they knew it.

I also talked to our Necromancer. He, too, was on vacation, and had decided to spend it exploring the world. He was learning how to negotiate the Internet and reading books, and he even took more trips to the zoo. Of course, now he brought guards with him, and took efforts to blend in with the public at large. True, this didn't always go well. Belmont, for example, tried to steal a parrot once. He'd become quite attached to the talking bird. Perhaps I'll buy him one if Vika continued to progress so swiftly under his tutelage.

I also call Willson. I had a large order for him. But the cheeky fellow tried to wriggle out of it. First, he pretended he didn't know how to use the phone. Right, as if an Artifactor could be such a moron. Usually anyone opting to work creating artifacts was by default smart, and they were always natural geeks. But then I realized what he was up to. First, I got an automated message saying something like "The person you're trying to contact is unavailable." And then I saw a couple of emoticons and Willson's voice saying he was busy now, but in case of an urgent need to reach him, he could be contacted by email. Or via his website. Or through this or that messenger. And he appended links and icons to this message. I myself was rather baffled by it all. Luckily, Victoria helped me out.

At least now I knew that Willson was no idiot, and that was good. He actually understood how to negotiate the technological landscape here better than people born and raised in this world.

But I was feeling disgruntled by his maneuverings, and so I messaged him along the lines of "aren't you overdoing it, Willie?" And he swiftly replied that "If you distract me now, my entire laboratory will go up in smoke. The tower too. And the castle would become a giant pit. So can we connect later?"

I couldn't argue with that. If your project is that volatile, well, I'll not distract you. But I wrote an email with a list of artifacts that I would like to see upon my return. And no, these weren't the standard protective or explosive amulets. My plan was for him to try to create something interesting, and later we'd attempt to combine technology from this world with offworld artifacts. I'd just finished my message to him when the phone rang.

"I heard you ran into some rough waters there, eh?" It was Vladimir Smorodinov speaking.

"It's nothing new, just the usual stuff," I waved off his concerns. Indeed, I'd encountered far more serious assassination attempts.

"True enough. Helicopters are shot down over the capital all the time; I can't even remember how many times I've been in a similar situation," he laughed

"Is that so?" I asked. "How many times has your helicopter been shot down?" This was interesting stuff, and I was glad that I wasn't the only one.

"Let me think....Hmmm....Ah! Never! Never has it gone down! Since the time of troubles, no one has ever taken a helicopter down here, not once!" he exclaimed. "I dare not go to Arkhangelsk now in light of how calm you are in light of this," he laughed. "But since you've been deprived of your transportation, I can provide you with a ride. Nobody would shoot it down....Or no, that's not exactly true."

"No need to bother, Vladimir. I've already dealt with the problem. All I need is to wait a couple of days," I responded. Anyway, I would have refused his offer. After all, I still had a cargo helicopter.

"Oh, then you'll be staying around for a while?" asked Vladimir, clearly delighted. "Then allow me to invite you over for dinner! I won't take no for an answer!"

No worries, though. I had no intention of refusing. It's not that I really wanted to visit him, but to decline his sincere invitation would be, at the very least, rude. And so I had to spend a little more money on a new dress for Vika. As most of what she'd brought with her had perished with the helicopter, I didn't even object. And so that evening we made our way to Vladimir's place.

What to say? His mansion wasn't particularly luxurious or large. Yes, real estate inside the city limits was exorbitantly expensive, but he was by no means a poor man. My impression was that he simply didn't require an ostentatious mansion. His was around four hundred square meters on a modest-sized plot of land with a low wrought iron fence separating the house from the busy street. And while his estate looked modest from the outside, the interior was something to behold.

Right away it was evident that here lived someone who valued artifacts, art, and antiques. Old paintings, sculptures, and more caught the eye right away.

Vladimir met us at the door, and led us to a drawing room with a table that was already set.

"Mikhail, I didn't have the opportunity to thank you earlier. When I think about what you've done for us, words fail me," said Vladimir's wife upon meeting me.

I just smiled and said "You helped me then, too, so how could I not repay the kindness?"

Then, their staff served us dinner, and I had to admit that Vladimir's cook was truly gifted. It's not that we didn't have good cooks too, but the dishes we were served were beyond praise. Sparkling conversation and delicious food, the time flew by and then we turned to the wine. Only Vladimir and I drank wine, actually. His wife abstained. I asked Vika to join her in drinking compote by way of supporting her. Why not, really? Vladimir could drink a lot, and while I could remove excessive alcohol from my blood, well, it would be onerous to have to constantly monitor Vika's intake. As it was, we'd been drinking too much in the capital.

"Listen, I want to show you something," Vladimir said, draining the second bottle of wine and dragging me somewhere. "You are the first of my friends to see this, by the way. I just bought it the other day..."

I was intrigued by then, and so went along with it. We proceeded along a lengthy hallway and then downstairs to a large basement, which was, it seemed, a real museum. Evidently not all of Vladimir's rich collection was on display upstairs.

"Behold!" he said, pulling a white sheet off of a rather large statue. "How do you like it?"

Well, it wasn't a bad piece of sculpture, if not for one small "but"...It depicted a large man sitting in a pensive pose. It was truly skillfully done, with the folds and wrinkles in the clothing rendered perfectly in the black stone with red veins. It was, in fact, mesmerizing.

"This piece, by the way, cost me twenty-seven million!" boasted my host. "Just so you know, an invasion group brought this from the offworld. It's a trophy. Offworld art! And do you know how few there are of such groups in our country?"

I didn't respond, and, approaching the statue, I poked it, and confirmed my suspicions.

"Well, it is quite the find, isn't it?" asked Vladimir, still admiring the statue.

"Yes, indeed it is. How very nice," I smiled wryly without any enthusiasm.

"That's an understatement! If you only knew the chaos at the auction. Never before did I have to fight so hard for a piece! Ha!" he said with a laugh, but he soon noticed how underwhelmed I was. "What's wrong? Don't tell me you're jealous; anyway I wouldn't believe it. You're not the type to envy; I'm a pretty good judge of character."

"Nothing, it's just..." I spread my hands. "I find it strange to see someone bring an infected item into his residence."

"What?" Vladimir was taken aback. "What do you mean?"

"Did you carry out an analysis? A scan?" I

asked, and he nodded in response.

"Yes, I tried but I couldn't scan it. The material is something else. It emitted so much radiation that the equipment burned out."

"Let me share something rather confidential with you. I happen to be an aficionado of anything from the Interface world and have studied their history and also interrogated prisoners. As you know full well, there are plenty of portals around our part of the world," I said, leading up to what I needed to say. "The point is that you don't need to know much to comprehend what this thing is. This black material blocks virtually all energy. But no, this is not a statue, rather, it is a man walled up in stone. Moreover, he, and those like him are usually walled up alive."

"What, what can I say? Art requires sacrifice!" chuckled Vladimir.

"You got that right. But not when a person is rotting alive from dozens of deadly and especially dangerous diseases. They walled him up so that he wouldn't spread the infection around the world," I paused, recalling how some duke on TV boasted about his achievements in battles in the offworld, and I couldn't help but chuckle. "And the ones who found this probably boasted about their legendary assault, saying that they took this statue from the king's chambers, right?"

"How did you know that?" asked Vladimir.

"I didn't know it. These idiots robbed the burial grounds and scurried off. That's all there is to it," I said, shrugging. No guesswork necessary. It was all clear. "It's better to keep it away from people. As is, from ten meters away I can tell that disease and death are emanating from this guy."

"Damn..." Vladimir muttered, looking apprehensively at the statue and stepping away from it without even noticing.

"Of course, you can believe me or not, as you wish. However I urge you to keep this statue away from your wife. And don't let the children draw near it," I said, as Vladimir clearly thought about what I was saying.

As well he should, actually. Of course, I'd told him too much. Better for me to not reveal all I knew, but that being said, it would have been wrong to leave him and his wife in danger. They were both fine people, which was quite rare among the aristocracy, and they certainly did not deserve the fate suffered by this poor fellow, imprisoned in stone.

"I'll sell it tomorrow," Vladimir nodded.

"Better do it, play it safe," I said. "I, as a Healer, can see the radiation of a deadly force, but of course, it's your call what to do with it."

"I'll have no trouble offloading it. I bought it for twenty-seven, and five people have already tried to buy it from me for thirty-five to forty. But I'll sell it to some jerk for thirty..." he rubbed his palms and laughed, and realizing how it looked from the outside he added, "Believe me, this bastard deserves more than just death. The things he does are so dark that I hate to even talk about them. If he were to lick this statue, the world would be a better place for it."

"Well, you know best," I shrugged. Actually, if my pigeon were a little bigger, I'd have him drop such statues on the heads of my worst enemies.

"Okay, then I'll have this rubbish removed from here," Vladimir covered the statue with the sheet again and shook out his hands. "Now then, I'll show you what else I have."

I readily assented to this, because there really were a lot of interesting items here. Fortunately, Vladimir's other statues were made of ordinary stone. I also looked at several paintings and stared in surprise at an inconspicuous-looking old, dirty, dilapidated fountain. It was the kind you drink water from.

"What's this?" I asked, and Vladimir gestured dismissively.

"Oh, someone gave it to me a long time ago. It's useless, really. It has no value. But it complements the collection because, well, it's obvious that it's ancient," the merchant walked past me and began to show me some old cleaver, but I stopped at the drinking fountain and began to study it carefully.

"I advise you to hook it up to a water source and wash your face every morning in it. And you should also drink from this fountain," I added, to Vladimir's astonishment. "Mind you, it's just advice," I smiled at him. "The water, you see, will be healing, but its potency lasts for about thirty seconds, so you couldn't sell the water, for example. I know you merchant types."

Vladimir laughed heartily, but he took what I said into account and looked at me and the fountain with a newfound appreciation. In fact, I'd like to install such fountains in my castle. And I would, but it was a difficult and tedious process to make them. This nondescript piece of stone, more like some kind of shell, contained a powerful healing spell; the water would have a beneficial effect on the body, charge you with strength and keep you young longer, at least on the surface.

Moreover, this wasn't really an artifact, it's just that the spell was hidden and embedded in the stone. That's why no one noticed its beneficial properties. And of course, I copied this spell. In my world, these were created a little differently, so it would be interesting to study how it was implemented in this fountain.

The rest of the evening flew by, and soon Vika and I were back in our room. She left to change as the dress, it seems, hadn't been the most comfortable. I, in turn, retired to my room. But before I could relax Cherepanov called me.

"So why are you treating me this way, huh?" he said, immediately complaining. "Off you go to the capital without telling me? Aren't you ashamed?"

"Please, just don't tell me that you're here too..." I sighed, to which Nikolai laughed.

"Yeah, right. I'm sitting and rotting in your bottomless hole!" he said, a hint of sadness in his voice. "Listen, you and I are business partners, right? And off you go, without a clue about how many clients there are in the capital!" I wanted to protest, explain that I had other matters to deal with, but Nikolai wouldn't hear it. "Okay, write down the addresses. If you show up, they'll receive you, for sure. I'll make sure they know you'll be coming."

What could I do? I wrote down the addresses. A few rich clients wouldn't hurt me, but I had to take care hide my abilities.

"But I don't work openly, you remember. So maybe next time... I'll get my mask, and come back. As it turns out, the capital isn't all that far from Arkhangelsk."

"Oh, all they want is silly stuff, nothing special! Just a little healing, and I've already told them all a lot of good things about you. Trust me, you've already got an excellent reputation among the Families there," gushed Cherepanov. "You can trust them, don't worry. They won't tell anyone."

"Yeah, right. A Healer who can cure anything with the snap of his fingers, no one's going to talk about it, of course not," I said, employing sarcasm.

"You just don't get it. Do you really think that you are the only one out there working in the shadows? No truly skilled Healer would ever reveal his abilities to people! This is normal practice, and the aristos would never give you up, even under torture. Only an idiot would share a good Healer with others!"

This was actually news to me. I'd been studying this world for so long, and yet I'd never heard anything like it. As it turned out, if an "aristo" were to blurt out too much, no other Healer would work for them. Who needed chatty, unreliable clients, after all? And so, in light of this, I agreed to see Nikolai's clients, and went to the first address the next day.

The illnesses, in truth, were not the most difficult, but sometimes the cases were rather challenging. For example, on the second day of making the rounds I cured some old duchess. She was nearly ninety years old, and the blood vessels in her brain flatly refused to let blood pass through. I'm exaggerating, of course, but when the old lady, who had been a vegetable that morning, walked into the drawing room and started chasing her relatives with a dirty broom for all their sins and mistakes, I hurried off. I doubted that they'd want me to come back.

I also cured a little girl. She touched some artifact and the metal melted into her hand. It was quite difficult to get it out, because it had melded with her body, causing a lot of pain and suffering. But over a couple of hours I extracted all the fragments by pulling the metal into my own body.

And so it was, in just three days without too much effort and taking plenty of breaks I earned around three hundred thousand! Vika and I also managed to walk around exploring the city some more, and I studied the societal makeup of the capital. Perhaps I should think about relocating here? No one in this city was out to kill me, the clients were plenty in number, and they paid well. I could live here without any trouble. So what if my helicopter was shot down. Who doesn't have that happen from time to time? And this city was full of good restaurants, with shops that sold you whatever you wanted.

For example, I spent one hundred and twenty thousand at one bookstore. I simply couldn't stop, and almost went cross-eyed trying to take in all the literature that interested me at one glance.

"Um...I, well..." Vika looked at the check and the happy me. "I didn't want to have to ask, but...I, too, want something!"

"Is fifty thousand enough?" I asked.

"For cosmetics, perhaps..." she hesitated, and I laughed.

"Why do you need cosmetics? I am your source for cosmetics. Do you want me to make your neck like a giraffe's? Or would you like a D-cup breast size?"

"Oh, okay, I'll just spend it on dresses," she said, snatching the money. "But you can't replace my lipstick, so I'll be buying that much, at least."

Good thing our hotel provided storage. Otherwise we would have had to rent another room. As it was, we had to hire loaders to transport it all when, on the fifth day our new pot-bellied transport roared up with its massive turbines and landed on the roof of the building. Our guards could never have managed it all on their own. And no automated loaders could have made it to the roof.

An entire delegation emerged from the new flyer. Men in suits quickly set up tables and chairs

and swarmed over me like flies, shoving documents under my nose for me to sign. Like, I had to
affirm that it wasn't them who tried to kill me, and
I had no claims against them. Under the cover of
the noise, they tried to give me more documents to
sign, for example, one of them obliged me to return
the plane upon completion of the investigation if it
was confirmed that the corporation was indeed not
guilty.

How very insolent. Good thing that I always
read documents in their entirety, including the
small print and footnotes. Especially the ones
marked by an asterisk.

Yes, we bought a lot of things. But this was
only the beginning. The pilot, fortunately, had previously operated such aircraft. Just the same, I'd
had him spend these past few days practicing on
a simulator. I didn't want him to press the wrong
button midflight, sending us into a death spiral.

And the capital was full of all kinds of markets, shops, and massive shopping centers. All the
best, a huge selection for every taste. So yes, we'd
spent all kinds of money. We bought some of the
best generators, enough for the entire estate, with
some extra. In this world, electricity was of vital
importance. I hoped that the offworlders didn't
fully understand how important, because then
they'd start hitting more power plants and also
fuel storage facilities right away.

Yes, for some time now I'd been thinking
about coming up with something with Willson's
help. An artifact generator could be of great help

to us and to all of the inhabitants of this world. But we didn't stop at generators alone. I called Georgy, and he sent me an extensive list of everything we needed. Approximately five tons of medicines, another seven tons of medical equipment. I feel like Roman really let loose with his demands.

Moreover, at first they didn't want to sell us such big lots. They said that you had to be a distributor to buy in those quantities, as I might be planning on reselling all this stuff, even to other countries. But Vladimir helped me with this. With one call, all of my problems were solved — he personally vouched for me with the suppliers.

And just as we were about to fly away, Chernomor called me.

"Are you still there?" he boomed.

"Well, yes, we're about to lift off," I said, eying the plane, which was parked now in the parking lot of a huge shopping center. I didn't know before that that it was even possible to land a plane in a parking lot designed for cars. But nobody ran up to us complaining, so I guess it wasn't anything new. But why were the guards cowering in the building? Well, it didn't matter.

"Don't fly away anywhere."

"As you say, sir!" I chuckled, and Chernomor grumbled under his breath. Did I hear him wrong, or was that an apology. It was hard to make it out. "I hope you're not about to tell me that the estate no longer exists, the lands have been destroyed, and we have nothing to come home to."

"No, you just need to drop in on a certain

address."

"Er...Alright then. I'll serve as your courier. Who should I say hello to from you?" I laughed. Although I had no idea what he was up to.

"I just called an old friend. He was once the commander of an elite mercenary unit," Chernomor boomed, "And he and thirty of his men, excellent fighters, I must say, are ready to join our guard. In a couple of hours they'll all assemble not far from you. About ten kilometers to the east of the capital, the town is called Dumpkin."

Okay, now this was interesting, as was the name of the town. Soon, he sent me the location and after we were done shipping I had the pilot take us there. Fortunately, Chernomor chose a place where even our iron monster could safely land.

Our Pathfinder landed in a field next to a rickety wooden house where our new fighters were waiting for us. Aha, now I understand what he meant by "old friends". They really were old. Each one was around seventy-five years old, if not older. It turned out that Chernomor wanted us to bring his old colleagues out of retirement.

"Okay..." I waved my hand at them, sighing heavily. "Pension guard, follow me," I had the old men head for the plane.

Many of them began to briskly follow me, but one stood frozen in place.

"What's going on!?" I turned to him, but all he did was shift from foot to foot.

"I can't fly off without Margarita!" he said,

indignant. "And usually, nobody lets me go any-where with Margarita. I won't part with her again."

"So you want to bring your old lady along, then?" I asked.

"No! What old lady?! I'm talking about Mar-gare-e-e-e-ta!" he almost sang the last word, rais-ing his hands to the sky.

"What is this Margarita, grandpa?" I was starting to get annoyed.

"I'll just show you!" he almost snarled, and ran into the old house. The rest of his colleagues shook their heads, one slapped his forehead, and they headed to the plane.

But we didn't have to wait long for Margarita's lover. There was a crash and a clang, and soon the door of the house flew out along with its hinges, and on the threshold appeared the happiest old man I had ever seen in my long life.

"Margarita!" he exclaimed, brandishing the six-barreled heavy machine gun cradled in his hands On his back was a huge backpack with a machine gun belt hanging out, and I could only guess how many rounds it held. "Margarita-a-a..." the old man drawled tenderly, stroking the friend from his youth.

CHAPTER 11

I NEVER THOUGHT IT COULD take so long to get everyone on board a plane. You'd think all they had to do was make their way up and through the hatch in the back, and sit down. But no, our old codgers weren't in any hurry. Groaning and muttering curses, the thirty ancient warriors clambered up the boarding ramp. It was slow going.

The first ones inside the plane stood in the aisle and started picking apart the quality of the outfitting in the state-of-the-art flier compared to back in the good old days. They blocked the passage to the others behind them, who started growling at them to get a move on. Crazy fun, really. Anyway, it was unexpectedly amusing. For example, the way one of the old guys negotiated the boarding ramp on his crutches. Even though his legs were practically buckling, he kept at it, even though he was clearly struggling. My guards wanted to help him, but backed off after receiving blows from his crutch. That took care of attempts to respect the elderly.

And if the one brandishing the crutches slowed down the boarding process, another more principled old man was even more of a problem. This was because he actually refused to use crutches, although his attempts to forgo them weren't getting him anywhere.

Out of curiosity, I scanned his legs, and was surprised. His joints were non-existent, replaced by disintegrating bone. In fact, none of his bones were fully intact, and the old man supported his frame through sheer willpower

However, the slowdown didn't end after everyone was finally on board the plane. We had trouble with the takeoff, too. I was used to this kind of thing, though. The pilot simply lacked the time to learn how to operate the plane, and he also needed a co-pilot. And so one of the guards joined him in the cockpit. Was it dangerous? Undoubtedly! But it made the flight even more interesting.

As soon as we took off, two of the old men had health emergencies. The blood pressure in one of them plunged, and the other had a massive stroke that threatened to kill him. But it wasn't time for Victoria to raise him from the dead, as I was right there and not about to allow a new recruit to die of old age. Indeed, it was child's play for me, dealing with a cerebral hemorrhage. The fact is that old people have tissue that can handle oxygen starvation much better. Their tissues have long been accustomed to this, so there are significantly fewer problems resulting from a disrupted blood supply.

The good thing was that, in contrast to when I treat my guards, it attracted little notice when I tended to these old guys. With the disabled or old, it just had to be done, after all. This was one reason I didn't often accept the young and healthy into my ranks. Why should I? After all, seasoned warriors who'd been wounded in battle had a wealth of experience. They wouldn't be cowed by yet another injury.

I started getting to know our new guys, and realized right away how pessimistic they were. And I mean all of them. And on top of this, they didn't seem to know where they were headed, and why.

"Don't be offended, count," said a tall, broad-shouldered old man with a white, lush beard that reached all the way to his waist. He had a deep, harsh voice and kept pulling out a hand-rolled cigarette, but then he'd stop at the sight of my disapproving glare. "It's just that I gave my word to Commander Chernomor, not to you. I am responding to his summons, but doubt that I'll stay long."

"But why not? Chernomor, I'm sure, promised you'd find it to be interesting, at least," I asked. I wanted to hear why they were so unenthusiastic about this venture.

"He didn't share much information with us. My impression is that he wants us to train new recruits. But that's not my thing. I want to see some action in the field, lead men into the fire!" he said, his eyes sparkling before dimming again. "But all I can do now is crawl..." he sighed.

So, Chernomor hadn't told them much. That was just fine. Later they'll find out that their lives weren't yet over.

"So where are you going, old man?" I heard someone chuckle, and again noticed the guy who'd refused to use crutches "Why don't you use a wheelchair? You'd get there a lot faster."

"What, maneuver a wheelchair into that closet they call a bathroom?!?" he shot back. "No way! I'll drop dead first!"

"But what if you can't wait?" snickered the other guy, a thin, crooked old man. He was the most mobile of this bunch, though.

"I left in plenty of time to avoid accidents," he snapped as he hobbled towards the bathroom, occasionally reaching for the wall to keep from toppling over.

Incidentally, it was a sheer pleasure to travel in the Pathfinder. Vika was absolutely delighted. Although the pilots were still learning how to control this iron beast, it cut through the air incredibly swiftly and smoothly. No shaking, no rattling, and we could walk about with ease.

But there were downsides, as well. It was originally a fighter jet, but then CRAP couldn't legally hand it over to me. Models such as this were supplied only to the Imperial Forces and also a couple of very powerful Families. I would have to procure special authorization from the emperor to have the combat version. But maybe this was for the best. My Pathfinder was tricked out to serve as a fine form of transportation. It had an enormous load capacity, generous luggage compartment, vertical takeoff capability and comfortable passenger cabins, just to name a few of its attributes. It was also fast and, for its size, was economical in terms of fuel consumption. This meant that I could fly back and forth to the capital far more often.

"Look, we even have a big clothes closet!" Vika crowed, jumping up and down, she was so delighted. And yes, they'd installed a huge closet in one of the cabins, along with a couple of massage chairs. Moreover, all of Vika's clothes fit into the closet.

By the way, there was no reason we couldn't convert the Pathfinder back into a combat craft. All we'd need, really, was ammunition. I already had all the weapons because near our castle a plane close in design to this one was buried underground. We could easily unearth it and remove the weapons systems. Although... It would be better if we had professionals do this work.

"So then, what's up with you two?" I chuckled, seeing a couple more of the old guys looking green-faced. They'd neglected to take their medication, so I intervened to help them. I relieved one of them of his diabetes, and, as for the other, I returned his intracranial pressure to normal.

Looking around, I saw that they'd all finally settled in well. There were all seated, and some stood around the mini bar. One was even serving part-time as a bartender, as there seemed to be a vacancy in the position. The Pathfinder's crew consisted of eight people. Two pilots, a mechanic, and a cartographer were essential. And, of course, a bartender.

"I had no doubt that you would order a Margarita," I nodded at the machine gunner, who was now sipping a cocktail. He grinned and took another sip. "Okay, listen up now," I addressed them all, clapping to draw their notice. "Do you know any mechanics? Anyone who could work with aircraft. It doesn't matter how old they are, ten to a hundred and thirty years old would be fine."

"Don't jump the gun, count," said their commander. "We're off to see our "warlord," and don't even know you. Don't think that just because we're old farts, we're at you beck and call. If Chernomor says so, I'll personally find you six of the best mechanics I know. And if you don't mind if they're disabled, I know about twenty guys who could answer to the call."

"How is it you know so many disabled men?" I asked. It's not like mechanics took part in battles, after all.

"Stuff happens even to mechanics," he shrugged. "How am I supposed to know the details...?"

Right, it was like with trees. The age of a tree can be determined by the number of rings on the cross-section of the trunk. And you can tell the rank of a lumberjack, say, by how many fingers he had left.

"Sir, we're almost there!" I heard the voice issuing through the intercom. "Where should we land?"

That's right, I completely forgot. And now, here we were already. How long had it taken us? About an hour and a half? And this was taking into account takeoff, so the speed of the Pathfinder was truly impressive.

I almost laughed as I looked out of the window. The plane was already hovering over the castle, and everyone inside had rushed out into the courtyard. That was my bad. I'd told only Chernomor about the new acquisition. He wasn't exactly the talkative type. However nobody would gun us down without his order, so I didn't need to worry about "friendly fire." As for where to land, I'd thought everything out in advance. As soon as I found out I'd be given a Pathfinder as compensation, I had the Earthbenders get to work.

"Well, open Sesame!" I said, having called Ludwig, and right away he did as told. A huge hole began to appear between the castle and the outer wall.

Stone slabs began to slide apart, revealing deep down below us a platform for the Pathfinder. It had to be some twelve meters down. Several meters of the strongest reinforced stone would cover this space. To destroy this beauty, our enemies would have to empty their entire arsenal. And even then, in all likelihood it would be futile.

The plane slowly began to descend, and even from the cabin I could hear the pilot's teeth chattering. Judging by his heartbeat, he could be going into convulsions, even. But our landing was smooth, with no dings on the plane's shiny surface. Just the same, Maxim seemed to be frozen in the cockpit. He said that his hands were clenched so tightly on the control wheel that they'd become one with it, and it would take him an hour or two to pry his fingers off.

We left him there and disembarked, only to face a hurdle. Of course, our earth mages were great. They thought of everything. They'd created steps for us, so that we might leave the hangar. But with me were thirty old men who moved along even a flat surface only by the grace of the gods above. Forget about them climbing steep stairs. But beside the stairs were some elevator shafts, although they were still unfinished. The thing is, in Arkhangelsk there were only two companies that supplied elevator equipment, along with installation services. Both of them were owned by local Families, of course, so forget about turning to them for our needs.

"We also made a magic elevator," Giovanni suddenly remembered. "That was when Toren got so drunk that....ahem...He couldn't even walk up the stairs. So I had to come up with something."

Ah, well, it's not like I didn't know that they'd drink in my absence. Especially Toren, because he allegedly discovered new facets of his talent every time he was "plastered." And so, I had no reason to complain. What mattered was that these guys did good work, and so I was happy to rejuvenate

Toren's liver.

Meanwhile, the gaggle of old men rose to the surface on the magic-infused stone slab in a matter of seconds. True, one of them broke his legs from such a swift ascent upwards, but that would be no problem.

Right away Vika left to manage all of our purchases. After all, besides numerous garments, we'd picked up scores of things for both our peasants and our guardsmen. Not to mention construction materials and tools for our renovations to the castle. In general we'd picked up most, if not all of what we needed.

And so I found Georgy and tasked him with a mountain of work.

"As you see, we can now fly to the capital," I said, nodding at the Pathfinder. "So now we have more for you to do."

"Yep, I see that," he said with a sad smile.

"Good. There won't be any problems negotiating purchases there as I have a contact in the capital who can sort everything out for us. So compile a list; I'll give you a couple of days to do it," I said. "Remember, we need elevators in the tower and the hangars, and don't forget to consult with our people about what kind of supplies we need for our electronics."

"No worries. I put together a list already, long ago," Georgy said with a smug smile. "Look!" he said, thrusting his cell phone in my face. Again I congratulated myself for buying all of my people these devices. They'd cost me a pretty penny;

ordinary citizens in our country couldn't afford them, no matter how much they longed to possess one. They weren't cheap, but now I could call them whenever I wanted, and they could also access the Internet, which significantly sped up their work.

And Georgy had, in fact, made a list already. However, the first items on it were prosaic things, like pillows and blankets, rather than specialized gear and equipment. Apparently we needed a whole lot of bedding.

"Well, you're the one who told me that our peasants should have all of the comforts of city life," said Georgy. "And I've been around to all of the stores, and have to say it's not easy finding sheets and blankets and so on in the quantities that we need! Also, what's out there is often cheap, bad quality, and overpriced," he said, beginning to sputter in indignation.

In fact, this was all sort of comical, our situation. Not long ago, we provided several peasant households with normal beds, quality soft pillows, blankets and mattresses, but the peasants... In short, they stashed everything in their attics and were afraid to even touch such "luxurious goods." They were afraid of repercussions from the master. And no matter what our guards said to tell them it was okay, the mattresses were for them to use, half of the bedding was still up in their attics, still wrapped in plastic bags.

"So you're suggesting we fly a plane worth fifty million to the capital for twenty tons of pillows? Is that what you're telling me?" I again asked

Georgy, who again shrugged.

"Well, if we try to buy the pillows here, we'll just get the usual runaround."

"Okay, let's just hold off on this, then. If you can get hold of this kind of thing in the city, do it."

The rest of the list was relevant. Timothy had helped draw it up, and thus, we needed to fill a few staff positions as quickly as possible. Fortunately, although I couldn't spend money with abandon, I did have some reserves. And in a pinch, well, I could probably sell a couple of artifacts to Vladimir. I just had to make sure they were the kind of artifacts I'd likely score. Nothing extraordinary.

Days flew by, one after the other. I was up to my ears in work, Chernomor was busy with his own concerns, Vika was making up for missed classes, and Belmore was enjoying bullying her, his student, forcing her to do the impossible.

I also worked with my Artifactor on how to continue to ensure that our aircraft were safely housed. We also came up with several plans on how to shoot down enemy missiles while they were still approaching. To this end, we'd use a powerful magical impulse. But it wasn't finished yet, as Willson needed to complete many, many more magical calculations. If he were to make a mistake, the magical impulse could actually take down the plane, which would be most unfortunate. This was a difficult, slow endeavor, and thus, I couldn't rush the process. Let him take as much time as he needed.

Meanwhile, the war with my neighbors went

on almost unnoticed. Of course, I knew exactly when the emperor's immunity would end, and I didn't waste time. I had my pigeons conducting reconnaissance in enemy territories day and night, assessing where and how many enemy fighters were out there, preparing to attack, tracking the movement of combat equipment, and also eavesdropping on conversations whenever possible.

Of course, eavesdropping was an iffy proposition, because it depended on being in the right place at the right time. In other words, learning anything of value depended on serendipity. Thus far, we hadn't been very lucky. The pigeons transmitted only a few telephone conversations between Baron Grishanov and his forces, and they also spied on the circles in which the new owner of the Snegirev lands moved. Khorkov Jr was in charge there, as I expected, and instead of rebuilding the destroyed villages, he spent most of his time drinking in the city, having squeezed all he could out of his subordinates.

My impression was that his war with me was the last thing on his mind. But this wouldn't last forever, because his father was no doubt a far more responsible person. So when "dad" eventually intervened here, I'd have to sweat a little. Or, rather, my pigeon squadron would have to get to work, while I watched the destruction via the screens as I sat in my cushy chair sipping wine.

Speaking of destruction, the pigeons did not use explosive amulets during the "ceasefire" imposed by the emperor. But an improvement to their digestive system had opened up opportunities. They didn't kill anyone, they just did all sorts of nasty things to the enemy. A couple of liters of bird shit might manifest in someone's porridge, for example, or the wiring in their tanks might fry out, for some reason — fun stuff like that. None of it was big stuff, but when minor irritations like that are constantly occurring, the enemy combatants might start wondering what their beef was with the Bulatovs, and was it worth it? Really, probably not!

But as soon as the truce ended, again our power went out. I assumed this marked the start of an attack, but I was only partially right. Not only I, but the baron and Duke Khorkov also lost power. And again the territory of the power plant was a hotbed of action.

Apparently the offworlders decided to repeat their stunt by opening numerous portals there. And they'd just launched repair efforts and upgraded the power plant, including by expanding the supply of electricity to the city. This time, though, I was prepared for something like this, and, thanks to the brand new generators I had brought from the capital, which were all rattling outside, our electricity was swiftly restored. My people weren't going to suffer any inconveniences because of this trifling attempt by the offworlders, and we had enough fuel to power the generators for at least a month, even without economizing.

That being said, I wasn't the only one who was ready for this. At the power plant itself, a big surprise awaited the offworld forces. As soon as the first invaders burst out of the portals with bloodthirsty cries, the full might of the Imperial troops stationed there fell upon them. Tanks roared and combat aircraft soared overhead. I could see the steel birds of prey combing the fields from the castle windows, releasing dozens of rockets that left behind scorched earth and tall columns of flame and smoke.

Too bad for the offworld landing forces really. But seriously, what did they expect? Did they actually think that we were all total idiots? I watched a short report on TV. There they showed colorful footage of a detachment of hundreds of heavy horsemen breaking out of a portal, and forming a wedge, and powerful horses trying to tear to shreds the cannons stationed at a distance. But instead, the detachment ran into a minefield, and therefore only two dozen soldiers reached the guns. Along with some infantry, of course. They were then mowed down by heavy machine guns, which then took out the next offworld detachments.

And so the attack this time didn't go down at all like the first time they shut off the lights. The offworlders didn't expect such a pushback, but the homeland forces were well-prepared. Thus, unlike last time, I didn't have to contend with a stream of wounded, as the regular hospitals managed without me.

But it turned out that this was just the prelude...Ten minutes later, we all realized the true aim of this stupid attack by the Interface world.

This was when a huge portal opened in the port district, along with dozens of smaller portals. Hordes of hunters, well-armed warriors, and mages started pouring out into the streets. Really, what to say? Sure, I could simply sit back waiting for the wounded, but the longer I did that, the greater would be their numbers. And I had Roman to handle whatever patients made it to our infirmary. After all, he was now well-stocked with medical supplies.

"Okay, you old codgers," I entered Chernomor's office, and it turned out to be quite crowded. If before I always found the commander of the guard hard at work tinkering with weaponry, now he had a real workshop set up!

One man was filing away at the barrel of a machine gun — why? Who knows! Another was hammering a fragmentation grenade for some reason, and a third was drilling a hole through an artillery shell. Were they out to blow up the castle, or what?

These were Chernomor's old friends who had by now all joined the ranks of my guard. No one apologized for how "uppity" they'd been with me earlier, but once they took an oath to serve the Bulatov Family, I got no more of that attitude from them. They accepted me as their leader and swore to fight for the Bulatov Family until their last breath. But I hadn't yet had time to work on their health issues. I just removed major conditions that had been ready to take out half of them. I left the less urgent problems for later. And so now, the 'relic squad' wasn't yet ready for prime time action. This, despite the fire in their eyes. The oldsters would soon give experienced warriors half their age a run for their money. And this was in part because, at their age, they'd lost their instinct for self-preservation.

"Look, commander!" said the one with the most impressive beard after setting aside the weapon he was working on. "I want to be a part of this, I don't care what you say!"

I looked over at him and saw his weapon, and slapped my forehead with the palm of my hand.

"Okay, Chernomor. Gather the guard, and I'll go and call the others..." — what else was there to say? This dude had actually created a new weapon. He called it a disposable hammer. In fact, there wasn't anything particularly innovative about it. He'd simply welded a pipe to the side of an artillery shell. You could only use this ad hoc hammer once.

Chernomor understood what we were up to, and activated a siren that filled the castle grounds. All of our warriors assembled and Chernomor started issuing orders. Some would stay behind to guard the castle, others would be charged with artillery and combat machinery and they'd head straight for the city, while still more were now in the hangar loading weaponry and ammo into our Pathfinder.

I was with our trinity of earth mages. What was remarkable was that none of them were concerned about having to fight against people from their world. They had many different countries over there, and they all fought with each other just like over here. Meanwhile, the mages hadn't sworn fealty to any single kingdom. Thus, they had no problems with joining the defense on our side.

Belmore, too, volunteered to join us, as well. He said that this was a great opportunity for Victoria. Knowledge is consolidated many times faster in the heat of battle. Moreover, spells would be imprinted in the subcortex, and from then on it would be much easier to use them. And Vika, too, wanted to take part in battle. Last time, she thoroughly enjoyed collaborating with me to repel the offworlders. She especially remembered the battle with the vampires. She'd grown noticeably stronger, although she realized how far she still had to go.

Now, we had two pilots operating the plane, so our takeoff and flight was smoother. They hadn't been wasting time in practicing with the Pathfinder, and I'd also bought the two brothers some books on these types of aircraft. They'd practically memorized these books, so now they could not only operate this plane, they could carry out maintenance on it, too. At least, theoretically. We had yet to test it in practice.

The Pathfinder gained altitude, turbines roaring and we rushed toward the city, awash, now, in columns of smoke. We were there in a matter of minutes, and had to seek out a landing site. This didn't take long. In the port district there was a plaza just right for use as a landing pad. But it was currently occupied by offworlders. A dense line of armored offworld infantrymen stood in a neat square, and a mage in their midst was preparing some kind of vile spell, looking straight at our plane. No, I definitely won't let you knock down my beauty...

"Chernomor!" I called, pointing at the mage. "Take him out..."

* * *

He'd spent his entire life preparing for this day. He, a junior mage knew it: his moment in the sun had come. This was it, his first mission in this strange, weak world!

He, Grallus, the fourth son of Arun of Caross, was born to kill. His path upward had been long and difficult, but, by hook and by crook, the mage had overcome all obstacles in his way. And now, what lay before him was glory, wealth, recognition!

He was a fire mage, still young, the best in his class at the academy, and he showed a lot of promise. But being only the fourth son, he could not claim his father's title. And thus, Grallus had killed all his brothers, and then his arrogant father. He took the estate, the castle, the army, and immediately responded to the king's call to take part in the invasion. After passing through the portal, Grallus and his squad of heavy swordsmen met only weaklings who squealed and begged for mercy. But why should these weaklings be spared? These were prey, not people. But then, that iron bird had appeared in the sky. It was swiftly approaching, and, seeing it draw near, Grallus smiled in anticipation. Here it was, the chance to enter into the legends by destroying the enemy's iron bird, capturing prisoners, taking the artifacts from this techno-world to his world and use the money from selling them to assemble an even larger army!

All of this flashed through his mind in seconds, and he then focused on his next moves. The roaring winged machine was close enough for him to deploy a complex spell, the Fiery Lasso. Few were those who knew how to create something like it, but it could be used to seize rather than destroy heavy machinery, which could then be taken back to their homeland, even if in parts. The metallic bird drew ever nearer, and now his warriors relaxed, because they could see that there were no weapons mounted on the wings. This meant it couldn't shoot at them, and functioned solely to land more feeble soldiers for their entertainment. This world, after all, had no formidable forces.

But just when Gallus was almost finished casting his spell, the flying machine swiveled around in mid-air and a hatch opened up in back, and standing in the hatch was an old, hunched over man. What was he doing there when he should be lying under a quilt ready to meet his maker? And his eyes were glittering as he wielded a heavy weapon.

"Close the shield..." Gallus's infantry commander tried to shout, but it was too late.

"Margarita-a-a!!!"

*   *   *

"Why are you sad?" I asked.

"Of course I'm sad! I wanted to go at it for an hour or two...but...but.... ten seconds, and that's it, I was done..." — the machine gunner lamented. "Oh, Margarita, I'm sorry it was so fast. I wanted to last longer, but no...no..."

He sat there, dejected. But I knew how much the cartridges for his Margarita cost. And I knew full well that even ten seconds weren't cheap when translated into rubles.

But it was all good. The detachment of armored infantrymen was blown away in no time. And then, the fire mage stopped creating his spell as he had to focus on saving his sorry self. But all in vain. While he might have escaped all thousand of the massive bullets that flew out of Margarita's rapid-fire drum like a fiery hailstorm, he failed to notice a single crossbow bolt. Nobody noticed, because all eyes were fixed on the crazy old man.

And he would have kept going, except that, fortunately, he ran out of bullets. So now he sat there mournfully cradling his Margarita, promising to last a little longer next time. Meanwhile, we managed to land. The bodies, torn to pieces by massive bullets, along with pieces of armor and surviving artifacts, were immediately transferred to the luggage compartment, and my guards began to disperse across the square.

The mages immediately created simple fortifications, while Belmore, just in case, activated several spells to raise the dead in advance, and Vika... Vika simply smiled sweetly as she clutched a blade charged with death energy.

"Well, shall we?" Something about the way she was smiling gave me the chills, sort of.

"Let's get some intelligence data first, shall we?" I said. "First we give orders to the troops, and then we'll set off."

"Ehh..." the girl sighed and, crossing her arms, sat down on a bench. Fortunately, there happened to be a lot of them in the square.

The pigeons had already explored the area, and now the operators were creating a detailed map of the portals. I could feel them, yes, but, just the same I wanted to have a good idea of which forces were emerging from which portals. For example, a team of catchers had come from one portal under the guard of a couple of warriors. Some of our oldsters headed their way, along with a dozen of our young guards. In no time they took care of the offworlders, collected the trophies and dragged the corpses to our Pathfinder. Right, we were taking it all, even the bodies.

Belmore wanted them, especially as these offworlders could be morphed into excellent bone guards. The thing is that some twenty corpses of strong warriors or mages were needed to make a single bone guard. But hey, we weren't here to sit back and watch the show!

Our detachments each went their separate ways, and then I, Vika and Belmore, along with our trio of earth mages, set off to close the most difficult breach in our area. You see, I'd gone online to officially book this area and the territory around it, conveniently claiming it as "ours." Now, no one else would be sent our way, which meant that we could unleash all we had. Just the same, though, I donned my signature mask, and also had the mages hide their faces. What we didn't need was major publicity. Even Vika wrapped a black scarf around her face, and I must say that our little detachment was imbued with an aura of mystery.

Horsemen were flying out of the portal. Twenty heavily armored knights were to clear the area so that their masters could safely enter this world to wreak havoc with their magic. But as the knights galloped down the street at full speed, a stone wall suddenly shot up in their path. Five of their leaders crashed headlong into it, falling off their horses; the others barely succeeded in "braking." But then, another wall shot up behind them, and red crystals started bursting out of the ground under their feet, piercing their armor, and damaging their protective artifacts. Only the strongest warriors, who had personal shields, were saved from instant death. But did anyone ever promise them a swift end?

"Arise already!" Belmore was irate. He was trying to create a monster out of a dead horse, but sorry. I'd used the beast's blood, and also all of the energy contained in the carcass. And I was now diligently extracting the red bone marrow. I could use it for blood magic, as well, and it was also a useful ingredient in some interesting spells.

So it was no surprise that Belmore wasn't able to take control of the corpse.

"Hold on, Belmore! Focus on those two for now," I said, indicating a couple of fallen knights. "I'll be done in a minute!"

"I don't want knights!" shouted the impudent Necromancer, stamping his foot. "I want a horse! I'll deal with the knights later on; I don't want to deal with them now!"

I see. Well, I was almost finished. Once done drawing what I needed from the horse, I began drawing complex symbols in the air. All around, stones thundered as they broke off from buildings and rained down on the heads of the enemy. Meanwhile, Vika was winging black sickles at the enemy and also taking control of the dead and forcing them to fight for us. And Belmore finally got his toy. The withered, terrible, wrinkled horse knelt down, allowing the Necromancer to mount it.

And I....What did I care about these knights? They're weaklings. But hey, a delayed spell using platelets...Uh huh, I'd read a lot of medical literature, and so here I was, ready to show off. In any case, now the offworld badasses I was expecting were about to make an appearance.

"Ha! Know the power of the great..." No, that wasn't the one. What was this clown doing? Some kind of loser mage stood in the portal, screaming out the titles and ranks of his master, who was about to majestically emerge. But before he could finish reading off the list of titles, I shut him up with a crossbow bolt in the mouth. His standard protective artifact didn't help him.

"Good, here comes the great one," I chuckled as the portal flared up again.

It was an imposing man draped in golden robes. He held the usual golden staff, but this one was topped with a crystal globe filled with light energy. Should he start casting spells we'll all get tired of squinting.

Looking about him with disgust, he stepped forward and...*oops*! Put his foot right into a sticky puddle.

"What the..." he lifted his foot up and even greater contempt and horror appeared in his eyes.

"A thrombobomb!" I'd just come up with it.

There was a red flash, but no explosion as such followed. Only a muffled pop and a dark red haze, inside which all blood will coagulate in just a couple of seconds. It wasn't the most epic spell, but I prized efficiency over showiness. And my thrombobomb worked as it should. The haze cleared, and in its place remained the pale corpse of a gold-clad light mage. He didn't even know what did him in until his final moment, when he surely felt the power of the massive amounts of energy in that ooze.

And now, the portal was silent. This, even though according to Kooky, a considerable army had gathered on the other side. It seemed that upon learning that their primary strike force had been taken out, the rest of the enemy thought twice about the need for riches and glory. Good for them for understanding that this way lies only death.

We walked past a few more portals, where my Necromancers honed their skills, the Earthbenders buried offworlders in tons of stone and metal, and I killed all and sundry with my crossbow. Behind us our detachment of fifty guards continued to collect anything of value, hauling it all to the Pathfinder.

And when the heavy artillery showed up, the rest was child's play, practically. Thus, before I knew it, hours had flown by. The portals were closing, one after the other, and as night drew near, the offworlders finally abandoned their attack. By then, so many detachments of defenders had converged on the city that it was time for us to leave. After all, we could no longer openly plunder artifacts and corpses. And so we boarded our plane and headed home. As I stared out the window, I went over our haul today. We'd scored corpses, offworld metals, armor and weapons. And since my guard had procured it all in the course of defending the homeland, we could openly sell whatever we wanted. My fighters, I had to say, were strong, and that explained our successes.

I sprawled back in my chair and felt for my phone, which was stashed in my pocket. I recall that it had vibrated in the midst of the battle. Of course, I'd ignored it then. Only now could I open my mail and read the message:

Congratulations! You are invited to the annual Healers Symposium! Mark your calendar! It will be held in two weeks at the Imperial Palace.

That was all. No details. So I turned to the Internet to find out more. It turned out that some three hundred of the best Healers in the country would be invited to this event. And attendance, as usual, was mandatory, at least for those who chose to stay home and heal people rather than go off to war. The symposium was a forum for Healers to simply network, and exchange best practices, expand their knowledge base and so on.

However, I liked the capital. I just had to stop with my jocularity. I'd almost blown my cover last time.

CHAPTER 12

IT IS TIME, I THINK, to renovate my study. Of course, I'd already had normal carpenters make improvements, and before meeting Ludwig, I was satisfied with what they'd done. But because I found myself spending more and more time in this space I wanted something more.

For example, I was like a warehouse inventory specialist, I had so many trophies from our plunder to organize. Here I was, sitting and sorting through the artifacts that we'd scored in our recent encounter with the offworlders. We'd collected quite a lot of items, although most of them weren't worth keeping. Some were empty dummies, the disposable kind, some of the amulets were also depleted, and so on....What a disappointment! I'd just love to walk into an offworld storehouse and plunder it instead of scoring crapola like this stuff.

I'd be ashamed to give it to my own guard, even. Moreover, why would I? My people should be armed with the best protection, along with my unparalleled healing methods. Why endanger their wellbeing with rotten artifacts that would fizzle out after a single bullet hit them? That bullet could kill, of course, but it was offensive when it did so despite the victim wearing an artifact that should protect against twenty or thirty hits. That would be needlessly endangering my forces.

So then, since I couldn't give this junk to my own people, I might as well offload it elsewhere.

"Vladimir?" I called the best merchant I knew. It wasn't easy to reach him, as his phone was busy for about ten minutes.

"Oh, hello there!" I heard his joyful, if tired voice. "What are you up to, Mikhail? Or did you just call to chat? By the way, I sold that statue to the right person, if you get my drift. And that fountain is miraculous! My wife just loves it! She says that she no longer needs to wear makeup."

"Well, I told you so," I shrugged. And, in fact, I had. "I'm calling on business. I have a batch of artifacts for you."

"Ah, is this by any chance connected with that most recent Interface in Arkhangelsk?"

"Absolutely," I chuckled. "Do you know any other sources of artifacts?"

"Well, what can I say?" Vladimir responded coyly. "But do keep in mind that any business through me is above board. I need all of the documentation, licenses and certificates. Just so you know, I send all of this stuff to the Imperial Chancellery."

Of course. The emperor was trying to oversee the circulation of artifacts in the country. I didn't yet know to what end, though, as what was the point of tracking the movement of artifacts that are used up during military operations? These were mostly disposable, and so rarely had a resale value.

"If you'd like, I could show you the corpses from which we took these artifacts," I said. Of course, we'd reanimated many of these corpses by morphing them into different creatures, but if he wanted, we could undo these changes, no problem.

"Um, no, that won't be necessary," he said. "Er, so you what? Brought the corpses to your place? Whatever for?"

"Well, I wanted to clean up the mess we'd made," I said. Yeah, a lame excuse, but how else to explain why I'd been collecting corpses? It just wasn't standard practice here, which was a big problem for the Empire. Yes, they took some of them for experimental purposes, but simply burned most of them "So then, what kind of deal can we make?"

I knew that compared to ordinary aristocrats, I'd made quite a haul, altogether worth more than a hundred thousand. And so Vladimir promised to send a helicopter over with a team of appraisers. After they took a look at the artifacts, he'd asses their value and then we'd draw up the documents for signing, shake hands, and I'd find the agreed-upon amount in my account. That would be that.

I then sent Vladimir photos of the artifacts to give him an idea of what I was offering. I did not describe the properties and effects of each, since in theory I myself wasn't an expert. However his appraisers could handle that end of things.

And so we agreed on his helicopter with his staff arriving tomorrow morning, and my servants could handle the rest. I just set aside the artifacts for sale, and left them to figure it all out. My work here was done, and I saw no point in wasting any more time on it.

"But my advice is to not sell it all at once," Vladimir added just as I was about the hang up. "It might attract unnecessary attention. For example, a baron in one provincial town was killed, just like that. Portals began to open there, and he made a good profit from extracting and selling artifacts, and suddenly his body was found in his own bed — apparently he'd somehow suffocated. And, small surprise, his mansion was ransacked."

However, he didn't need to warn me about this. In fact, I'd shown him far less than what I'd actually picked up from the Interface world. What I was offloading was only the especially cheap stuff. I'd get several hundred thousand for it all, hopefully. But hearing his words, I again recalculated it all, and decided to sell only half of what I'd been planning. I'd let the rest languish among the mountains of much more valuable artifacts for now, which I'd eventually sell in the capital.

Now done with business matters, I decided to relax by taking a little walk. And I might as well also check out how everything was coming along. For example, I'd recently allocated a whole barrel of aviation fuel to pilot training. Our other helicopter was finally falling apart and so we'd buried it underground by the other downed plane.

Our poor pilots had their work cut out for them. Our planes and the helicopter had completely different controls! What a surprise, at least for me. But they were managing just fine, and their skill set was definitely expanding. I was confident that in another week I'd have two aces capable of masterfully piloting both helicopters and planes. After all, was that not why I'd accelerated their intellect during their training? Now, they could retain knowledge far better, and their acumen was enhanced. Too bad they'd have to grapple with severe headaches later on. I'd neglected to tell them about that bit, though, lest they balk at the changes I made to their headspace.

"So Willie, how are you?" I said, having dropped in on him in his tower. This required my activating the heartbeat search, because the scoundrel again tried to hide from me, this time in the basement. We had some empty rooms there, and he was sure no one would find him below ground.

"So how did you find me?" my Artifactor was astonished. "I've installed shields against scanning in this room."

Oh, I didn't even notice. But yes, the room

was protected against any search spells. However, I wasn't searching for him at all. I merely listened to the beating of hearts around me, that's all. How to stop the beating of your heart, after all? The old runologist could have installed a more advanced screen, although it wouldn't have functioned for more than a couple of hours. He'd have to refresh it after that. These days, though, old Arnold was always dead drunk in the sidecar of a motorcycle, living the life.

"So why are you hiding?" I said, and looked at him suspiciously. "Are you shirking work? Did you not fulfill my order? Is that it?"

"I did, so just take it already," he said, throwing a bag at me, which I deftly caught. "Monster..."

"Why am I the monster now?" I was taken aback. He was slow at getting the job done, but quick to take offense.

"Well, you're forcing me to do things I don't want to do. What's with all these simple artifacts? I long for a challenge! Do you want me to build a natural energy concentrator and set it up to grow cacti?"

"What!?" I didn't understand what he was proposing. Why would I need a cactus, and even if I did, why would I need it ASAP?

"Oh, forget it!!" he waved, and plopped into a chair. "Just check the work and leave me alone."

I poured a dozen new charged artifacts out of the bag and began looking over the magic chains contained in them. And I have to admit that Willson always had an interesting approach. It was wrong of me to right away assume that he was stupid. I mean, he might be, but he anyway knew his craft inside out.

I had in my hands now a dozen disposable attack artifacts. Seven were fashioned as rings, and the rest were bracelets. One was a lightning strike, and could hit a target at a distance of up to twenty meters. Another, when activated, could release a powerful stream of flame over a large area, while the third, on the contrary, could create a narrow beam of fire that could melt, say, a metal door in a matter of seconds.

The rings were imbued with the Quicksand spell. This might not seem like much, but, in fact, it could have many uses. It was a spell that made even concrete crumble, after all. Likewise with a wall, and if you used it on the ground beneath an adversary's feet, he, or his tank or whatever would get stuck.

"Excellent work!" I said to Willson, who finally broke into a smile. So then, he appreciated praise. "Make more of these!" I showed him a ring.

"How many?"

"A thousand should do, at least for now," and the smile vanished from his face, which suddenly turned pale.

"What do you mean...a thousand?" he asked as one eye twitched. "Why so many?"

"Well, I have an army, and they need to carry out combat missions," I shrugged. "Okay then. Get to work. I'll stop distracting you. You're a busy guy, after all," I smiled, and ducked out of there.

Once my words fully sunk in, I figured he'd try to finish me off. I didn't want to have to take measures to shut him down should that be that case, such as "modifying" his body a smidgen. No reason to let it come to that.

Next, I dropped in on Chernomor and his comrades. It was all easy with them. Chernomor had them line up right away, despite the fact that after the big battle half of them could hardly walk.

Surprisingly, none of them said a word; they simply followed the order and prepared to listen. Then, Chernomor looked sternly at his old friends and said that I could rejuvenate them, and also cure them of what ailed them. He put it just like that. They, however, didn't even bat an eyelid. They just nodded to indicate that they'd registered what he said.

"These people will never divulge classified information, don't worry," Chernomor told me. But I knew this already, because once they'd all sworn fealty to me, right away I'd ascertained what was going on in their heads. I could discern no hidden agendas. These old guys were simple and pure as the driven snow, accustomed to following orders without question, and mindful of what honor and dignity were all about.

This time, I'd come to them for a reason. I'd thus far only dealt with the most threatening maladies, and now I could begin the rejuvenation process. No, I wasn't going to fool around with their external appearances. This was difficult and time-consuming, and also not relevant, even. But I could do something about their internal state. They'd still look like decrepit old men, but they'd be able to jump about as if they were twenty.

"And so I'll flutter like a butterfly, sting like a bee, but still look like an old fart?" chuckled their commander, and I shrugged. "Yes, which is even better!"

By now these guys were fully behind me, thanks to Chernomor, who'd had a brief conversation with them. In contrast to when we'd first met, they now readily carried out my every order. Of course, I had to make allowances for age and health.

On the downside, the old men asked for an indecently large salary. But I opted to meet them halfway, because, after all, these were rare specialists. And, moreover, they had numerous grandchildren to feed. And they also needed funds for knitted hats, because things now stood, only five of them were wearing the products of a certain enterprising little girl. Apparently the rest couldn't yet afford hats of their own. Thus, I knew where their first paycheck would go.

I spent a couple of hours launching the rejuvenation processes in their old, almost dead bodies. This would take time, as organisms couldn't be upgraded just like that. I figured that, in a week, they'd already be able to keep up with the young guards, and in a couple of weeks, they'd even be able to outperform them. Being old and seasoned, they were better trained already, so all they needed was youth-like vitality.

Next, I looked at how things were going at the front. The truce had ended not long ago, and the offworld invasion then took place, and so my enemies had no time for me. But it was worth noting that Duke Khorkov was beginning to stir. He hadn't yet made moves against me, but his lands were abuzz with activity. He'd launched a massive construction project, involving lots of expensive equipment, materials, and personnel. I didn't know what he was planning yet, but figured that all of this was a plus. I'd be taking over his lands someday, and so the more infrastructure and buildings the better.

In contrast to Khorkov, though, the baron was still riled up. He was assembling more and more troops at the border, and had even eschewed contributing to repelling the offworld attack. He could have at least sent a detachment so as not to ruin his reputation, but no, he decided to sully his name in the hopes of destroying his neighbor. Did this do him any good? None whatsoever. Worse still, his troops were now so concentrated that they were an excellent target for my light aerial forces.

"Kooky," I said to my scout, who was on a perch polishing off a pretzel. The crumbs fell on the sofa, where other pigeons were sitting. They eagerly pecked at the bounty. "Hey, aren't you the cheeky one now!?"

"*Cooo!*" he shrugged.

"I see, your spa is closed now for cleaning." Right, once a day his retreat was gone over until sterile clean, and that water in the Jacuzzi and fountains was changed. Yes, his was a five-star spa, no less. The only inconvenience for everyone was that during the cleaning all the pigeons were scattered throughout the castle. This meant more cleaning would ensue. "Okay, I have a mission for you."

I pointed out the coordinates on the map, and gave him the bag of artifacts. The feathered one purred for a while, but then waved his wing, calling two assistants, and went to carry out my orders. First to Khorkov and then to Baron Grishanov, to keep both my enemies on their toes. I didn't want them to forget about me.

After all, the truce was over and they had yet to attack us. They must be waiting for me to take the first step and stumble. I must say that this was folly on their part. Now they were destined to see their combat aircraft go up in flames.

And ten minutes later, Kooky reported mission success. He and his team had dropped explosive artifacts onto Khorkov's heliport. Three choppers were totally destroyed, and a fourth was damaged. And next, they did their thing at the baron's estate. Grishanov had only two helicopters, though, so the explosions weren't as colorful. Not that I was aiming for visual effects. I got what I wanted, and that was to ensure that my hostile neighbors couldn't swiftly transfer enemy forces onto my territory, or strike the castle with bombs or missiles. It would take them some time to acquire new helicopters.

Of interest is that as Kooky was flying over

Khorkov's land, our Combat Suits were also out and about and they noticed a strange large clearing covered by camouflage located not far from our borders. I sent the pigeons out there to take a look, and now I and the Combat Suit operators were smiling as we looked at the resulting footage.

"Sir, as I understand it, we need to call Chernomor. Right?" asked one of the operators, marking something on the maps.

"Yes, and the pilots too," I smiled. "For now, stick to surveillance, and alert me right away if there's any activity."

Currently, there was a lot of construction work going on all over Khorkov's new holdings. However, Kooky took note of this particular project. It wasn't just a workshop or village being built there. Rather, it was a military base, which they were constructing right under my nose. Moreover, it was nearing completion. While the only military hardware there was primarily for security, of concern was the long convoy of trucks heading toward the base. I didn't have to guess what they were carrying. There's no such thing as too much ammunition, and I wasn't used to having to purchase it. On the base were several new container buildings housing five hundred fighters, and also there were around a hundred sentries on patrol. Basically, nothing we couldn't deal with.

"Don't tell me that we'll have to hide in the shrubbery again while you charge into the enemy camp on your trusty horse?" Chernomor glared at me. I just smiled and nodded.

"More or less you're spot on. Kudos for your perception!"

"But...wouldn't it be better if we busted onto this base and put a swift end to their plans? We could seize the heavy machine guns and cannons. They clearly don't expect an attack," Chernomor checked the data from the operators and shrugged, not understanding why I always chose this particular tactic.

Okay then, why was I always electing to go it alone?

"It's not easier, your approach," I said, shaking my head. "Just be prepared. Have the Pathfinder overhead, and put together a convoy of trucks. Today, we'll replenish our supplies. Moreover, we might even have surplus for sale."

Chernomor nodded, and started assembling the guards. As for me, I mounted my Corgi horse, and prepared to head out.

"Mikhail!" Victoria called out as I passed, and I stopped. "Why can't I come with you?" Okay then. Like I said, she could get ready quickly when she wanted to. In a flash, the countess had donned her combat gear, buckled her sword on, and even put on a little makeup. Her war paint, by the way, looked pretty good on her. Perhaps I spoke too soon when I criticized her cosmetics.

Ah, but no, this wasn't cosmetics. It's just that she was so excited about this venture that she'd lost control of her necrosis, and so it was seeping from her eye sockets. Cosmetics were a waste after all.

"Vika, you stay here," I said. "Your job today is to sit at the monitors and enjoy the show."

Victoria paused and looked confused. "But aren't you planning on killing them?"

"Well... Not exactly... And not all of them..."

Now the girl was completely confused and I, taking advantage of this, spurred my horse on.

I didn't have far to go. What an impudent duke this Khorkov was. I don't know which of them ordered the placement of a powerful and obviously expensive military base right on my border, but this person clearly underestimated my strength and cunning. It was most likely the father who'd given the order for this, and that was the only reason his son got his butt off the bar stool. However, they hadn't yet finished building the base.

Although there were several fortifications up already, these weren't enough yet, although it was only a matter of days before they'd all be in place. It was a solid camp, with a perimeter fashioned from pre-fabricated modules wired for electricity via lines on the roofs. Kooky personally verified this by pecking at said wires. The resulting jolt of electricity melted his feathers a tad. He wanted to pour acid on the generator for payback, but for now I forbade him to do so. We didn't want to reveal to Khorkov that we were aware of his new base.

It was stationed in the middle of the forest some distance from the roads. Thus, it could only be seen from the air, and even then only if the reconnaissance aircraft was flying at low altitudes. They'd strung camouflage nets all over the roofs, and had their vehicles travel at night without headlights. During the day the camp was quiet. In essence, they were planning something majorly big here, and it was most fortunate that they hadn't yet finished constructing and equipping the base. Even so, the equipment on site had to be worth millions, and the crates constantly being delivered there also had to be full of costly supplies. If this included ammunition, it had to be far from the cheapest.

I left Corgi a couple of kilometers from the base, and I proceeded to make my way around it a couple of times. I carefully studied every centimeter, scanning the barracks and the booths in which the sentries stood, monitoring heartbeats. I also ran a sonar scan so as not to miss the underground spaces in the military camp.

I did not discern any hidden passages. As Kooky and his team told me, this camp was a work in progress, and now I could see how huge the duke's investment in this operation was. He'd sunk a lot of moolah into this. A lot. I couldn't say exactly how much, but clearly the demolition of this place was going to strike an unpleasant blow. It could inspire the duke to throw all he had into retaliating, but I already had a plan should that be the case. One thing I was sure of was that soon we'd get to see what the Khorkovs were made of in battle. And as this wasn't a local Family, they weren't likely to get any support from the others.

As I traipsed about the territory, I prepared a number of interesting spells and also loaded my crossbow. I then fired a bolt through the neck of the sentry stationed at the main entrance to the camp. Then I rapidly fired off several more into others on guard, and after quickly pulling their corpses into the woods, I activate the dissolving process.

Now I could move deeper into the camp. Some of the enemy were sleeping in tents, but most of them were in the barracks. This consisted of two two-story wooden buildings that looked more like warehouses. But the actual warehouse was a little further off; this I knew. In fact, it had more guards around it than there were at the barracks.

"What?" the guard didn't have time to think twice before a large red crystal hit him in the face. But he'd almost detected me....or, rather he'd almost detected a corpse. You see, the soldier thought he saw a drunken comrade who had fallen asleep outside his tent and walked right up to him. And I simply used his blood to kill the curious soldier. I dragged the two bodies into the tent, although it was occupied by five more sleeping forms. But their sleep was so sound that even if I was to slug them in the face, they wouldn't awaken. That was my doing, the deep sleep. I didn't need to kill them, after all. As I was hiding the bodies, I heard footsteps.

"Hey! I heard something!" That was a whispering voice right outside the tent.

"Okay then, raise the alarm," chuckled

someone else. "What? Not so sure now?"

"You know yourself what we'll get for a false alarm," the first guy said, offended. "Okay, so maybe it's just someone taking piss, so why scare him?"

Good for him to trust his own senses. Good for me, actually; not so much for those two. Next, two muffled clicks were heard in the ringing silence of the night. That would be me. My crossbow bolts flew right through the tent walls. I hit them straight in the heart, because that was all I could feel, and the shells, loaded with sharp, powerful pain, didn't even permit the poor sods to scream.

Thus, I made my way from tent to tent, and then moved on to the barracks. I had to expend a fair amount of energy to ensure the peaceful slumber of the guardsmen. I programmed it so that they would all wake up at once, in three and a half hours. Then, I turned my attention to the warehouses. I had to use up my entire arsenal there. The soldiers guarding the place weren't sleeping on the job, and I could tell they were suspecting trouble that night. They'd called the men in camp a few times already, and after nobody picked up, they sent a group of five out to see what was going on. But then that group of men fell silent. You see, they ran into the Dose rune, with delayed activation. First, one of them stepped across the activation zone for the rune, triggering a quiet pop the released a bloody fog that engulfed him and his comrades. This spell wasn't like the one that produced hundreds of sharp crystals. What happened was that this fog simply blocked all sound, so no one could hear the cries of the small detachment.

The next two sentries to be sent were taken out by bloody spikes. These were small little spikes, but I had complete control over them. And so I could hit the enemies in the back, although one of them managed to fire a short burst into the air.

I waited for the siren to sound, but it didn't happen. By now all that remained were twenty men, and they all took to their heels and ran towards the forest. Five managed to jump over the fence, but I intercepted the path of the rest of them. Then, drawing my sword, I rushed forward into the attack. With one swing, my blade doubled in length and turned red. My two targets didn't expect this and couldn't block the blow. Blood gushed from the wounds like a stream, but I immediately took control of it, using it against them. Another swing, but this time my enemy was more cunning. He managed to throw himself at my feet and plunged a dagger into my thigh. Mmmm... poisoned. Good thing I'm a Healer.

Before he knew it, I grabbed him by his combat vest and hoisted him up like a shield against the machine gun fire coming at me. It was a powerful weapon, as the bullets pierced the guy's body and pounded my diamond armor. Then, I heard the tell-tale click — the enemy had run out of ammunition. I tossed the body at the two machine gunners and took cover behind a tree. A bloody explosion knocked them off their feet, and miniature red crystals pierced several more, causing severe bleeding. Yes, thromboembolism can not only clot blood, but also deprive it of this ability.

The fight was quick, but just the same, five of them got away. They could have retreated to a safe distance and contacted command, but no, that was not meant to be. After all, once in the forest they were chased and kicked by one extremely aggressive horse. And Kooky hadn't been derelict in his duties, so the network connections to this camp were down.

"Okay, now you can start up service again," I said to my feathered scout, who was plopped on the ground pecking at something.

"*Cooo....*" he muttered, ignoring me to concentrate on what mattered.

"So what you telling me is that you cannot turn the connections back on here?" I said, realizing that my pigeon had gone overboard when carrying out this task.

"*Erp...*" he shrugged.

"Okay, then you fly off and tell Chernomor yourself to haul ass this way! We don't have much time!" I said striding up to the bird to give him a demonstrative kick in the butt, but he figured out what I was aiming at, and my foot swished through empty air.

I had to wait about twenty minutes. First he had to get there, then he had to transmit my order, and finally the Pathfinder arrived. And before long we started cleaning out the warehouse. Crate after crate and box after box...All sorts of lettering on them. Some held shells, some held cartridges, and in others were machine guns and rifles neatly laid out in rows. We also found new electronics for jamming communications and for the communications themselves... In general, there was something to profit from here, but we weren't going to fit everything on the plane. I had a big convoy arrive a little later for some of the ammunition and weapons.

"Get it done!" Chernomor barked to his slightly surprised guards, who headed to the barracks, where some four hundred enemy soldiers were still fast asleep. It was only after making sure that he had been understood did the commander of my guard turn to me. "Mikhail, I understand that orders are not to be discussed. But why would we load sleeping men onto a plane and then give them weapons?"

"Maybe they'll sleep more soundly holding guns?" I smiled, and Chernomor waved dismissively as if to say "do it your way."

And, of course, that's what I was all about. I wanted every one of Khorkov's men to be dressed for the weather, armed with a quality weapon, and provided with a bulletproof vest and helmet. They should be fully alert when they woke up.

Thus, in a few hours, the four hundred armed sleeping fighters were on board the plane, and it took off. I was on the Pathfinder, as well, and enjoying the sight of the trucks loaded to the brim heading toward the castle. At this rate, we'd soon have to build a new warehouse, and the parking garage would be replenished today with two dozen new armored vehicles. What a shame that we couldn't get the tanks over here. I really appreciate a good tank.

And Willson was absolutely delighted. He kept asking to be freed from his work to tinker with the technology a little. He wanted to understand how everything worked so as to improve on it. I, too, wanted this, but first he needed to close the holes in the supply of artifacts. I wanted all my fighters to be protected and well-armed.

About fifteen minutes later the Pathfinder began its descent and I headed for the exit. Yes, this place was perfect, and nobody noticed us. And if anyone did take note, they got a pigeon slap in the face.

"So then, do we unload these guys now?" sighed Chernomor. "Right here in this field?"

"Why not? It's warm outside, they won't freeze. And hurry up, in half an hour they'll start to wake up!" I indicated the exit, and then I and Kooky began to monitor the area. As well as the unloading process.

Four hundred men — that's a good-sized crowd. It took a while, but my pigeons assured me that no one noticed us. About twenty minutes later the turbines howled, the Pathfinder took off from the ground and at an extremely low altitude we rushed towards the castle.

I didn't waste time hurrying over to our drawing room, for some fun viewing. Quite a few of us had already gathered there. Vika, Belmore, the earth mages... We had a large screen displaying the live stream from the surveillance cameras, and we all seated ourselves on the sofas and popped open some beverages. Yes, sometimes a cold beer was just the ticket.

"Look, one of them woke up! See!" exclaimed Vika. She realized now what my plan was and was now eagerly awaiting the outcome. "Another one, too!"

"In five minutes they'll all be awake," I smiled. I made a slight mistake with the calculations, but this was even better.

We all fell silent at once, because we could not only see what was going on, we could hear, as well. You see, we had a pigeon with a camera hovering above the field, and another feathered creature with a microphone flying right above the heads of the Khorkov Family's guards. And thus, we could listen in on the newly-awakened soldiers. Needless to say, they were surprised, and that's putting it lightly.

"Hey! How did we get here?" asked the command officer, but the man beside him just shrugged.

"Do you have service?" And the other just shook his head. "Phone? Radio? Anything?"

"Right, as if I'd have left you a radio!" I chuckled, reaching for a dried anchovy and tossing it into my mouth. "Come on already! Take a look around you! Go towards the lights!" In fact, not too far off was a searchlight and several light posts.

"I think we should head over there," said the

officer, motioning toward the lights. "We'll get an idea of where we are, at least."

"Listen up, men!" barked his adjutant. "Check your weapons and move out. Employ stealth!" he said, stressing the last word.

Soon they'd all assembled and started out, and fifteen minutes later they began emerging from the thickets near a fortified checkpoint manned by other fighters. The opposing sides were attired in different uniforms with different coats of arms, and both forces were very surprised to see the other.

"Who are you!?" both sides shouted in unison, grabbing their weapons.

"We are ..." the officer responsible for this checkpoint did not have time to finish. A stream of concentrated acid fell on his head, and the man clutched his skull and screamed.

All hell broke loose.

Shots rang out, resulting in a massacre. I, in the meanwhile, enjoyed my beer and smiled. Later on, how would they ever find out how a detachment of four hundred Khorkov fighters had ended up on Baron Grishanov's lands? Being from the capitol, the duke had yet to form any alliances with anyone. Could it be that he was out to seize more land? It was anybody's guess at this point, and who would believe anything he said?

CHAPTER 13

"I COULD WATCH THIS forever," said Vika, smiling as she stared at the screen. Yes, there was a reason I'd dispatched so many pigeons armed with cameras there. I wanted to see everything in detail.

And there was a lot going on. First, the four hundred involuntary paratroopers woke up and set off to find a means of communication. Of course I'd deprived them of phones and radios just so they'd have no way of knowing where they were.

And the baron's guards might have been open to helping the duke's men out, but just then Kooky unleashed a stream of acid piss, and everyone opened fire. Indeed, four hundred armed men were enough to launch a local war. They were well-trained and quickly jumped into action, and it didn't take long for them to take the checkpoint.

But that wasn't the end of it. They couldn't

find a telephone, and the radios were also unresponsive (big surprise), and so the duke's men headed for the nearest village. And since none of the vehicles would start, they had to proceed on foot, pausing now and then to exchange fire with the baron's forces.

Yes, it was tough going for them. And it was nice witnessing their confusion. The officer picked up a phone, hope in his eyes, but in the center of the screen he saw a neat hole. He no doubt thought it was a bullet, but, actually, it was created by the beak of a certain nasty pigeon. Ha!

And thus, the duke's throng of men moved on, rolling over any who tried to stop them, gradually acquiring heavier weapons. In response, the baron sent more and more of his forces into the fray. If at first they were paralyzed with surprise, they then pulled several large detachments with heavy equipment from our borders to protect their rear.

All fun, but Kooky wasn't omnipotent, and, anyway, sooner or later we had to give them the opportunity to contact the outside world. And so, once the Khorkov forces captured a fairly large village, we allowed them to find a telephone, with which they called their headquarters.

Good thing that I'd armed one pigeon with a microphone instead of a camera. This particular avian eavesdropper was in the attic of the house where the officers had assembled, and listened attentively to all they said. It was hilarious. We all laughed and laughed at their astonishment at what had happened. How could four hundred men end up like that deep within the territory of this baron?! He wasn't an enemy, or, rather, he hadn't been before now. No, Khorkov had some explaining to do; he'd have to conclude some kind of peace treaty with the baron, or resolve matters by force.

As the fun was unfolding on the baron's lands, another flock of pigeons was watching Khorkov's territory, where they were just beginning to stir. In fact, for whatever reason, all of Khorkov's troops had been put on alert as they began to investigate what was going on. And half an hour later, six large transport helicopters were sent towards Grishanov's territory to evacuate their lost boys. The latter was in real trouble, as the village they'd occupied was now practically surrounded. A battle involving tanks and hundreds of people was on the verge of breaking out.

"Action flicks like this are my favorite. I can't resist them," said Chernomor. "Great plot twists in this one, and realistic graphics. But something is missing..."

"Maybe some romance" I mused. "Let's send a love bird to Kooky. That might help the plot."

"Eeeew! Don't spoil this for me!" Chernomor shook his head. "Let's just watch the show."

Well, okay, no love story then. Anyway, he was pretty busy. His forces were all occupied with shitting and eating, and shitting and pissing. They'd drop their shit bombs right on the enemy's heads, and they didn't have to worry about hitting any of our guys. Everyone on the field of battle was fair game.

Could I let six transport helicopters get through? No way! Since I'd failed to steal them, I was obligated to at least hinder their progress. Thus, I had a squadron of fighting pigeons intercept them. They were awaiting their moment now, filling their bellies with the best grain. Mixed with a laxative, of course, although this was unbeknownst to them.

Some ten minutes later, thanks to a major infusion of energy, the "special avian forces" managed to catch up with the helicopters. And they proceeded to unload all of their organic "bombs". Explosions thundered, acid hissed, and two choppers fell like stones. Another started smoking and began a slow descent. And the remaining three were even less fortunate. The commanders had ordered them to do whatever it took to evacuate the stranded men, and so they'd powered on. One, though, was shot down by Grishanov's troops, and the others had to land right away, and the crew jumped out and took up defensive positions.

I have to say that we'd done well with this. And not just me, no. Thanks to the well-coordinated work of our pigeon reconnaissance, we could see the action unfold in living color, and even hear everything that was happening on Grishanov's lands. And the pigeons worked hard to provide the best footage possible, flying about to get the best angles from their little cameras. I'd also sent two pigeons with microphones to the enemy camp.

And then the baron managed to surprise me. I was certain he no longer had any Combat Suits, but then another one appeared in the sky. It flew out of Grishanov's mansion heading towards the battlefield, but fell short by some five kilometers. So much bird shit landed on it en route that it was forced to land. Meanwhile, I found a flaw in this technology. They'd disabled much of the ability of the Suit operator to see by pooping all over the lenses. And they'd used both acid and ordinary bird droppings, but were still unable to totally blind the operator.

But even if we hadn't destroyed the Suit, we did force it to land, and the operator was confused by what had happened, and made one serious mistake. He assumed that pigeons weren't dangerous and that they were, in fact, stupid, and had emptied their bowels out of fear at encountering him. That's what he assumed, and so after making sure that there was no one around except the pigeons, he exited his Suit to clean the lenses. Kooky was waiting for him to do this. And I passed an order on to Berg and his Combat Doves, who sped toward the Suit on their bikes. I had no idea how they were going to manage to drag the huge metal behemoth off, but somehow they'd manage to do before the baron's men got there.

For several hours I watched the battle. My pigeons flew back and forth in a continuous stream to procure more and more artifact shells to drop on the heads of the enemy. They needed to do this to ensure the continuation of the hostilities. When the baron's men had almost pushed the duke's forces out of the village, my birds started raining bombs and acid on them. And when Khorkov's guard began to gain the upper hand, they dropped explosive artifacts on them.

It was fascinating watching the overall confusion and chaos and how each side grew ever weaker. Better still was that now, there were no longer any troops on my borders. Khorkov and Grishanov were too busy with each other now, and so for the time being had no time for the Bulatovs. This, actually, was what I was trying to achieve, generally speaking.

And so, just as dawn was breaking, this exciting action movie finally reached the end. What a pity, yes, but anyway we'd done more than I hoped for. I hadn't expected the four hundred soldiers to hold out for so long, but in the end, they simply ran out of ammunition. And this despite the fact that my pigeons tirelessly carried filled magazines and dropped them near the guards' positions.

"Vika," I woke her up. She'd fallen asleep right next to me on the sofa. "You should go to your room..."

"I just wanted to see it...." she yawned. "But you're right. And thank you for the great show. It's the best movie I've ever seen, almost," she smiled.

"I liked it, too," I said with a chuckle. It had all worked out so well that I couldn't imagine how the two sides would ever come to terms with it. "I have something to do now, so for the next 24 hours

I don't need any distractions. Deal?" I said to Vika and to the snoring Chernomor.

"Okay!" nodded Victoria. She asked me no questions about what this was about. But in fact, she'd know soon enough. She'd see it with her own eyes.

On my way I summoned a certain twenty loyal guardsmen to join me, and off we went to the infirmary. It was empty now, and so I could cut loose with my abilities.

"I chose you because you are my most loyal and experienced fighters," I said to this, my future special forces unit, looking around at them. Several of them had hailed from the special forces in the Imperial army. Others were from my old guard. They'd served the previous head of the Family and had displayed their loyalty over and over again. Also here was the driver of the car in which I rode when it was hit by a hail of machine gun fire during Snegireva's assassination attempt. I'd fully healed him already, but now I was going to make him the head of this unit.

"Sir, I cannot speak for anyone else, but my health is excellent!" said one guy. "Can I ask what we're doing in the infirmary?"

"You have excellent health, but it's still far from ideal," I smiled. "I want to make your bones and skin stronger, improve your senses, and improve your regeneration and metabolism. This is voluntary, of course. I won't judge anyone who wants to opt out. It's a grueling process, painful."

Silence ensued, but as I expected, none of

this crew was afraid of pain. Nor would any of them mind being stronger. So they dispersed to the beds and prepared for treatment while I extracted the spells I had prepared in advance from my energy pouch.

Yes, I'd decided on this course of action whilst watching the shitshow on the baron's lands. I was inspired by the realization of how many problems could be caused by even a small detachment located behind enemy lines. And these were untrained ordinary guards. They weren't hiding, and didn't know where they were. But what would happen if, instead of those four hundred soldiers there were experienced specialists, seasoned in dozens and hundreds of battles, who knew exactly where to go and what to do? That would be a big headache for the enemy, to put it lightly. And my special forces wouldn't just be regular men; rather, they would have enhanced abilities.

And so over the next twenty-four hours I neither rested nor slept as I went from one bed to the next. I'd done something like this before when I created security for the king. My brother was a strong fighter himself, but just the same, I always worried about him and therefore provided him with the best security. Did I regret it? No, he used to be a completely different person back then.

The infirmary was filled with green flashes, and a magic circle woven from threads of vital energy began to shine right below the ceiling. My enhancements had to be comprehensive, as all bodily functions were interconnected. And thus, my changes impacted all of them. And when all these changes came into force, I'd have a universal squad for reconnaissance, sabotage, and powerful pinpoint strikes both behind enemy lines and on the battlefield.

Their skin was now much tougher, and the only way to break their bones would be to drop them from an airplane. I also focused on their vision. They had perfect vision, but now they could see even better in the dark and would even be able to briefly zoom in on something in the distance. This latter feature could hurt them, but in a pinch they could use it, and afterwards I could then heal the damage. I accelerated their ability to react significantly, which would be extremely useful in close combat. Already they were skilled warriors, and I'd had them all hone their skills in sword fighting. Ammunition, after all, could always run out, and so the ability to fight both with and without weaponry was a must for any self-respecting fighter.

In addition to all this, I added a few other little things to my elite fighters' arsenal. For example, I upgraded their digestive systems to enable them to eat tree bark, or even go without food and water for some time without losing strength.

I didn't turn them into super soldiers, but now they were stronger than other humans, and that was more than enough. These enhancements, along with what they already brought to the table in terms of experience, was just the right mix.

Of course, I could have done this sooner. At

least, that's what Chernomor thought as he watched me working so hard on creating my pigeon warriors. But it had taken me awhile to turn to Chernomor's fighting force.

Candidly, I myself wanted to do this sooner, but what can I say? I've been busy. And enhancing warriors required careful preparation, not only when it came to creating enough spells and storing enough energy, but also in terms of preparing the men for the process.

For it all to work out, they had to be in excellent health. And yet one thing or another always came up. Yes, I ensured they were in top notch condition, removed ailments, attuned their bodies to receive large amounts of energy, and they did their part, too. But of course, if any were wounded, it took time and effort to remove the resulting damage. Rehabilitation and some time for full recovery were unavoidable.

And one or another of these twenty men were always wounded, except that now that we'd enjoyed a long break in the fighting due to the truce and lull in fighting, I finally was able to treat them all.

After finishing my part of the process in the infirmary, I took them all down to the Lazarus font. The magical pool would ensure that their bodies accepted my enhancements, and it would also help them rebuild the structure of their magical channels, which would help them survive all this. In fact, it took a lot of effort on my part to ensure that these men didn't die from this treatment.

I'd known Healers who would enhance their servants. The latter were ungifted, of course, because mages could simply level up all on their own through grueling training and practicing their magic. But with the servants, the issue was that all people's bodies are different, and so if they were treated all the same, some simply wouldn't be able to withstand it and would die.

And yet, few were those who rejected enhancements, though they risked their life for them. The opportunity to grow stronger was irresistible to them. And so because these Healers gave their underlings a choice, and didn't force them to accept enhancements, I didn't intervene. But even though I didn't come down on them, my view of them didn't improve. Lazy, themselves lacking in talent — there was no other way to describe such Healers.

My approach to this process was completely different. I started by creating a medical record on their magical status for each of them. I studied their bodies up and down, drew up a detailed plan of their magical channels, blood vessels and weak points. This was very important, because it was fundamental to generating enhancements for the body.

Some people are naturally endowed with thin membranes, others have overly thick and inelastic walls for their magical channels, and still others can boast of great energy conductivity in their main channels. All of them required a different approach.

In short, it was a complicated process, and I had to adopt a unique plan for each of them. Now, though, seeing what I'd done, I was completely satisfied. None of the fighters underwent rejection to the changes, and although the end result would be different for each of them, what I'd created was a truly powerful detachment.

Ten of them had bones that were three times stronger. Five of them were now able to jump from the fourth floor without breaking their legs, while the rest were a little less fortunate. But this was just the beginning, so they need not despair.

To build a mansion to last the ages, you had to start with a solid foundation. That's what I was doing, metaphorically speaking. The ensuing upgrades would take far less effort and time, and, best of all, I could treat the fighters one by one rather than all at once. This was the only time I needed to create a single binding spell like this.

The vision enhancements went particularly well. It's no coincidence that in my youth I'd written extensive studies on providing a third eye to the ungifted. This enabled them to not only see magic, but to also cast weak spells. I also was deeply involved in studying ordinary eyes back then, so I had undergone a lot of training.

By the way, the ungifted can indeed perform magic, but at the expense of spiritual energy. True, this magic is primitive and differs strikingly from real, classical magic, but the fact is that it is better than nothing. This kind of thing was mostly practiced by Orders who worshiped an entity or a thing. All sorts of priests, shamans and clerics quite easily passed off their spiritual magic as miracles.

By the way, many people call this energy Prana. But that's not quite what it was, although I wasn't one to argue about it with them. It was far easier to nod and agree with such idiots than it was to try to talk seriously with them.

Two days flew by in a flash. In the morning I visited my patients, carried out the necessary manipulations and continued the enhancement process, and in the evening Vika and I sat in the drawing room and watched on the big screen what was happening with the neighbors.

They'd yet to conclude their hostilities. I didn't know what the problem was, but it seemed that every attempt to settle differences between the aristocrats would lead nowhere. Maybe the connection would break, or one or the other party would violate the terms of a ceasefire....whatever. It's not like pigeons were dumping explosives at the most inopportune moment, was it?

Finally, as the second day was drawing to a close, the fighting between the two sides began to subside. And I didn't like this at all, so now I sat in front of the screen and watched as my troops penetrated Grishanov's territory and swept away his flimsy checkpoints on the border.

Chernomor personally led this detachment into battle. He took a lot of equipment, a hundred guardsmen, and as cover the sky above had a host of pigeons flitting about armed with explosive artifacts. We didn't forget about reconnaissance either; practically the entire enemy territory was now under 24-hour surveillance, and two pigeons with microphones were constantly flying near ground level to eavesdrop on all conversations held by the enemy's command staff.

One of them was even spotted, endangering the entire operation. An enemy soldier accidentally noticed an overly curious pigeon and managed to snap a photo of it. The photograph turned out to be extremely interesting, as there was a pigeon sitting by the window and holding a microphone in its talons, right against the glass. But the soldier didn't manage to inform his officers, much less show them this photograph. He ran off helter skelter once acid fell from the sky onto his head. Kooky had waited several hours to relieve himself, to deadly effect.

Chernomor wasted no time in swooping into a village and capturing it, and then fortifying it with our forces. To this end he brought along our trio of earth mages, and thus, in just twenty minutes they'd created bunkers, and barrier walls with loopholes, and trenches to hinder tanks, and many other obstacles to advancing enemy forces. That is when the baron began to move his troops. He'd heard that Chernomor himself was directing this attack, meaning it was a serious matter. And he also heard about all of the military hardware Chernomor brought in, and thus, the baron had even more of his forces head for the captured village.

Soon, a battle of sorts was raging, although the baron's guardsmen were struggling. Of course, it didn't help them that explosives were falling right from the sky onto their tanks and vehicles, and their infantry was constantly caught in acid rain. Meanwhile, my people simply fired at them from their fortified positions. Small wonder that little headway was made by the baron. His tanks then rolled into quicksand that formed right under them, and the infantry, too, was unable to break through the defenses. And so, Grishanov had to summon large detachments from all over his lands, along with more artillery and heavier combat machinery.

"Okay, now's the time!" I clapped my hands and headed out. "Vika, Belmore. Would you like to join me?"

"No need to ask!" exclaimed Vika. "I'm almost ready!"

"Are we going on foot, or do we have a ride?" asked Belmore. "You see, I get carsick pretty easily."

"Don't worry, you won't get sick," I said, wondering why he never mentioned this before. After all, we had motion sickness pills on hand, not to mention me and what I could do. I could fashion a steel vestibular apparatus for him that would prevent him from ever getting sick.

In any event, we were going to be traveling by plane. Along with us would be thirty old men, twenty younger guards, our two Combat Suits for loading — that was it.

We'd planned all this in advance, and thus, the earth mages had already opened the stone slabs over the hangar. We all boarded the Pathfinder, and, turbines roaring, we took off. But we maintained a low altitude.

We flew just above the treetops as, according to the pilots, this made it more difficult for radar to detect us. Whatever. This kind of thing wasn't my forte, so I took their word for it. I simply sat back and enjoyed the flight as I pondered the canopy of pines and fir trees right below the belly of our metallic flying beast.

Our pigeons had mapped out a route for us in advance, as stealth was vital to our mission. We weren't going to join the battle. In fact, Chernomor had staged it for the sole purpose of attracting as much attention as possible. And he was doing a great job. That village was a hotbed of action right. It helped that we had plenty of ammunition now, thanks to cleaning out Khokov's big warehouse.

We flew over our lands, dropped into the territory of a neighbor with whom I was not yet at war, and then we reappeared over Grishanov's lands in the most unexpected place, and immediately began our descent.

My plan was, in fact, rather simple. Chernomor had forced the baron to concentrate almost all of his forces on the captured village. And the time was right because, as the baron was also still tangling with Khorkov, he was in no position to deal with a hundred guardsmen.

Thus, we landed right next to a military camp.

We were in the depths of the camp, where the artillery was stashed, along with something else of interest. I learned about such devices completely by accident, when Timothy was fantasizing about acquiring one. He'd seen the car in a photo taken by a pigeon. It didn't look like much to me, but he said it would nice if we could get something like it. Okay, if Timothy said so, why not? And I'd also inflict pain on our enemy, so yes, again, why not?

As soon as we landed, our hatch opened and the Suits flew out. They drew the brunt of the attack to ensure that no one would fire at the Pathfinder. Then, our guardsmen quickly ran out. Margarita, though, had to stay behind this time, which made her lover look very sad. I saw no point, you see, in providing him with ammo. This operation would be very expensive, plus we weren't out to destroy the camp and everything in it. The thing was that Margarita's old man didn't know how to do anything but aim and pull the trigger until the gun belt in his bulky backpack ran out of bullets.

In a matter of minutes we cleared the camp. Nobody expected a powerful enemy detachment to suddenly show up deep in the camp, so the baron's men didn't even have time to raise the alarm. Anyway, there weren't many of them about; just around fifty artillerymen who didn't even have their guns at hand.

Too bad for them that here we were. And now that we'd secured the process, we opened the luggage compartment up and started loading what we came for. Our Combat Suits rolled the devices inside -- two shiny trucks were driven into the huge compartment. I never would've noticed them if I hadn't found out what they cost.

What these innocuous looking trucks did was jam communications by interfering with the electronics, even from afar. They could also do other cool stuff, too. They were called something like electronic warfare stations. What this meant was that these stations could make even our Combat Suits malfunction. The feed to their monitors would quit working, and other functions would shut down altogether, thereby taking them out of action. And the closer Combat Suits or planes got to them, the more effective was the interference from the jamming stations. And not to mention mobile communications, which, as it turns out, could be completely blocked within a radius of half a kilometer.

And now, these jammers were mine. All I needed now was to find the specialists to operate these stations, and then our castle would be safe from any attacks. They couldn't even target me with missiles, and any sabotage groups that decided to drop in for some dirty work would find they had no way to communicate with the outside world, and so no, they couldn't tell anyone about me and what I could do.

The operation to steal the jamming stations went off without a hitch. Of course, I hadn't directly participated in it, perusing the screen on my tablet as my men, assisted by the corpses raised by Vika and Belmore, loaded the plunder onto the

Pathfinder. I was watching the footage from the pigeon cameras, and coordinating the actions of my fighters. For example, Chernomor was soon forced to retreat.

The baron had assembled a large strike force comprised of many powerfully Gifted, and with one blow they swept away almost all our defensive lines, bringing the rest of the soldiers with them. But by now it didn't matter, as he'd held out long enough. Thus, he retreated with a clear conscience and was glad that he'd managed to avoid losses. There might well be a truckload of wounded, but Roman could take of them. I didn't see any critical cases among them.

Then the picture changed, and the pigeons showed me a video from the enemy's side. The baron's men had by now occupied the village and were celebrating at vanquishing the enemy forces in a serious showdown. But they were really planning on a celebration after they got back to their base. And once that happened, what fun to see their faces! Everything was gone! We'd even taken the corpses with us. After all, they'd helped with the loading, and it wouldn't have been right to leave them behind. All that work to just be buried in the ground?! Bad optics, that.

Back at the castle I headed straight for the infirmary to check on the wounded. As expected, Roman was doing a great job at stabilizing the condition of the seriously wounded, and was also treating the less severe cases. I helped him out for a while; not wanting him to overextend himself. He hadn't slept much of late, and had spent a lot of energy on his studies and practice session.

"By the way, don't you want to become a magister?" I asked him when we had a respite in the residency room. This was, it turns out, what they called the lounge for doctors. It was where they could rest up a bit. Shut the door and get a break from the patients. Ignore them, even, unless it was urgent.

"A magister?" Roman raised an eyebrow. "What's that?"

That's right. I hadn't yet initiated him into the intricacies of the hierarchy of mages from my world. The ranking system in this world was, how to say? Superficial, meaningless. It didn't have anything to do with the real powers wielded by mages, or the Gifted.

"So then, do you want it, or not?" I asked him again, not wanting to explain all the details right then. It would take at least a day, and that would be the abbreviated version.

"Sure, why not?" he shrugged. "What do I have to do for it?"

"You have to attend the Healer's symposium in the capital!" It was important that I be up front with him about the extra work I was planning on dumping on him for the privilege of becoming a magister. Why not? He'd be willing to agree to about anything right now.

"No, then," he shook his head. "I'd rather not become a magister then."

Damn, my little ploy failed this time.

"But why not? How about if you just accompany me, then? Would that work for you?" I tried to find a solution, but Roman remained adamant.

"Yeah, sure...We'd fly there together, but then, all of a sudden you'll just disappear, leaving me alone with those old codgers."

Right, he was onto me yet again.

Except that I'd have disappeared before even boarding the plane. It really was going to a venue at which old, wizened men got together to boast about their feats. I knew myself well enough to know that I'd get sick of it, and, then I'd end up revealing too much about my own capabilities. I just cannot stand it when some wise guy starts promoting misguided medical practices. I always had to intervene. As cruel as it was, I'd end up revealing my powers right away...Better for me to simply slug them in the face or something.

And I hadn't yet come up with a plan to get out of attending the symposium. Anyway, once done with treating the wounded, I went up to my study to sort through piles of documents.

Incomprehensible letters, intelligence reports, stuff from Timothy and also Georgy....Kooky distracted me from this incredibly boring activity. He, as usual, landed on my table and began strutting from side to side, glancing sideways in my direction.

"Come on, spit it out," I said, tossing aside some expense reports. "I see you've got something to say."

"*Cooo,*" he said, shrugging. "*Cooooooo-coo.*

Coooo"

"What's that?" He fell silent in mid-sentence for whatever reason. He said that he had important information, and I would be very interested to hear it, but... But what that "but" was, we could only guess.

"Coo....coooo," he said in a snarky tone as he spread his wings.

"Fifteen kilograms of white grain from the Interface world?" My eyebrow shot up in surprise. "You won't burst by any chance? The greed won't bust right out of you? Come on, tell me what you learned there!"

"Cooo. Cooo-coo..."

"Are you sure you want to fight me?" I asked, looking seriously at him, but he decided to go all the way. And he stood in a fighting stance, ready to fight me.

"Eh..." I sighed sadly. "What am I going to do about you, huh?"

* * *

Yes, Kooky really did have some interesting information. He recently flew into a portal on my lands and conducted reconnaissance there. He'd discovered that the offworlders had finally acquired some smarts and now, an army was heading for the portal. I had no idea how they were funding this venture of theirs, since Kooky had almost completely cleaned out their treasury. He must have hidden the coins somewhere in the castle.

The enemy decided to come in with all his troops at once, to sweep away the defense at the portal with a single strike force, and, after then, having secured their presence in our world, they would rebuild the fortress. Otherwise, without an army, construction just wouldn't happen, as their earth mages seemed to vanish with enviable regularity.

The attack would begin very soon, tomorrow or the day after tomorrow, which meant we had to jump to it in terms of our own preparations.

"Listen, what's going on? And why?" Vika distracted me by walking in.

"What are you talking about?" I asked.

"It's just strange...why is that bald pigeon of your running about in a panic?"

"How should I know? No doubt he was trying to engage in blackmail and extortion again. This makes his feathers fall out by themselves, I've seen it more than once," I shrugged and smiled, and Vika laughed. It turned out really well, a short haircut suited him, even a buzz cut. And now Kooky could get a sense of what it felt like to serve as an infantryman, if only for a little while.

CHAPTER 14

"YOU HAD AN ASSIGNMENT for us?" asked Ludwig cautiously upon walking into my study. The other mages had already assembled and were looking at me almost suspiciously.

They knew I had something in mind. There they stood, stiff backed and staring at me as if I was about to lower the boom on them.

"Yes, that's right," I smiled and leaned back in my chair, appreciating the escalating tension in the room.

"Well?" Giovanni couldn't stand it. "Mikhail, we're now fully aware of your impossible demands on us, so you can't surprise us."

"Wonderful!" I exclaimed. "So you won't flip out when I tell you to erect a township near the portal."

"A town...." repeated Toren "I won't ask you why you want a town. To be honest, nothing surprises me anymore. My concerns are that it would take....weeks...to create a small town from scrap materials....Weeks..."

"You have a day! Tomorrow, I expect a town near the fort. You can work in shifts," I snapped as the Earthbenders blanched.

"But...but..."

"Tomorrow, and not a day later," I shrugged. "Well? Hop to it! You don't have much time! Keep in mind that as you're building the town you may be attacked by your former fellow citizens."

"I quit!" announced Ludwig. He was clearly on the verge of hysteria.

"No, Ludwig, you're not quitting. And you'll carry out my order. Don't you remember the eighth clause in your contract, which lays out the consequences of violating construction deadlines?" I said, almost smirking.

And my ploy worked. He believed me, although there was nothing about deadlines in the magical contract. Or, rather, yes, there was, but it didn't contain anything about consequences should the mages unintentionally miss a deadline. Anything could happen, after all.

So why did I want a town near the enemy's fort? I had to have it there, that's why. I wanted some modest, three-story buildings, narrow streets, with a central town square. Also, all of the structures should be constructed from clay and stones from the ground. No frills, just a regular town in which no one actually lived, but which would look like an actual settlement from the outside.

The mages finally recovered enough to totter off and figure out how to carry out my order, and I headed for the basement. What was sad was that one of my projects had to be destroyed because of these offworlders. They had to launch this attack at the worst possible time, the absolutely worst time. But that was just the way it goes, after all. No escaping it.

I descended to the first level below ground. We had a number of caged cells in one room. I had a number of pets here that were cared for by servants.

I had peasants who regularly supplied me with new animals. I would pay them for this. For some time now they'd managed to supplement their income by catching these rats. And they were happy about this, which is why we had a significant population of the creatures in cages now. I estimated their numbers to be around five thousand! Of course, this was also due to their impressive reproductive abilities.

At first, my plan was to give these rats to Vika. Her birthday was coming up, and I thought the rats would be the perfect gift. She could use them to create a serious bone monster or plague golem. There were many options, actually. I didn't want to just throw money at a gift. I wanted something special. Plus, it would make the Family stronger, although I'd give up my army of rats.

Oh, well. I had to use the rats myself, but this was going to be interesting. I was certain the offworlders would fall for my provocation, and all I needed was to wait for the town to be in place. But the mages were already at work on this. I'd provided them with energy crystals, and I expected they could finish by my deadline of tomorrow.

And it didn't matter that nobody knew why. All that did matter was that the mages were capable of building a town. I had to be sure that the offworld forces wouldn't be able to resist my new town, and I also had to have the mages create several underground passages to access the town. People had to freely enter it.

Belmore, by the way, understood what I was up to as soon as he saw me working with the rats. He laughed, while Vika stood there, clearly puzzled about what I was up to. But I didn't enlighten her. I wanted her to see it for herself.

"Why don't I raise some zombies to feign ongoing activity in the town?" suggested Belmore. "They could walk around with boxes and move them from one building to another. What do you think?"

"Well, why not?" I gave him the go ahead. "Sounds like fun. Maybe have them dance about in a circle and make rude gestures toward the portal."

"No need to suggest that," said Belmore, somehow offended. "I thought of that already."

The earth mages cursed non-stop, but nevertheless managed to erect an entire town in literally one night. By the time they were finished they looked worse than Belmore's zombies, but they'd done their part and could now sit back with a clear conscience. To express my gratitude I poured some energy into each of them, and right away they felt much better. Sure, this was all just the way they felt. In reality they were in lousy shape, but what mattered was they felt just fine. I did what I could to help.

But the offworlders let us down a little. They didn't appreciate our haste and anticipation and attacked us not that day, but the next. But Kooky had alerted me. He'd grown even glossier, simply beautiful feathers, which he needed for his reconnaissance work. Ludwig was impressed, and before turning in he sketched Kooky in his notebook. I expected he'd be setting about sculpting pigeons in the walls again.

The strange thing was that the offworld army was not at all hindered by Kooky's plundering of their coffers. Kooky had stolen over two thousand coins, several artifacts, and all kinds of trinkets from them, but just the same, the offworld lord had the means to pay for the services of warriors and mages. Just as I suspected early on, he must have a reserve treasury that the pigeon never managed to get to. It must be stored in his castle in that room that had rather powerful magical protection. And his army was quite impressive. According to our aerial scouts, the offworld forces had recently swelled in number, with new recruits from distant lands. All in all, it looked like this lord had thoroughly prepared, and didn't plan on retreating.

And although we were expecting the invasion, when it started, we anyway were caught by surprise. What happened was that all of a sudden the offworld soldiers lined up in tight columns and began swiftly filing through the portal. Hundreds of fighters penetrated our world and immediately occupied pre-selected positions.

Thus, in a matter of minutes, the half-ruined fort erected in turn by my three earth mages, was occupied. And before we could fire on them, translucent energy domes began to flicker over the fort. Right, their mages were ready to act, swiftly protecting their infantry from earthly shells.

And with good reason, because in no time the domes began to ripple from the massive projectiles that fell on them. Our guys were firing the cheapest shells, just to announce their presence. We'd discussed our tactics in advance, and so far we didn't have to change the plan. Meanwhile, the offworlders were elated. Of course, all our efforts did not bear any fruit; no one was the least bit hurt by the shrapnel.

The portal glowed and flickered as more and more enemies entered our world. Heavy infantry, armored cavalry, entire detachments of battle mages, and even catapults and other contraptions for a siege. I also noticed light horsemen armed with crossbows and bows. They were dressed in furs and skins and were strikingly different from the other offworlders.

It was my understanding that these were offworld mercenaries. This meant the lord had enough funds to hire elite warriors, which was why his army was rather motley.

"Mikhail, I understand you've got a plan, but this isn't going well. Let's at least call Konakov," said Chernomor, looking unusually tense. He was nervous about all of the enemy combatants pouring through the portal into our domain. "This is no ordinary battle; let's call for reinforcements!"

"Oh, come on now. It's just one lord with a bunch of mercenaries. No big deal," I waved my hand. "And we've got a foolproof plan. They don't have a prayer of succeeding," I said. In fact, my plan was a good one. First, I'd torment the enemy, and then deceive him, and finally I'd deal him a decisive blow.

"Yes, I know. But we have two hundred people, and they have seven thousand!" Chernomor was still uptight. "You can clearly see that the odds are against us..."

"Two hundred people and five thousand rats!" I raised my finger. "You must not forget about our assistants. And Belmore also raised a couple dozen zombies — they're helping, too."

"They will help, yes..." Chernomor sighed. "But maybe you could at least alert Konakov? Or else contact the Imperial Chancellery, who could help."

"And then we'd have to share with them! No way!" I shook my head. "I want all of the offworld steel, and the artifacts."

Really, why share? What would be the point? I mean, nobody ever shared anything with me. The

Empire never helped me, and my neighbors only worked to inflict damage on me. Yes, the duke could indeed help with ammunition, and perhaps even warriors, and completely legally. He could even show up in person to help repel this attack. But hey, these lands are my lands, and it is on me to protect them. Just like I've always protected them. And I'll do it again, this time, too. It was my only option.

As the enemy continued to pour through the portal, we, too, kept busy. Our artillery tirelessly pounded the energy shields, and our pigeons kept watch over every nook and cranny in the fort. With the possible exception of some shielded rooms. The lord had finally learned from some of his egregious mistakes, and had not skimped on magical protection. Thus, it was impossible to get inside to find out what was in there. I'd have liked to do just that, but this time it was off the table. Thus, the scouting work carried out by Kooky and his team was vitally important.

The offworlders occupied their fort and began preparations. To everyone's surprise, this took them four days. They brought in even more troops, tried to assemble siege weapons, loaded artifacts and planned their big attack.

"I don't understand what's taking them so long!" Chernomor said, ever the more nervous with each passing day. "They should have struck immediately!"

"Why do you think that?" I asked. "What if they need to prepare first?"

"Who needs to prepare when they can over-whelm us with numbers? Look!" he pointed at the screen on which the feed from the pigeon camera was displaying what was happening inside the fort. "How many mages do they have in there? Do you see?"

"Yes, but almost all of them are busy support-ing the dome," I shrugged. Of course they had pro-tective artifacts, but these were costly, even in their world. I, too, had a stash of such artifacts, but all they could do was protect a tank. Or per-haps an artillery installation. In any event, it wouldn't be possible to cover the entire fort with artifacts, so the mages had to do it the old-fash-ioned way by creating and maintaining a magic dome.

And that is why we'd been continuously pounding them with artillery shells. We didn't have many specialists, having only managed to re-cruit ten, but that was enough. All of the guns we'd acquired as trophies were being used. As long as they could shoot, they were being fired, even if it was hit and miss, more or less

Chernomor was furious, in part because I hadn't provided him with all the details. But Bel-more immediately understood why I needed the rats and a town built the day before the invasion.

First of all, we completely changed the land-scape of the area. The offworlders had planned on fighting in an open field, and their mages prepared special spells in advance, but here you go, you have to fight in narrow alleys and clear out houses.

Offensive, right? I'd be upset in their shoes.

But that wasn't all. There was a reason why it took a long time for them to prepare. After all, their life mages wasted no time setting up tracking spells that sensed sources of life. They were idiots for not foreseeing my trick. So now they were sure that there were some five thousand warriors in the new town, because they sensed life in almost every building. What they didn't know was that these were rats.

So now they were preparing to clash with a five-thousand-strong army inside a town. I told Chernomor about this, and he laughed. Which was weird, actually. I'd only seen him smile a couple of times. I guess my tactics here really got to him. But that wasn't all. Even though the life mages had confirmed to their command that there were people in the city, the lord still sent out reconnaissance squads from time to time. There they saw zombies dragging boxes from one place to another. Just for appearances. However, whenever the lord's scouts showed up, these boxes turned into throwing weapons

True, the zombies were destroyed quite quickly, because the lord sent a detachment of chasseurs. These were crossbowmen with high-quality weapons and enchanted ammunition. And their explosive crossbow bolts were no joke. They could bust apart a stone wall, and had no problem taking out zombie bodies.

But this was why we'd created underground passages. As soon as the rangers penetrated the town, they encountered serious resistance. I went myself, taking Belmore and Chernomor with me, and together we showed the offworlders that they needed to do their homework.

How to get the job done when you can't even find the nuts to assemble a ballista? You sit there, assemble a siege weapon, and don't bother anyone. But as soon as you put a bolt or nut on the table and turn away, it immediately disappears. And the vile pigeons, cackling maliciously, carry it all off and drop it into the cesspool.

The offworlders were bewildered at why it was filling up so quickly. Little did they know that it was primarily full of tools, food, and nuts and bolts and such for siege weapons. Our pigeons even managed to damage the runic inscriptions on the weapons. First, they doused them with acid, and then they used their talons to scratch other patterns on the weapons, destroying the magical enhancements formerly embossed on them.

But the pigeons were doing even more than this. They didn't neglect their reconnaissance duties, and that was how one of them noticed that the magical protection had noticeably weakened in one area. The mage there was nearing total exhaustion, and was drifting off to sleep now and then.

So that is where we sent five artillery shells. And although three of them missed, and one simply crashed into the exhausted protective dome, the last one hit a concentration of fighters, inflicting serious losses. After all, they were so jam packed in there that this was inevitable.

"Ah, I think it's begun..." Yes, clearly the enemy camp was stirring.

True, they didn't all of a sudden rush into an attack, but their mages stepped out onto the walls to create some intricate spells, and a couple of minutes later a real storm of magic came falling down upon our newly built town. Meanwhile, I sat in my drawing room, sipping wine whilst enjoying the show displayed on our viewing screen.

I loved watching magic attacks. Every single element and type of magic was unique in how it was rendered, but almost all were vivid and bright. One was from a flame mage, and another must be a wind mage, as together they'd created a fiery tornado. A nice spectacle, yes, but nothing special. The reddish hues and showers of scorching sparks rose into the air as the wind mage spun them around creating a funnel which he sent down to earth. They'd managed to inflict maximum damage, so I had to applaud them.

The tornado danced down the fictional town's main street, lightly touching the buildings. There were other mages focused on bringing the structures down. For example, a pair of combat earth mages took down five building at once as if slapping a house of cards, and then they compressed the ruins to finish off anyone trapped in them. And another flame mage sent a blaze of fire into another building, roasting alive any living being inside. All that remained behind was now a heap of ash.

Good going, mages! Use up your energy. I'm all for it. As for the rats, I felt sorry for them, but far better for them to perish rather than my people. And so I watched as the enemy mages mindlessly spent their already depleted reserves.

It was for this that we'd spent all this time pounding the enemy, preventing them from taking a breather. We'd kept the mages on their toes using up their energy to maintain their canopy, and now we had them triumphantly tearing into our town of rats.

What was funny was how, at their command headquarters, every time new losses were reported they would celebrate. For example, a building went up in flames, and supposedly twenty enemy troops were killed. A water octopus pierced another building, taking out ten more. This was, then, their strategy. The offworld command sat in their headquarters counting all the foolish enemies their mages were taking out spending only energy, which would be restored the next day.

Or would it? That was up to me!

What a shame about the rats. I didn't expect any of them to survive. I'd fed them well and tenderly cared for them, and their last weeks of life had been a rodent paradise, yes, but still, I felt badly for them because, after all, they, too, were living beings. But I had no other option.

I also felt badly for the zombies, who'd worked so hard lugging boxes about all day, and for this, they got nothing but a barrage of magic. Many of them had already turned to ash and ice, but this was just at first. Before long they'd be further broken down into molecules, which was also part of the plan.

Okay, the offworlders were happy. I got it. After all, in their mind, they were demolishing an entire town without suffering any serious losses. Sure, they'd had to sacrifice a few reconnaissance units, but that was all. Finally, the flurry of magical attacks began to subside, and then the gates of the fort swung open, and a host of detachments emerged and lined up. Looks like the next phase of the invasion was about to start, and I was sure the offworld lord expected me to cower in fear, and, perhaps, bite my nails with chattering teeth.

Sorry to disappoint, but that's not my way. What I did do was smile, and pick up my radio to give the next order.

* * *

Meanwhile
Inside the offworld fort

"Master Commander, we've taken out another fifty! Our sand mage unleashed a dust storm that swiftly killed them!" The warrior delivering this report didn't bother masking his delight. "Your strategy is brilliant!"

"Indeed, now you see why I insisted that we take our time before invading," intoned the commander, raising his finger to emphasize the veracity of his words. "This is why it is going so well."

In fact, it was. At least, that's the way it appeared. The enemy had failed to bust through the dome, try as he might. A single shell had made it through, taking out almost three dozen soldiers. But this loss was negligible, and not even worth recording. Thirty out of five thousand — that was nothing.

And everyone present was now lauding the commander. At first, some had disagreed with his plan, but now, it was clearly bearing fruit. And this was thanks to the stupidity of the enemy, who had opted to not immediately attack. That would have potentially saved them, but now, they had no means of resisting their onslaught.

"As soon as I saw that town, I knew our enemies were idiots," chuckled an officer. "But it was only later that I realized they were stark raving mad. I wonder if everyone in this world is stupid?"

"Probably. And this is why they will lose in the end," said the commander with a smug smile.

They'd prepared so well for a reason. And though from the outside it might look like an easy win, in fact, it had required effort. Everyone contributed to the victory, and they'd done well, despite the enemy's attempts to stand in their way.

And now, the buildings in the foolish town were a heap of rubble. Flames were raging through the streets, demolishing any signs of life. Hundreds were perishing by the minute.

"From my calculations there are around a thousand left in the town. Their army has been decimated, master!" continued the Healer upon checking the data from his life-detecting artifact. "You are a mighty leader!"

"Thank you, Zulfrid," the commander nodded gratefully. "Well then, gentlemen!" He looked around at the men assembled around him, who all rose to their feet. "It is time of us to launch the second phase. Go now, and return victorious!"

A loud "hurrah" shook the walls of the headquarters, and the officers rushed to lead their detachments. The gates of the fort swung open and the commander watched with pride as his army rapidly approached the town in which the remnants of the enemy forces were cowering. As a dense formation of infantry conducted a pincer movement, shock troops began to clear the streets.

"Sir!" — the communication artifact flashed with light, and the voice of the commander's chief adjutant issued from it.

"Speak!"

"Sir, there is no one here. The city is empty, and all that remains are..."

Suddenly his voice broke off. The commander's eyes widened in horror, and the ground shook beneath his feet.

"Get the hell out of there!" screamed the commander, but it was too late.

*   *   *

Well, they finally made their move. I thought they'd never be done with their preparations. All that endless assembling and disassembling their siege contraptions, lining up in columns, stacking arrows, and wasting all that energy to feed their defensive barriers.

But finally they'd gone on the attack. They poured out of their fort and rushed to the town to overwhelm it and come down on it like fist right on the hordes of rats and several zombies, who'd settled in to take a last stand. A valiant group, indeed.

But what the offworlders weren't expecting was a deluge of rain pouring down on them from the clear night sky. It's not like the weather forecasters had predicted inclement weather. But the strange thing was that these offworlders hadn't learned anything from the past. Apparently they needed to repeat the errors of their ways. Also strange was the rain, which smelled funny, not at all like water.

But although most of the army had already been doused with the foul liquid, the offworlders continued their advance as if nothing was amiss. Meanwhile, the Pathfinder hovering high above the town had practically emptied its tanks. After which the team began to empty the luggage compartment, which was almost filled to the brim with boxes bearing the emblem of the Khorkov coat of arms.

Do I feel sorry for throwing away expensive shells like this? Yes, it hurt to see the abandon with which we were wasting this expensive commodity. But then again, we had nothing to use these shells on. All we had was the ammo for special guns and rocket launchers that had yet to be brought to the camp by the Khorkovs. The plane's hold contained quite a few of these shells. They were neatly packed into boxes, and carefully placed in a steel container that barely fit through the mouth of the luggage compartment. And we sent the entire container down, down, onto the town below.

I once saw fireworks on TV. The capital was celebrating some kind of milestone date, and to mark this occasion they launched special rockets into the air that exploded in the sky into thousands of multi-colored lights. Beautiful, of course. Festive. But our Arkhangelsk fireworks surpassed that of the capital's. We produced more dazzling lights and claps of thunder. Better still was the fiery mushroom cloud now rising above the battlefield right where the enemy fort used to stand.

"How... beautiful..." I heard the sleepy voice of an earth mage. Ludwig couldn't miss such a spectacle, and so had joined me.

So now I could expect frescoes of mushroom clouds along with flocks of pigeons adorning the walls.

"Chernomor," I said, ignoring Ludwig. "Tell me. Why did we waste so many powerful shells?" Yes, they really were powerful. I felt the shock wave from here in the castle. I can only guess what it felt like on the ground.

Our pigeons were blasted to earth by it, and now most of our cameras were out.

"Why did you have to crater the fort?" I shoved Chernomor on the shoulder. He was staring fixedly at the screen where footage from the only working camera was displaying the aftermath. "You personally calculated how many shells to drop on the fort, right?"

"Yes, I did..." muttered Chernomor. "But....but...," he stuttered, pointing at the screen. "I didn't expect that."

Gradually the pigeons recovered and ascended into the air, showing us the scene. And, what to say? No more town. No more fort, either. Nothing remained. Gone, too, was the portal, unable to withstand such a powerful release of energy. All that remained was a crater, some 24 meters deep, and surrounded by a lot of fallen trees. Now, a steppe would take the place of the former forest, as what remained was essentially scorched earth.

And looking at the magical field, I began to understand how the explosion had transpired. In short, our attack was even more effective than I ever thought it would be. Under my plan, we were to lure out the troops, set them on fire and blow them up, and finish off their main forces with artillery. And then I'd enter the action by capturing prisoners and demolishing their command.

But it didn't pan out that way. First, we'd released all that jet fuel onto the mages, who did nothing to shield themselves from it. Why bother when it was just some kind of liquid? Sure, it stunk, but they weren't about to drink it. Too bad for them that their protective magic was unable to flag jet fuel. They lacked anything like it in their world, and thus, suspected nothing.

After dumping the fuel, we followed it with that massive container of explosives. I had no idea how many tons were contained inside it, but it busted right through the nearly depleted magic dome. Again, nobody expected it. Planes usually fire off bullets and shells, after all. But this was nothing of the sort, and their magic dome simply burst. All they had maintaining it at the time was a single mage who was by then exhausted. No surprise, as he'd been pouring his energy into the shields for four days straight, almost non-stop.

And then, the explosion. More precisely, two explosions: first, our container blew up, and then the shock wave caused the magic projectiles they had in there for the catapults to detonate. They exploded, too, as was to be expected, causing their stash of combat artifacts to explode. The column of flame rose high into the sky, perhaps a kilometer upwards. I hoped that nobody would ask me what the weapon was that I'd tested here, and to what end. This might come later. Now all that remained for us was to celebrate our victory, because our squadron had flown over the crater several times already and nobody detected any surviving enemies. Nor did they discern any surviving artifacts...Right, we'd lost more than we'd gained in this battle. The neighboring mountain was also destroyed. It is worth mentioning that this mountain was magical and thus, was impossible to simply demolish.

I went out there myself to see with my own eyes the consequences of the destruction. I walked along the edge of the crater, looked at the plain that had recently been a town, and helped the wounded guardsmen. Yes, a few of our men had suffered damages, even though they'd been standing at a safe distance. Needless to say, some of the peasants' houses in nearby villages were impacted by the blast wave. At least the chicken coops survived; they were designed just for something like this.

"Well, gentlemen, I congratulate you," I smiled and nodded towards the crater, "this portal will no longer cause problems!"

"Sir..." one of the officers standing in front of me pointed at something over my shoulder. "Look at....well, see for yourself."

Right away this sort of spooked me, but I turned around anyway. And there... A new portal had opened...

On principle I didn't pass through it, although I really wanted to. There could be another army there, or another lord hungry for riches. To hell with it. It had opened at the very edge of the crater and, right then, nobody was exiting from it.

"Well then, don't go anywhere," I shrugged. "Aim at that portal, and if anyone emerges from it, fire."

I also ordered my people to install thermal imaging cameras in case invisible entities tried to penetrate our world, and I had sappers mine the area around the portal itself. No one would pass through from the offworld now; in fact, I myself would have trouble reaching the portal without the help of the sappers.

I headed home, and as soon as I had a shower, a quick dinner and was about to collapse into bed, the phone rang. Cherepanov... He probably wanted a drinking partner... But anyway I had to answer.

"Not asleep yet, eh? I knew it!" exclaimed the count, clearly excited.

"No, I'm not sleeping; you're very perceptive," I muttered. "If you want someone to drink with, I can offer you the earth mages, but then I'll have to treat their livers."

"What are you talking about? Don't you know what's happening?" shouted Cherepanov, and right away I recalled the kilometer-long column of fire from the explosion.

"It's no big deal. It could happen to any-body....You do realize I'm at war with my neighbors and anything can happen, don't you?"

"What? Are you raving now?" Nikolai was confused. "Turn on the news!"

What, I made the news!? But how? I hadn't done anything illegal. So I detonated a bomb on my own lands, what of it?

But anyway I turned on the news. I went to the drawing room, poured a glass of compote, lounged on the sofa and pressed the button on the remote. Vika had been sitting by the fireplace and reading a book, but she joined me as soon as the broadcast was on.

"Ugh..." I sighed, turning up the volume and leaning in toward the screen.

"The Imperial Observer TV channel presents you with exclusive footage!" the announcer spoke in a brisk tone, and the footage displayed a bird's eye view shot. Columns of black smoke rose over some cityscape." "I repeat, breaking news! Severodvinsk has been totally overrun by offworlders! A massive invasion has taken place."

"What's that!?" Victoria asked, moving closer to the TV to point out a strange building to me. "I've never seen anything like it..."

"It really does look like a magic tower..." I looked closer. There was now a new building in the center of the city's central square. It was a very, very tall tower that extended all the way up to the clouds.

"There are no longer any network connections functioning in Severodvinsk, all lines are down, and no power is reaching the city! We've lost one helicopter during an attempt to fly in closer, so now all we have access to is this footage," continued the announcer.

What we saw in the footage was dismal. Every now and then we could see flashes of spells and we heard the roar of artillery. The magic tower couldn't block good old gunpowder, but as for the heavier combat machinery, well, the planes were taken out right away and the tanks, well, they might be able to hang in there for a while longer. The footage also showed huge crowds of refugees. People had fled their homes with whatever they could grab on the fly, and some were running barefoot across the frozen ground towards

Arkhangelsk as columns of military vehicles headed their way.

"The latest reports are that the city's defense has been completely destroyed! Reports allege that around a hundred aristocrats have died, and the offworld invaders have captured the inhabitants of entire districts and are forcing them through the portals!"

"Unbelievable!" I shook my head, disgusted. "Get ready, we're heading out there, now!" I said, rising to my feet. This was not the time to catch up on my shut-eye.

"You're right! We have to help!" agreed Victoria, also jumping up. "Give me a minute and I'll be ready!" she added, not understanding why I was laughing at that. "We are going to help people, right?"

"Yes, sure we are. Why else would we go there?" I nodded, but now Victoria was even more suspicious. "Really, we're going to help the refugees. And we'll do this by cleaning out the now abandoned military bases! Look, on the news they clearly stated that the entire army was swept away, half of the aristocrats are no more. And so all that military hardware has been abandoned!"

"Not to mention the people!" protested Vika.

"Yes, them, too..." And I hadn't forgotten about them. Why not do it all? "That's right, Vika, you can help us recruit them. We'll find places for many newcomers."

Vika left then to get ready and I went to find the earth mages. They were still resting and didn't want to let me in. But it had to be done. I simply reminded them of the bald pigeon and hinted that its feathers could easily grow on them. In the most unexpected places.

"So then, something's come up," I said right away once I was in their common room. They'd fashioned quarters in which they all had their own apartment, but also shared a common room. It was set up for rest and relaxation. "I need you to build at least six full-fledged villages. It needs to be done well, the fields need to be demarcated... Well, who am I talking to? You already know the drill. They have to have underground shelters and other delights of military villages."

"We'll need a month..." Toren began to say, but I interrupted him.

"A week, no more. You can start right now!" I smiled, and spinning around, I headed out the door. We simply didn't have any time to waste. Of course, as soon as the door closed behind me I heard the earth mages start whining.

"Guys, how do I quit? Let's maybe read the contract again, shall we?"

Perhaps I wasn't going about this right. I'm talking about the way I treated my people. And maybe there would be those who might accuse me of dancing on the bones of the fallen aristocrats of the Severodvinsk Families, and others might call me a marauder.

But no, this wasn't the case at all. These six villages would be built for ordinary people who have lost their homes. I could protect them, and their life here will be much better than ever before. And to this end, yes, my plan was to take from the dead their property, and so what of it? What did they need tanks, helicopters, shells and cartridges for? Nothing, while I could still use them. And I was going to do what it took to get them.

I gave everyone the necessary orders, and while they were preparing to leave, and others were getting the plane out of the hangar and rolling the equipment and gear into it, I decided to take a little rest and think. Although... What was there to think about? A city that was almost as large as Arkhangelsk had been captured. Totally and completely! The offworlders fully understood how very important technology and electricity were to the locals. Moreover, they have learned how to take out the main trump card of the technological world. This was truly dangerous.

These were troubled times. And they called for difficult decisions. I smiled. My smile was predatory, wicked, and boded ill for the enemy. I then closed my eyes, inhaled deeply, and concentrated on my soul.

"Remove the fifth seal!"

E N D   O F   B O O K   S E V E N

Want to be the first to know about our latest LitRPG, sci fi and fantasy titles from your favorite authors?

Subscribe to our **New Releases** newsletter:
http://eepurl.com/b7niIL

Thank you for reading *The Healer's Way!*
If you like what you've read, check out other sci-fi, fantasy
and LitRPG novels published by Magic Dome Books:

NEW RELEASES!

Crossroads of Oblivion
a portal progression fantasy adventure series
by Dem Mikhailov

Gakko Academy
a portal progression fantasy adventure series
by Evgeny Alexeev

War Eternal
a military space adventure LitRPG series
by Yuri Vinokuroff

The Hunter's Code
a LitRPG series by Yuri Vinokuroff & Oleg Sapphire

The Order of Architects
a portal progression series
by Yuri Vinokuroff & Oleg Sapphire

I Will Be Emperor
a space adventure progression fantasy series
by Yuri Vinokuroff

An Ideal World for a Sociopath
a LitRPG series by Oleg Sapphire

The Healer's Way
a LitRPG series by Oleg Sapphire & Alexey Kovtunov

A Shelter in Spacetime
a LitRPG series by Dmitry Dornichev

The Village
a LitRPG progression fantasy series
by Dmitry Dornichev & Alexey Kovtunov

The Dark Healer
a historical progression fantasy series
by Alex Toxic & Nadya Lee

Ghost in the System
An apocalypse LitRPG series by Alexey Kovtunov

The Last Portal Jumper
a LitRPG series by Konstantin Zubov

Lord of the System
a LitRPG progression fantasy series by
Alex Toxic and Furious Miki

Kill to Live
a LitRPG progression fantasy adventure series
by George Bor and Yuri Vinokuroff

Kill or Die
a LitRPG series by Alex Toxic

The Strongest Student
a portal progression action fantasy series
by Andrei Tkachev

Living Ice
a portal progression alternative history series
by Dmitry Sheleg

Law of the Jungle
a Wuxia Progression Fantasy Adventure Series
By Vasily Mahanenko

Reality Benders
a LitRPG series by Michael Atamanov

The Dark Herbalist
a LitRPG series by Michael Atamanov

Perimeter Defense
a LitRPG series by Michael Atamanov

League of Losers
a LitRPG series by Michael Atamanov

Chaos' Game
a LitRPG series by Alexey Svadkovsky

The Way of the Shaman
a LitRPG series by Vasily Mahanenko

The Alchemist
a LitRPG series by Vasily Mahanenko

Dark Paladin
a LitRPG series by Vasily Mahanenko

Galactogon
a LitRPG series by Vasily Mahanenko

Invasion
a LitRPG series by Vasily Mahanenko

World of the Changed
a LitRPG series by Vasily Mahanenko

The Bear Clan
a LitRPG series by Vasily Mahanenko

Starting Point
a LitRPG series by Vasily Mahanenko

The Bard from Barliona
a LitRPG series
by Eugenia Dmitrieva and Vasily Mahanenko

Condemned
(Lord Valevsky: Last of The Line)
a Progression Fantasy series
by Vasily Mahanenko

Loner
a LitRPG series by Alex Kosh

A Buccaneer's Due
a LitRPG series by Igor Knox

A Student Wants to Live
a LitRPG series by Boris Romanovsky

The Goldenblood Heir
a LitRPG series by Boris Romanovsky

The One Who Changes the Future
a dystopian portal progression fantasy series
by Boris Romanovsky

Level Up
a LitRPG series by Dan Sugralinov

Level Up: The Knockout
a LitRPG series by Dan Sugralinov and Max Lagno

Adam Online
a LitRPG Series by Max Lagno

World 99
a LitRPG series by Dan Sugralinov

Disgardium
a LitRPG series by Dan Sugralinov

Nullform
a RealRPG Series by Dem Mikhailov

Clan Dominance: The Sleepless Ones
a LitRPG series by Dem Mikhailov

Heroes of the Final Frontier
a LitRPG series by Dem Mikhailov

The Crow Cycle
a LitRPG series by Dem Mikhailov

Interworld Network
a LitRPG series by Dmitry Bilik

Rogue Merchant
a LitRPG series by Roman Prokofiev

Project Stellar
a LitRPG series by Roman Prokofiev

In the System
a LitRPG series by Petr Zhgulyov

The Crow Cycle
a LitRPG series by Dem Mikhailov

Unfrozen
a LitRPG series by Anton Tekshin

The Neuro
a LitRPG series by Andrei Livadny

Phantom Server
a LitRPG series by Andrei Livadny

Respawn Trials
a LitRPG series by Andrei Livadny

The Expansion (The History of the Galaxy)
a Space Exploration Saga by A. Livadny

The Range
a LitRPG series by Yuri Ulengov

Point Apocalypse
a near-future action thriller by Alex Bobl

Moskau
a dystopian thriller by G. Zotov

El Diablo
a supernatural thriller by G.Zotov

Mirror World
a LitRPG series by Alexey Osadchuk

Underdog
a LitRPG series by Alexey Osadchuk

Last Life
a Progression Fantasy series by Alexey Osadchuk

Alpha Rome
a LitRPG series by Ros Per

An NPC's Path
a LitRPG series by Pavel Kornev

Fantasia
a LitRPG series by Simon Vale

The Sublime Electricity
a steampunk series by Pavel Kornev

Small Unit Tactics
a LitRPG series by Alexander Romanov

Black Centurion
a LitRPG standalone by Alexander Romanov

Rorkh
A LitRPG Series by Vova Bo

Thunder Rumbles Twice
A Wuxia Series by V. Kriptonov & M. Bachurova

More books and series are coming out soon!

In order to have new books of the series translated faster, we need your help and support! Please consider leaving a review or spread the word by recommending *The Healer's Way* to your friends and posting the link on social media. The more people buy the book, the sooner we'll be able to make new translations available.

Thank you!

Till next time!

Made in the USA
Coppell, TX
27 October 2024

39256259R00193